FATEFUL VOYAGE

Recent Titles by Pamela Oldfield from Severn House

The Heron Saga
BETROTHED
THE GILDED LAND
LOWERING SKIES
THE BRIGHT DAWNING

ALL OUR TOMORROWS
EARLY ONE MORNING
RIDING THE STORM

CHANGING FORTUNES
NEW BEGINNINGS
MATTERS OF TRUST

DANGEROUS SECRETS
INTRICATE LIAISONS
TURNING LEAVES

HENRY'S WOMEN
SUMMER LIGHTNING
JACK'S SHADOW
FULL CIRCLE
LOVING AND LOSING
FATEFUL VOYAGE

FATEFUL VOYAGE

Pamela Oldfield

This first world edition published in Great Britain 2007 by
SEVERN HOUSE PUBLISHERS LTD of
9–15 High Street, Sutton, Surrey SM1 1DF.
This first world edition published in the USA 2008 by
SEVERN HOUSE PUBLISHERS INC of
595 Madison Avenue, New York, N.Y. 10022.

British Library Cataloguing in Publication Data

Oldfield, Pamela
  Fateful voyage
  1. Great Britain - History - Edward VII, 1901-1910 -
  Fiction
  I. Title
  823.9'14[F]

  ISBN-13: 978-0-7278-6582-3   (cased)
  ISBN-13: 978-1-84751-042-6   (trade paper)

All Severn House titles are printed on acid-free paper.

Typeset by Palimpsest Book Production Ltd.,
Grangemouth, Stirlingshire, Scotland.
Printed and bound in Great Britain by
MPG Books Ltd., Bodmin, Cornwall.

One

Wednesday, 6th November, 1907

The church clock struck midnight. The sound echoed through the silent London streets, where only the barking of a dog or the wail of a cat disturbed the dark alleyways, and the clatter of a hansom cab was less likely. Still awake, Hester closed her eyes, determined that somehow she would make sleep come. It was the third night in a row that she had remained awake until the early hours of the morning. Around her she heard the familiar sounds of the little attic room. The flutter of the curtains as the wind reached them on its way past, the regular tick-tock of the small brass carriage clock that had been Alexander's first gift to her, and the occasional sound of the wooden rafters that always contracted as soon as the fire turned to ash and the temperature of the room dropped.

Beside her in the bed, Alexander stirred.

'I can't sleep,' he grumbled. 'Thinking about that damned man, Drummond! He undermines me at every turn and I won't put up with it any longer.' He turned on to his back, wide awake and simmering with anger.

Hester said nothing. The past six years had taught her when to keep quiet.

'He thinks he's getting away with it,' Alexander muttered, 'but I've got his measure, and I'm going to break him! He'll be very sorry he crossed me.'

Frank Drummond, Hester knew, was a colleague with connections to people in the Home Office. She also knew that Alexander hated him for some reason she had never understood.

'He won't know right from left once I've finished with him,' he threatened. 'No man treats me like that and lives to tell the tale!'

She laughed dutifully. 'Poor chap.'

She wasn't sure what the man had done to anger Alexander, but she knew better than to ask. He kept his professional life remote from his personal life, and she had no wish to share such problems.

'He's gone too far this time, damn him, and I'm going to nail him.' He sat up, sighing heavily to let her know he was less than happy. 'It's stuffy in here, Hester. Is the window ever opened?'

He was fanatical about fresh air.

'It won't open properly, it—'

'Don't remind me. It sticks. My fault, I suppose.'

Hester remained silent. It *was* his fault. She had offered to arrange for a carpenter to adjust it, but he had refused, saying that *he* would see to it.

He broke the silence abruptly. 'How would you like a trip to New York?'

'Together?' Foolishly, for a moment or two, she allowed herself to hope.

'Don't be ridiculous! To accompany my aunt. What time is it?' He reached for his pocket watch and squinted at it in the moonlight which filled the room. 'A trip on the *Mauretania*,' he elaborated. 'Her maiden voyage, no less.'

Knowing that without his spectacles, Alexander could not see properly, she said, 'It has just struck twelve.'

The *Mauretania*, she thought, her eyes widening. His aunt must be very wealthy. She was a brand new transatlantic steamship which doubled as a liner, sister to the *Lusitania* which had sailed for the first time a couple of months earlier. The maiden voyage sounded wonderful, but it also meant being apart from Alexander which made her hesitate.

He slid from the bed, walked into the lavatory and returned a couple of minutes later. Standing by the bed, he rubbed his eyes and then ran fingers through his hair, a mannerism he had when he felt guilty. He was eating too well, she thought a little critically, and becoming a little grey on the temples. Soon he would look like any other middle-aged man – not that it would bother him. Alexander had too much confidence to worry about how he might appear to others.

He swung his arms: forward, up and down, sideways, then up and down again. The 'loosening up' exercises he had learned as a boy at his very expensive private school.

'I told my aunt you would accompany her.'

'Not . . .' Her face fell.

'Yes. Edith. She's still nervous of the sea and refuses to travel alone. You've never been to New York so I said you'd go with her.' He sat down on the edge of the bed. 'She has to see a specialist there. Her friend has recommended him. Dr Guy Stafford.'

'What's wrong with her this time?'

'Goodness only knows. I don't.'

'What happened about the kidney trouble?'

'Nothing as usual. It went away as soon as she lost interest and turned her attention to a heart problem.'

'She suspects heart trouble now?' Hester shook her head. Travelling with a cranky old woman held no appeal. 'Why doesn't she advertise for a travelling companion? She can afford to pay well. Some women would jump at the chance.'

Hester considered what she knew about Alexander's elderly aunt. Edith Carradine was a widow – a silly, bad-tempered woman with more money than sense, according to the nephew she adored. She apparently thrived on imaginary illnesses and enjoyed the attention that came with medical consultations.

Alexander laughed shortly. 'She did advertise. No one would take the money.'

'I'm not surprised. From what you tell me, I can imagine her interview technique!'

Alexander touched his toes ten times, then straightened, puffing slightly. 'I told her it was settled. You have to go.'

Annoyed at being manoeuvred, Hester began to resist. 'Why can't one of her daughters go with her? That makes more sense.'

Alexander snorted. 'Because they both produced convincing

excuses the moment the idea was mooted. One is apparently nursing a sick friend, the other is preparing for an exhibition of her watercolours. It has to be you, I'm afraid. It's not too much to ask, is it? A favour to me. I'm very good to you.' He leaned forward. 'I make you happy. I buy you beautiful clothes, I . . .'

'I make *you* happy in return.'

'I don't deny it.' He kissed her hand, her arm, her neck. 'Say you'll go. Please, Hester.'

She was wavering. A trip on a liner to New York and back would be an adventure, but Edith Carradine was a definite fly in the ointment. The other reason for Hester's hesitation was a permanent worry that one day Alexander would find another woman. It may be that leaving him for several weeks would be too great a strain for him. He might find someone, intending only a brief fling, but then . . . She frowned. He was still an attractive man, despite his age, and he was influential and comparatively wealthy. Few women could resist his charm if he put his mind to it.

'How long would we be gone?' she asked.

'As long as it takes. She might be over there for several weeks. Five or six, perhaps. It would do you good, Hester. You lead a very uneventful life. I'm a selfish brute, keeping you all to myself. Aunt Edith will probably sleep a lot. Early to bed, afternoon nap and all that. You can enjoy life at sea.'

'Five or six weeks? Then I definitely won't go.' Hester propped herself up on one elbow. 'Are you trying to get rid of me? Is that it?' She tried to sound light-hearted, but she was actually very nervous now. Was she being naïve? Was he trying to tell her something? Was he tiring of her after all this time? She suddenly saw a frightful image – herself returning from the trip to find the flat was no longer her home. Would he do that? She didn't think so, but the hateful vision made her draw a sharp breath.

He stood up, crossed to a chair, and began to dress himself. 'I don't want to argue,' he said. 'I've said you'll go. That's the end of it.'

Defeated, Hester gave in to the inevitable. To annoy him, she asked, 'Who did you tell your aunt I was? Your mistress?'

He gave her a withering look, sat down, and began to pull on his socks and shoes. He combed his hair without looking in the mirror and shrugged on his jacket.

'The question was a serious one, Alex,' she insisted. 'Who will you say I am?'

'I told the odd lie!' He grinned and suddenly looked much younger. 'I said you were once the dressmaker to the wife of a friend of a friend . . .'

'I can't sew for toffee!'

'And that I know you to be utterly reliable and of a dutiful disposition.'

'Dutiful!' Pushing the negative thoughts aside, she laughed. 'Oh, Alexander! You didn't!' She hoped she was not dutiful. It sounded horribly submissive.

'It was what she wanted to hear, Hester. Don't fuss. By the time she finds out that you are *not* dutiful it will be too late. You'll be travelling on the finest ship ever built in this country. If she goes fast enough, she might take the Blue Riband from the *Lusitania*! It will be a wonderful experience. An elegant cabin, good food, games to play, a library . . .'

'Games?' She raised her eyebrows.

'Shove halfpenny, Ludo, deck quoits.' He grinned.

Since it was inevitable, Hester allowed herself to hope she just *might* enjoy it.

'When is this trip, Alex?'

'In ten days' time. You can go for walks on the deck.'

'Walks on deck? It's November!'

'Wrap up warmly. It will do you good. Blow away the cobwebs.' Ignoring her protests, he rushed on. 'I'll give you some money and you can buy a few new clothes in New York. You'd like that, wouldn't you?' He kissed her. 'Now, I must go. Marcia . . .'

'Will be wondering where you are . . . I know.' Hester drew up her knees and hugged them defensively. This was the worst moment, the one she always dreaded, when he left her with so little apparent regret. As though he had just completed a business transaction and was eager to leave the office and return to his other life. Perhaps, for him, that was exactly how it felt. The idea tormented her and she had to bite back a cry for reassurance. She had told herself many times never to reproach him. She had entered into their arrangement with her eyes wide open. It was swings and roundabouts. Often being with Alexander was a joy, sometimes a habit, but at other times it brought pain.

She said brightly, 'It's a good thing you don't have far to walk.'

He waited as she remained sitting on her bed. 'Well, don't just sit there. You have to lock the door behind me.'

'I will,' she said.

'I like to hear the chain go on. I've told you that London's a dangerous place. I ought to know – the streets are full of villains.'

He worries about me, she thought, slightly cheered, and slid from beneath the sheet, followed him out of the bedroom and along the narrow passage. He opened the door, turned back to give her a perfunctory kiss – and then was away, clattering down the stairs.

'That's right,' she muttered. 'Wake all the other occupants.'

Remind them that it's midnight, she thought unhappily, and you are hurrying back to your wife. Let them know, if they don't already, that I am merely a kept woman, to be abandoned every night on the stroke of midnight like Cinderella's slipper.

The street door opened and closed, and she hurried to the front window as she always did, and, with fear clutching at her heart, watched Alexander stride out along the street in the direction of his wife and their home.

'Don't betray me while I am in New York,' she whispered. 'Please don't betray me.'

As soon as he was out of sight, she went back to the empty bed and lay staring up at the moonlit ceiling. She was thirty-one, her youth was gone – and she needed him.

Marcia pretended to be asleep when her husband returned, but when he finally slid into bed beside her, she mumbled sleepily and opened her eyes.

'How did the meeting with Grey go?' she asked.

'So-so. He's an idiot, that man.'

'But did you get your point across? You were there for long enough.'

'Which point?' He yawned.

She breathed in through her nose and recognized the woman's perfume. No doubt she would again find red gold hairs on the collar of her husband's jacket and maybe a smudge of rouge on his shirt. Was he really so careless of discovery or did he think her totally unobservant? Did he think she was ignorant of the small flat he had bought in Chalker Street in which to squirrel her away?

Whoever the woman was, Marcia did not care. She was welcome to him. He would never leave her because she had brought a great deal of family money to the marriage and had made life easier for him while he climbed the career ladder to a senior position within the police force.

Alexander Waring had been a young police sergeant when they first met, mixing with the worst ruffians in the criminal underworld. He had claimed, laughingly, that he was on first name terms with all the best villains. He had thrived on the challenges, relishing the hostilities, the plotting and counter-plotting, frequently risking his life. He had succeeded where lesser men had failed, bringing a record number of miscreants to justice. It had been a long, hard struggle, and she was pleased and proud that, with her money and her social contacts, she had eased the way upward for him. He was now a detective chief inspector at Scotland Yard and she felt he deserved it.

But he didn't know everything. Marcia knew something he did not – though only forty-nine, she was seriously ill and would soon die. She was therefore grateful to the other woman who satisfied her husband and left his wife free to end her days in comparative peace. The drug the doctor gave her allowed her to pass many hours in a dreamy half-conscious state that was more than bearable. It was positively euphoric. Only towards the end of the evening did she allow herself to emerge into full reality, and accept the pain that went with it. She did it willingly to spare him unhappiness. When she died he would be free to remarry. By then she would be in another, hopefully better, place.

'Which point?' Marcia echoed. 'Why, the point about the increase in manpower. That was why the meeting was held. You knew it would be a late one – and then you were popping into the club.'

He had lied. She knew it. Not that the lies troubled her, but it riled her that he thought her so easily tricked. One day she might surprise him.

'Oh, that!' He recovered quickly. 'Yes. The manpower issue. He's going to consider it – or so he says. He made a half-promise, but he's a slippery customer. How have you been today? Any better?'

Instead of answering, she asked, 'Was Fanshawe there?'

'Fanshawe? At the club, do you mean? Of course he was. The old blighter's always there. It's his second home!'

'Last night you said he was ill and you'd had to take him home in a . . .'

'Taxi. Oh, yes. That.'

She smiled in the darkness. Poor Alexander. He was a hopeless liar – at home, anyway. He could never remember from one day to the next, but perhaps that was better than being a good liar. She was not complaining.

'Yes, of course,' he went on hastily. 'He wasn't ill as it happened. Just drunk. Paralytic, in fact. Stupid old fool!'

'I thought you said he'd collapsed and you kindly offered to . . .'

'I was being charitable, Marcia. One doesn't care to malign one's friends. He's practically an alcoholic.'

'Still, it was kind of you to look after him and see him safely back to his flat. It made you terribly late home.' She crossed her fingers and hoped she hadn't gone too far.

'I found a woman for Aunt Edith,' he said, changing the subject abruptly. 'She's travelled before and is eager for the trip.'

'Wonderful. What does she charge?'

'We didn't discuss that. I shall leave the financial arrangement to the two of them when they meet.'

'What's her name? How did you find her?' Now Marcia was genuinely interested. Years ago, as a young wife, she had been persuaded to travel with Edith and it was an experience she'd rather forget.

'Someone at the club mentioned her. Hester Shaw. She used to be a dressmaker and loves travel but cannot afford it.'

'Hester? I like that name.' Marcia yawned. 'Have you given any more thought to the carpet in your study? It's positively threadbare in places and Mrs Rice is always grumbling about it. It holds the dust apparently.'

'No, I haven't, and she should mind her own business and get on with her job. I've actually had more important things to think about than a worn carpet. That may surprise you.' His tone was caustic, a sure sign his wife had irritated him.

Marcia turned over on to her left side. 'Goodnight, dear,' she said, in a sickly sweet tone that she kept for such moments.

'Goodnight, Marcia.'

Her pain was murmuring already, agitating like a pet dog waiting for a treat, but knowing it would soon be over made it bearable. As soon as her husband was asleep she would go downstairs and take some medicine.

'Don't wake me if I oversleep in the morning,' she said. 'I've had a busy day and I'm tired.'

'Mmm . . .'

He was already half asleep. When his breathing changed she would recognize the sound. Marcia thought of the coming pleasure and smiled.

At three thirty that same night, Charlie Barnes was making his way through the silent back streets of Liverpool. He had just come from a late-night poker game in which he had lost the last of his wages, and his usually sunny expression had given way to one of disappointment and growing anxiety. At the corner, he turned into Marlin Row and headed for number five. Outside the door he paused to run his fingers through his curly brown hair which was more dishevelled than usual. He rubbed his grey eyes, which were smarting from the smoky atmosphere of the room at the Jolly Sailor, tugged down his jacket and fixed a carefree smile on his face. Instead of knocking at the front door, he tapped five times on the front window and, when nothing happened, he repeated these taps with a little more force.

Under his breath he said, 'Wake up, Annie!' and stared round at the neighbouring houses to see if anyone was watching from behind twitching curtains. After a few moments, while he tapped his foot impatiently, the door opened, a hand reached out and a young woman pulled him into the narrow hall.

'Charlie,' she whispered, as he pushed the front door closed with a practised movement of his right foot. 'I thought you was never coming. You know what time it is?' She was tugging at his jacket, trying to take it off.

'Course I know.' He pressed her against the wall and kissed her hard on the mouth. Annie was a pretty little thing – with blue eyes and fair hair which curled carelessly around her face – and she adored him. He'd been seeing her for more than a year and Charlie knew she'd do anything for him. She had no husband, jealous or otherwise, although poor Stan Holler had been after her since their school days and made no secret of his feelings for her. (Not that he stood a chance while Charlie Barnes was around!) So she had no kids to distract her *and* a place of her own. He was lucky and he knew it.

'Wait,' she said, wriggling free. 'We can't do it here. Someone might see.'

He followed her into the room which she rented from Mrs Fisher, who owned two other houses in the street and was considered a wealthy skinflint by her tenants. The room served as a bedroom cum living room and was sparsely furnished with a second-hand bed, table and two chairs. Within minutes they were both naked on the bed, eager for each other after the days they had been apart.

Afterwards, Charlie felt cheerful again and a little better about the money he had just lost. He had his arm around her and in the light from the street he saw that Annie was smiling too.

'I told you I'd be back,' he said. 'I promised and here I am.'

'Like a bad penny.' She snuggled closer.

'Not so much of the "bad", Miss Green.' He kissed her shoulder.

Charlie knew that whenever he was away on a trip, she worried that he would meet another woman and she would never see him again. Not that she had ever put her anxiety into words, but he knew. Charlie understood women. He loved them and would never deliberately hurt one of them. But he was good-looking and they buzzed around him 'like bees round a honeypot'. That was how his mother had described it when he was eighteen. Now he was twenty-five, and in love with life, he knew what she'd said was true and enjoyed himself.

Most of the time, that is. It was hard to enjoy himself when he was skint after a poker game that had robbed him of his last sixpence and left him with an IOU for a pound.

He sighed then quickly turned it into a cough.

She said, 'So where was you?'

She spoke lightly, but he sensed her unease.

'Here and there,' he said, hugging her. 'How many times do I have to tell you that I'm footloose and fancy free. Always have been and always will be. Not the marrying kind.'

'But . . . you weren't . . . in trouble again?'

'In trouble? When do I get in trouble?'

'You were in that fight once. Just after Christmas.'

He rolled his eyes. 'That was nothing. A bit of a falling-out, that's all that was. Me and Stan Holler. He was always on to me because of you. They never even fetched a copper!'

'But they threw you both out into the snow.' She giggled.

'It cooled us off. No harm done. We shook hands after-wards. You know we did.' He dismissed the incident with a shake of his head. 'A bit of a dust-up, that's all. A misun-derstanding, you might say.'

'You might have got hurt.'

'Course not! You shouldn't worry, Annie. You'll get wrin-kles.' He kissed her again. If he ever decided to settle down

– and it was a mighty big 'if' – it might be Annie, but
marriage held no appeal for him and he made no bones
about it. Annie knew the score.

'I'm off again on the sixteenth of this month,' he
announced. 'On the *Mauretania,* no less! Maiden voyage.
I'll earn more and there'll be lots of rich people so lots of
tips! I'll be rich when I get back. We'll go somewhere nice.
Blackpool maybe. See the lights.' He hugged her. 'Might
even stay the night!'

'Stay the night in Blackpool. Oh, Charlie! D'you mean
it? In a hotel? Oh, we couldn't, could we?'

He could hear the excitement in her voice.

'Why not? You're a good girl. You deserve a treat.'
Somehow he had to steer the conversation the right way.
He hated borrowing money, but if he went to New York
without settling the debt, they'd be waiting for him when
he got back and he'd probably face a beating. 'The thing
is, Annie, I'm a bit short at the moment and I want to book
the hotel before I go away. I don't suppose you could help
me out, could you? If not I'll chance it and try to book
when I get back.'

'Oh, Charlie,' she wailed. 'You haven't been gambling
again, have you? You still owe me two shillings from the
last time you lost.' The reproach in her voice was obvious
and Charlie counted to ten.

'Then I'll buy you something nice in New York,' he offered.
'You'd like that, wouldn't you? A present all the way from
America. That would be something to show your friends,
eh?' He idled his fingers through her blonde curls. 'I quite
forgot I owed you that two bob so you'll forgive old Charlie,
won't you? And as for the gambling, well, it's not real
gambling. Just the odd poker game. I'm trying to save up.'

'But so am I and . . .'

He sat up. 'No, Annie! Not another word. You're right.
I shouldn't have asked you. I only needed a couple of
shillings, but one of my mates'll help me out.'

She was silenced and he knew that now she felt guilty.
She thought she'd been mean, a poor friend and less
generous than his mates.

Charlie pressed home his advantage. 'That's enough about money. What shall we talk about now? I know, you haven't told me about that new job you went for – the one at the florist where they would train you to arrange flowers. Did you get it?'

'No.' She held his hand to her mouth and kissed it. 'They said I was not mature enough. I'm still at the laundry and Ginnie's still hanging on in the ironing room. If she'd go I'm definitely next in line for her job. The ironing would be better than nothing, but not as nice as the florist. Charlie, about the money. If you—'

He put a hand over her mouth. 'What did I say? No more about money. I shall manage, don't you worry. Not mature enough to work in a florist shop? But that's nonsense, that is. Suppose I have a word with them. Sweet talk them. How would that do, d'you suppose? Anything I can do to help you. You know me.'

'It's kind of you, Charlie, but it's too late. There's a new girl working there since Monday. But there's another job going at the greengrocer's and I might—'

'Which greengrocer is it? Suppose I come with you. A bit of moral support.'

'They won't listen to you. It's me they—'

'I could say we're engaged. They're not to know.'

'It's not just that, Charlie. They made me do some sums in my head and I got them wrong.'

He ran a hand gently down her body then up again until it cupped her breast. 'You do still love me, Annie, don't you?'

'You know I do!'

'Then there's something you can do for me. It's a lot to ask, but . . .'

'Anything I can.'

'Then make me a cup of tea! I'm parched.'

Her pretty laugh rang out as she cuffed him playfully. 'You are a one, Charlie! You'd get away with murder, you would.' She scrambled from the bed, pulled on her flannel nightdress and crossed the room to the corner she called her kitchen. A single gas ring stood on a wide shelf and a saucepan hung on the wall. There was a single tap and she half filled the saucepan and lit the gas ring. While she found two cups, tea, sugar and milk, Charlie waited, sitting up in bed with the blankets pulled up to his neck. The room boasted a small black iron fireplace, but the fire had long since gone out and the room was chilly. He had hurried through a damp fog to reach Annie Green and was thankful he need not go out again until six. He could then sneak away before Mrs Fisher was up and about next door.

Annie returned to bed with the tea and Charlie sipped his gratefully. He told her about the RMS *Mauretania* and about the preparations that were being made for her maiden trip.

'You should come to watch us leave the harbour,' he suggested. 'There'll be a band playing and the ship will be decorated with bunting – and you can watch all the toffs going on board.'

'I might do that, Charlie. Then I can wave to you.'

When they had drunk the tea Charlie slid down under the blankets and closed his eyes sleepily. Annie rinsed the cups and then crossed to the small wardrobe where she kept her few clothes. While Charlie dozed, she opened the drawer at the bottom and took out a small tin where she kept her savings. Annie extracted a shilling and two sixpences and counted what was left. After returning the tin to its hiding place, she tiptoed round to Charlie's side of the bed and placed the money on the small table which contained a candleholder and a dish of withered rose petals.

Charlie grunted and opened his eyes. 'Oh, you sweetheart,' he murmured. 'That'll see me through until I start back at work. Give us a kiss!'

The kiss led to another and then somehow he was not sleepy after all, but soon after, once the passion passed, flushed and satisfied, he forgot about the fog and the unsuccessful poker game and finally slept.

A few hours earlier, while Charlie Barnes had still been hoping to win at poker, an elderly lady had sat at her writing desk in an elegant apartment overlooking the small green area optimistically known by the inhabitants of Tessingham Terrace as 'the park'. Her thin grey hair was plaited and hung down to her waist. Her crumpled face shone with an application of expensive skin cream and the bony hand that held the pen showed signs of a professional manicure. Her faded grey eyes stared at the page through small, round lensed spectacles while her small mouth moved approvingly with each word that she wrote.

Edith Carradine, at eighty, no longer remembered her birthdays out of choice, and she also no longer remembered anyone else's birthdays. Her days, she told herself, were too full. She had to watch her wealth, monitor her servants, and ensure that she stayed healthy. All three aims were fraught with difficulties because she could not trust other people to do their work properly or get them to understand the quality of service she had been brought up to expect. Her father's family were descendants of landowners in Surrey where several large farms remained and were worked by tenant farmers. Her mother's money had come from overseas investments, mainly India – money that had been wisely invested in the City. She had married well, too, and her husband had left her a large sum of money when he died twenty years ago.

She had, she believed, two ungrateful daughters, who were more than willing to spend her money, but refused to allow her a say in how it was spent. They even rejected her advice whenever they could. After the death of her husband they had finally rebelled against her autocratic ways and the resultant relationships were fragile. Entries in her daily diary over the past years provided evidence of the many and varied quarrels and estrangements between mother and daughters.

She glanced back at the many and varied complaints she had confided about them. Dorcas had refused to take her advice on footwear, as usual, and had bought laced shoes instead of buttoned boots – and had had the audacity to suggest that at the age of forty-five she was old enough to choose her own shoes. Cheeky young madam! Evelyn had employed a housemaid from an agency instead of training a young girl straight from home. Lazy, that was Evelyn's problem . . . And only recently Dorcas had lied to her in order to avoid including her at a dinner party. Selfish creature. Her mouth tightened at the unhappy reminders.

This particular night, however, Edith Carradine had nothing unpleasant to record about either Evelyn or Dorcas. Her mind was on the approaching trip to New York on the RMS *Mauretania* and the woman her nephew had found to accompany her.

Wednesday, November 6th, 1907 – Young Alexander has come to my rescue, bless the boy. He has found a suitable companion for me who comes highly recommended by a friend of his. Her name is Hester (or possibly Esther) and he says she was once a dressmaker but presumably has now fallen on hard times. Not a 'fallen woman,' I hope! I said, being unusually flippant. I expected him to laugh, but he gave me a very odd look and changed the subject. Perhaps he found it somewhat out of character, which I daresay it was. Alexander describes her as 'biddable' (or was it dutiful?) so we should get along. I shall take no nonsense from her and at the first sign of unsuitability shall not hesitate to send her packing. I can always hire another companion for the return crossing when we reach New York. I shall take two of my dresses that need alteration since the Harley Street man (I forget his name) advises me to wear a less restrictive corset as he suspects that the present one is putting undue pressure on my digestive organs. A little sewing will keep Miss Shaw out of mischief. There will be no 'shipboard romance' for any companion of mine. I shall firmly discourage 'followers' and will keep a strict eye on Miss Shaw from day one.

Blotting her writing carefully, Edith reread her words with satisfaction, but as she replaced the pen she frowned at the backs of her hands which were liberally sprinkled with dark freckles. It seemed that no amount of lemon juice would fade them and that irritated her. She had plenty of time and money to spend on herself and enjoyed buying expensive clothes and cosmetics. She had once been a great beauty, and although she was now a mere shadow of her former self, she still had the satisfaction of having outlived many of her friends. Age was her enemy, but, she told herself, she was prepared to go down fighting.

Two

Annie Green would not have recognized her lover in the smart uniform of ship's steward. Charlie hurried through the public rooms of the *Mauretania* on a tour of inspection with his friend Chalky White. He had waved 'goodbye' to Annie on the quayside two hours earlier and had parted from her with real regret, but had forgotten her immediately. Now some of the crew found themselves with time on their hands because the boat train from London had been delayed and it would be another hour at least before the eager passengers reached Liverpool and could start boarding.

'A drawing room for the women. What next?' Chalky rolled his eyes. 'They're pampered, they are.' He stared round the large room in undisguised awe. 'Look at that! Oak panelling. What did that cost?'

'It's maple, not oak,' Charlie told him loftily. 'Wait until you see the men's smoking room. Their panelling's walnut.' He had overheard many useful facts earlier by loitering near to three of the ship's officers who were escorting important passengers around the new ship.

Although the ship was an express liner, her title was Royal Mail Ship since she had been designed primarily for the speedy carrying of mail to and fro across the Atlantic, but certain concessions in the way of comfort had been made to the travelling public and the interior decoration was elegant enough to impress them.

Chalky frowned. 'They say it's not a patch on the *Amerika*.'

Charlie rushed to the ship's defence. 'But the *Amerika* is slower, don't forget. We did twenty-six knots during the trials. Wish I could have showed Annie round. She'd have been knocked sideways. Be like a palace to her, this would.'

'It's like a palace to *me*!' Chalky grinned suddenly. 'When you going to marry this Annie, then, if she's so wonderful?'

'Don't rush me. We haven't mentioned wedding bells and I don't intend to. You know me, Chalky. Do I look like someone's husband? I don't want to end up like you with two kids and another on the way. You know what one of my lady friends told me? She said I wasn't husband material! Elena her name was. A real darling. Father was an Italian and owned his own restaurant. You can get to like spaghetti if you try hard enough and it's free!' He laughed. 'Not "husband material". I took it as a compliment and her mother took against me. But it's the truth. I want my money for myself.'

'To pay off all your gambling debts!'

'Who says I've got any?'

'You always have gambling debts. You can't play poker because you've got an honest face.'

'That's all you know.' Charlie tapped his chest. 'I'll be rich one day. You never will. Come on, let's take a dekko at the Grand Salon.'

They were not disappointed. In fact nothing disappointed them, although they were careful not to appear too impressed and passed semi-critical comments from time to time in order to appear blasé.

Half an hour later, the passengers began to embark and Charlie was back at his station in the bar reserved for first-class passengers. People swirled around him, mostly lost and asking for directions, but some were already settling into the comfortable chairs with a drink, determined not to miss a moment of the good life they had been led to expect from the publicity literature for the 'floating palace'.

Charlie slipped between them with practised ease, a tray of drinks balanced on one hand, a cheerful smile on his face. First day aboard the new ship, but he knew it didn't show. Like his colleagues, he managed to look entirely at home as he ministered to the passengers' every need and anticipated the tips he would receive when the crossing came to an end.

An elderly woman laid an imperious hand on his arm and stopped him in his tracks.

'How can I help you, madam?' he asked smoothly, his handsome face creased into a smile, his eyes on the powdered face and elaborately coiffed hair.

'You can show me the way to my cabin, young man,' she answered. 'All this muddle and confusion – it's a disgrace. First the train from London is late and now we are supposed to make our way through this frightful crush of bodies. It's quite unnecessary.'

'I wish I could help you, madam, but the bar staff are not allowed to leave the area. However, I . . .'

The woman turned to her much younger companion. 'What did I tell you, Miss Shaw? No respect for age or class these days. Standards are falling everywhere you look. We are paying for first-class service, but look what we get!'

'I'm afraid, madam, that on a maiden voyage the crew are not always familiar with the layout of . . .'

'Don't make excuses, young man. The fact that this *is* the maiden voyage is all the more reason why the trip should be superbly comfortable for the passengers. I shall write to Cunard as soon as the voyage is over and shall tell them exactly what I think of their efforts!' Her eyes narrowed. 'Where do you come from? You're not a Londoner. I can tell from your accent.'

'No, madam. Liverpool born and bred!' He smiled, but she refused to be charmed.

'A pity.'

Charlie gave a polite shrug and took a second look at the woman who he now knew as Miss Shaw. So she wasn't married. He guessed she was a little older than him, not beautiful but definitely attractive in a restrained way and with a just perceptible air of sadness about her that Charlie immediately found intriguing. He was also a great admirer of bright auburn hair, especially when it was allied to green eyes. He wondered if she had a fiancé. He thought it more

than likely. He could imagine her asleep in a silky nightdress, her hair tousled on the pillow.

She turned to face the old woman. 'Don't worry, Mrs
Carradine. We'll find one of the officers. Or would you like
to wait here with a glass of lemonade while I go in search
of our cabin?'

'Lemonade? In this weather? Certainly not.' She tossed
her head. 'However, I wouldn't refuse a pot of tea and a
biscuit while I'm waiting.'

Charlie tore his gaze away from the younger woman.
'You might try the Verandah Café, madam. It's a brand new
concept and we think . . .'

'Certainly not.' She turned to her companion. 'I shall stay
here and you may fetch me—' She broke off. 'Oh! I see
no vacant tables.'

'I'll find you one, madam,' Charlie told her. He leaned
towards her confidingly. 'I know the very place – tucked
away in the corner where you won't be jostled.' He smiled
at her and then at the red-headed woman. Was it his fancy
or did the latter brighten slightly under his attention? Women
responded to him, he knew. He had once boasted that given
time he could have any woman he wanted. It wasn't quite
true, but he did have a great deal of success with what he
called 'the ladies'. He put it down to being slim, handsome
and a smooth talker – and to loving them and letting them
know it. This young woman, however, was a different kettle
of fish altogether. He had never chanced his arm with a
first-class passenger but he was tempted. How would she
react, he wondered. She might be flattered or she might be
offended or consider him impudent. The more he thought
about it, the more he fancied the challenge.

The old lady agreed to the pot of tea with a show of
reluctance and the younger one went on her way in search
of their cabins. Charlie led his elderly charge to an empty
table and, with a slight pressure on her arm, helped her to
settle in the seat. Moments later he returned with a pot of
tea and a plate of biscuits.

'What is your name, young man?'

'Charles Barnes, madam.'

She gave him a condescending nod. 'Thank you, Mr Barnes.'

'Shall I fetch a drink for your daughter?' It was meant to be not-so-subtle flattery but it failed.

'My *daughter*? Don't be ridiculous. I hardly know the woman. Miss Shaw is my travelling companion. Nothing more.'

She gave him a dismissive wave of her hand and Charlie escaped. Silly old bat, he thought and gave a few moments' thought to the unfortunate Miss Shaw, until a trio of smart young women appeared and asked for his help, and the old lady and her unfortunate companion were at once forgotten.

Fifteen minutes later Hester was ushered into her cabin by Mrs Pontings, a kindly stewardess who confided proudly that she was the sister of one of the ship's officers.

'And if you need me, just press the bell and I'll come along right away,' she promised.

'When do you go off duty?'

'We're always available, madam, so if you're taken ill in the night don't hesitate to ring. That's what I'm here for.' She smiled. 'Enjoy your trip.'

She closed the door and Hester was left alone to get her breath back and marvel at her surroundings. The carpet was a pale green, as it was throughout the rest of the passenger areas. The hand basin was fitted into a marble surround. The bed linen was of a high quality and matched the curtains which framed the porthole.

Edith Carradine had booked them into adjoining rooms, solely for her own convenience, as she had explained coming down on the train from London.

'If you are in cheaper accommodation elsewhere, Miss Shaw, I should not be able to summon you so easily. There would be no point in paying for a companion who is not on hand if I am seasick or otherwise inconvenienced. I hope you appreciate my generosity.'

'I do indeed. Thank you.'

The truth was that being next door to her employer might prove more limiting, thought Hester, who had secretly hoped for some opportunities to explore the ship's facilities on her own. Still, there seemed little she could do about it, and she was certainly grateful for the luxury the cabin afforded her. It was a far cry from the small flat which Alexander had bought for her. Not that she wasn't grateful – she certainly was. He had met her at a desperate time in her life which she wished to forget.

Mrs Carradine might be an irascible old woman, Hester thought, but she knew how to do things in style.

Hester had also learned, on the train, of the garments Mrs Carradine was expecting her to alter. She would do the best she could with them, but if her employer found fault with her work, she planned to claim that her eyesight was failing. A lie but what else could she do? She could hardly betray Alexander who had lied on her behalf – albeit for his own benefit. Presumably he had thought Hester would enjoy the trip despite her responsibilities to her employer. Or had he? Had he perhaps been eager to get rid of her so that he could pursue someone else? The worry never left her. He had promised Hester that when his wife died he would marry her. Marcia was much older than him, but Hester realized she might live for another ten or twenty years. Her own situation was far from ideal, but the life into which she had been drifting when she and Alexander met would have been far worse.

Hester now went into the adjoining cabin to see if it varied in any way from her own. It looked similar but with the addition of a telephone on a stand in one corner. She shook her head in amazement and wondered who Mrs Carradine would want to contact. Her uncooperative daughters? More likely her nephew Alexander, to complain about the unsatisfactory companion he had found for her!

There was a knock on the door and when she opened it a porter stepped briskly into the cabin, wheeling a large trunk.

'Your luggage, Mrs Carradine,' he said with a smile. 'Will you need help with your unpacking?'

'I'm Mrs Carradine's companion and no thank you. I think the unpacking will probably fall to me.'

'Right, madam.' Deftly he manoeuvred the trunk into

position beside the chest of drawers and then loitered hope-fully. He did not outstretch his hand, but Hester realized that he was expecting a tip. 'I'm so sorry, I have no money with me. It's in my cabin next door. If you'd wait a moment.' He stepped outside and waited in the narrow passage as she found a sixpence and handed it to him. Hiding his obvious disappointment, he smiled and hurried away with his trolley.

Ten minutes later Hester had collected her employer from the bar and installed her in the cabin.

Mrs Carradine stared round with narrowed eyes. 'Where's the bathroom?' she demanded. 'Every first-class cabin on the *Mauretania* has a bathroom. There must be some mistake. Ring for the steward at once.'

Hester had also read the brochure. 'I think it said that *some* of them have bathrooms.'

'When I want your opinion, Miss Shaw, I'll ask for it. Please ring for the steward.' Her glance fell on the trunk. 'Who brought that?'

'A porter. I gave him sixpence.'

'More fool you!' Abruptly she sat down on the edge of the bed as though wearied by the day's events and Hester felt a sudden compassion. She was, after all, very elderly, but her habit of fighting everyone who tried to help her was inevitably going to drain her energy.

Mrs Pontings arrived, smiling, but Edith Carradine soon changed that by interrupting her introduction with a demand to know where the bathroom was that she had expected.

'The number of cabins with bathrooms is limited,' Mrs Pontings explained soothingly. 'But you'll find that . . .'

'Limited?'

'I expect they had all been snapped up by the time your booking was received. They do cost a good deal more and many passengers find . . .'

'I am not one of your "many passengers", Mrs Bunting. I am—'

'It's Pontings, madam.' Ignoring Edith Carradine's icy tone, the stewardess continued. 'My name is Pontings. Not Bunting.'

Edith Carradine looked at Hester. 'Get rid of this woman,' she snapped. 'I'll take the matter up with someone more senior.'

Hester looked at the stewardess apologetically. 'I'm sorry,' she stammered. A look of understanding passed between them before the stewardess withdrew.

When the door had closed behind her, Hester hesitated, then said, 'She's a very nice woman.'

'How would you know? She has no manners. She interrupted me.' Edith stared balefully round the cabin, but found nothing else to annoy her. 'Unpack my trunk, please, and then go next door and unpack your own luggage. I shan't eat this evening – it is already too late thanks to that stupid train driver. I will go to bed at ten o'clock. If I need you I shall knock on the wall. Let's hope for good weather. Are you a good sailor?'

'I don't know yet.'

Edith Carradine snorted. 'Well, don't expect me to look after you. You're the companion! If you want dinner tonight you will have to go down on your own. I shall rise at eight and will expect you to accompany me to breakfast in the dining room at a quarter past nine on the dot. Life, I have discovered, needs careful supervision, and time has to be properly disciplined. You will, I'm sure, find that out for yourself as you get older.'

The cabin was silent for the fifteen minutes it took Hester to unpack the trunk and stow away the various items of clothing. The long skirts and dresses went into the small wardrobe with the five pairs of shoes while the underwear and small garments fitted into the drawers.

Since the old lady made no comment, Hester decided her work must have met with approval, but when she turned to leave she was given a nod but no thanks. She closed the cabin door and hurried into her own room where she let out a sigh of relief. Exhausted, she sat down on the bed and covered her face with her hands. How on earth was she going to survive the rest of the crossing?

That evening it rained hard as RMS *Mauretania* pulled away from her berth at the Princes Landing Stage and only the boldest or more foolhardy passengers braved the outside decks to watch the departure from Liverpool. Hester was not among them. She had decided to explore the ship more thoroughly and then go for dinner at eight o'clock. She moved quietly along the passage between the rows of cabins, making little sound on the tiles underfoot. They had been specially designed to reduce noise and would ensure a minimum of disturbance from late-night revellers for those already in their beds. Hester began to enjoy herself as she blended in with passengers and crew, the latter busy about their duties, the former in the process of settling in. Hester found the library, it was almost empty, and then peeped into the men's smoking room before arriving at the bar where her employer had waited for her pot of tea.

At once a young purser appeared at her side, his tray at the ready, his smile broad. His dark hair was parted in the centre and smoothed down with what smelt like patchouli oil and his dark eyes surveyed her with obvious approval. But he was not Mr Barnes, she noted, and was ridiculously disappointed.

'Can I get you anything to drink, Miss Shaw?' he asked.

She blinked in surprise. 'You know my name?'

'Charlie Barnes mentioned you to me. He said to look after you if he was not around.'

'Goodness!' She laughed. 'That *is* good service.' She felt herself colour with pleasure at the idea that the young steward had spoken about her to a colleague. 'I'll have a glass of orange juice.'

'May I recommend a cocktail, Miss Shaw?' He indicated a menu standing on the table. 'A Tequila Sunrise might suit you. It's very pretty. Most ladies like it. Or there's the Manhattan. That's—'

'I think I'd better not,' she said reluctantly. 'I don't drink a lot of alcohol and it might make me dizzy.' Her employer would throw a fit if she thought her travelling companion had taken to drink!

At that moment, to her secret delight, Charles Barnes materialized beside them. He raised his eyes and turned to

Hester. 'This is Chalky White, Miss Shaw. Don't believe a word he says.'

Both men laughed at this.

'I'm only trying to advise her on a suitable cocktail.'

Charles Barnes tutted. 'If Miss Shaw wants any advice she will come to me. You go and serve the old gentleman over there. He looks thirsty.' With a nod of his head, he indicated a burly be-whiskered man who at once caught Chalky's eye and beckoned.

Chalky rolled his eyes. 'Must I?'

'Remember your wife and kids.'

'Oh, I do!'

Fixing a friendly smile to his face he moved away in the direction of his next customer.

Hester said, 'That was unkind, Mr Barnes.'

'I hope you'll forgive me.'

'I'm sure I will. He doesn't look old enough to have a family.' Goodness, she thought. Am I flirting with this man? How ridiculous.

'He made an early start. Married at twenty, regretted it at twenty-one. Not like me. No wife. No kids.'

'And no lady friend?' The words slipped out unbidden. Hester was appalled. Stop this, she warned herself. You're making a fool of yourself. You have absolutely no interest in this man or his friends.

'No special lady, if that's what you mean. So, now, if there's anything I can get for you . . .'

Hester took a deep breath and let it out while she made an effort to take her own advice. *This stops right now.*

'I was going to order a glass of orange juice.' She softened the words with a smile. 'I hope you're not also going to try and sell me a cocktail instead.'

'Maybe tomorrow,' he said, winking. 'No pretty young lady should travel on the *Mauretania*'s maiden voyage without trying one of our cocktails.' He moved smoothly away, unaffected by the ship's movement.

Hester felt the faint vibration from the engine room and was aware of a distinct lightening of spirit. Blow Mrs Carradine! she thought. She can be as awkward as she likes.

I shall still have some free time and I intend to enjoy myself. She felt like a young girl let out of school and then felt guilty. Being with Alexander was a permanent constraint, but that was not his fault. He could only be with her when work and his home life permitted and she understood that he had meetings to attend which occasionally lasted well into the night. They could never venture outside the flat together in case they were recognized, and even when she was alone, she did not feel free. She was constantly afraid of meeting someone she knew – an old friend, perhaps – who might ask her difficult questions about her present situation or ask for her address so that they could 'pop in' and see her. Casual friendships Alexander had forbidden because he hated the idea of finding someone there when he called in unannounced.

As she sipped her orange juice and watched Charles Barnes mingling with the other customers, she realized with a start that here on the *Mauretania*, if she discounted Edith Carradine, she was unknown and could move anywhere she liked without fear of being recognized or embarrassed. She could sit in the library, stroll on deck or scan the shelves of the on-board newsagent in search of a suitable magazine. She could then sit and read it in a sheltered corner of the deck, with a rug over her knees to keep her warm.

There was no one to point the finger. Yes! she thought, growing bold. Tomorrow I will choose my first cocktail.

With a faint smile on her lips, Hester plucked the list of cocktails from the table and gave it her whole attention.

The night passed smoothly as the ship's bow cut through the cold grey water on her way to Queenstown in Ireland. Twelve and a half hours later she docked, to the delight of her crew and those passengers who appreciated the speed she had maintained. At this rate, they told each other, the *Mauretania* might well equal the *Lusitania*'s speed record and that would be a matter for huge rejoicing as a friendly rivalry already existed between the two sister ships.

For a while Hester and her employer stood at the ship's rail with other passengers and watched the huge sacks of received mail being hauled upwards by winches. Once in New York it would be sorted and sent on its way, while mail destined for Great Britain would be taken on board.

A smart middle-aged man standing next to Edith Carradine turned to them, introduced himself as Dwight Leonard and asked how they had slept. 'It was a good run down,' he said, with a noticeable twang which immediately labelled him as an American, even if his name had not immediately done so. 'Cunard can be proud of her new ship. Yes, ma'am! This company doesn't cut corners. No expense spared on this vessel. Mind you, we still have to see how she copes with the Atlantic. The sea can sure be rough at this time of year, but the *Mauretania* will take it on the chin.' His laugh was a loud, proud bellow which made the two women smile. His face changed. 'But that can slow us down. That's the only problem. Nothing else to worry about on a vessel like this. You can rest easy. Yes, sirree! I slept like a baby last night. How about you two ladies?'

Before Hester could reply, Edith said frostily, 'We went to bed early and slept well enough, thank you.' Hester realized that she was not enjoying the man's well-intentioned conversation.

Undeterred he continued. 'Not that we need to break any records. The *Lusitania* has already snatched the Blue Riband from the Germans.' He laughed and Hester joined him, but Edith stared grimly ahead, saying nothing.

Below them the relentless activity proceeded at what appeared to be a snail's pace. Passengers were boarding – men carrying hand luggage, women with young children, elderly people helping each other up the gangway and disabled people in wheelchairs being pushed up by sturdy crew members.

The man said, 'Did you folks know we took on bullion back in Liverpool?'

Edith finally showed an interest. 'Do you mean *gold* bullion?'

'Indeed I do, ma'am. Twelve tons of it, so they say. Twelve tons of pure gold! Now, doesn't that give pause for thought?'

Hester said, 'A very expensive ballast!' This brought another bellow from Leonard, but Edith had once more relapsed into silence.

'Take a lot of slaving in a creek in California to pan that kind of gold! My granddaddy did a spell there back in '49 and thought himself lucky to end the day with half an ounce of the darned stuff. All he got at the end was a bad back and empty pockets, but he had to try. They all did. Some won out, the rest didn't.'

'It must have been exciting,' said Hester.

'You bet. Hard labour, too, but it was an adventure.' Making a final effort with Edith Carradine, he gave her a smile and said, 'It's a pity you turned in so early last night, ma'am. There was one helluva fireworks display as we passed the New Brighton pier – to wish the ship Godspeed.'

Hester expressed disappointment that she had missed it.

'Very over-rated, in my opinion,' Edith said. 'All that noise. I'm afraid I value my rest. In my state of health a regular and early bedtime is essential.'

Hester recalled what Alexander had told her and wondered what these ailments amounted to. Was her health really at risk or was it all in her mind? Maybe she should enquire. If Mrs Carradine were ever taken ill on board, her travelling companion should be able to offer some insights into the problem. If the old lady regularly took tablets, Hester ought to have some idea what they were and when she should take them and what the dosage should be. She thought about the ship's doctor and wondered how well qualified he was. For the first time she realized that being a travelling companion had its responsibilities and decided to approach her employer on the subject of her health at the first suitable opportunity.

Almost as though she had read Hester's mind, the old lady turned abruptly from the rail. 'We must go inside, Miss Shaw. I've seen quite enough. This cold damp weather is bad for the lungs and mine are weak enough already. We will go for breakfast and discover what sort of kitchen the *Mauretania* has produced. You can always tell by the toast. A decent kitchen will offer diners toast that is well-browned but not burnt.' With a brief nod to their American companion, she walked briskly from the rail towards the companionway.

After a moment, Hester said, 'It was nice talking to you, Mr Leonard.'

He doffed his hat. 'Your aunt, perhaps?' he asked, raising his eyebrows.

'Hardly,' Hester said. 'I'm her travelling companion. In other words, Mrs Carradine is my employer.'

As she hurried away from him in pursuit of the old lady, she thought, I'm actually being dutiful now! How terrible! But Mrs Carradine was paying for the trip, she reminded herself, and was entitled to her money's worth.

Fortunately breakfast – served in the dining room; an elaborate area built on three levels – satisfied Edith's high ideals in most respects. The porridge was free of lumps, the milk was fresh, the stewed apples were just sharp enough and the toast was the right shade of brown. Her only grumble resulted from the fact that they had to share a table with four other people. These were a mother and her twelve-year-old daughter and an elderly couple. As these four had turned up earlier for their breakfast, Hester and Edith only shared the table for twenty minutes and, to Hester's relief, her employer managed to restrain herself from making any critical remarks. However, as soon as they had left the dining room, Edith gave an exaggerated sigh of relief.

'What frightful people! I shall speak to the management. I had no idea when I chose the *Mauretania* that we should be forced to share a table with strangers.'

'I thought they were very pleasant. The girl was very well behaved . . .'

'She was sullen.'

'I thought her shy.'

'Believe me, Miss Shaw, I have two daughters of my own. The girl was sullen. Boys of that age are also sullen – with the exception of my nephew, who was perfectly capable of conversing with adults from a young age.' She spread marmalade on her toast and cut it carefully. 'And the mother's accent! Goodness knows where they hail from.'

Refusing to be drawn into the attack, Hester said, 'It

sounded like a West Country accent to me. Maybe Devon or Cornwall. The other two were cheerful souls.'

Edith gave her a withering look. 'Mr and Mrs Gutteridge? They never stopped talking, if that's what you mean by cheerful. Practically told us their life stories. So they run a successful grocery chain. It's of no interest to me. I'm not used to being bombarded with information over breakfast. It's bad for the digestive process. If we can't have a table to ourselves I shall write to Cunard and complain.'

Hester's mind was working fast. 'I'm sure you could have your breakfast in your cabin if you wished for privacy. The stewardess could probably see to it for you.'

This would release her from her employer's company for the best part of an hour each morning. Edith's company was already proving wearing, Hester reflected.

Concentrating on her boiled egg, she tried not to show her enthusiasm for the idea. She said innocently, 'I think you're right, Mrs Carradine. Doubtless many other like-minded people are making similar arrangements.'

Mollified by her companion's encouragement, and beginning to think it her own idea, Edith finally left the table and went in search of Mrs Pontings, leaving her travelling companion to enjoy a second slice of toast in peace. She was about to leave the dining room when one of the waiters came to her table.

'Miss Shaw?' he asked.

She nodded.

'I've been asked to give you this.' He handed her a small envelope and hurried away.

Startled, Hester opened the envelope with fingers that shook slightly. Who would send her a note? Unless it was from Mr Barnes . . . It was!

If you fancy a drink later and need an escort, I'll be at the Verandah Café at eleven tonight. Charlie Barnes.

'Oh, no,' she whispered as her insides tightened with a mixture of excitement and fear. 'No!' she insisted, as her pulse quickened. An assignation with one of the ship's stewards?

It was quite out of the question. Edith Carradine had made it clear that she was not to become involved. No shipboard romance. That was how she had put it. And there was Alexander to consider. Not that he had extracted any such promises, but there was such a thing as loyalty. 'Quite impossible,' she muttered and crumpled up the note impatiently.

But a drink sounded harmless enough. Probably all the crew members were trying to find a woman to flirt with to brighten up the crossing. Was that all it was? Maybe all the single women were hoping for a mild flirtation to while away the time as they crossed the Atlantic. Perhaps it was normal. Perhaps she was being paranoid.

Only one quick drink. She told herself she was making a big deal out of nothing.

Adrenaline was coursing through her at the idea of a late-night meeting with Charlie Barnes, but, perversely, she wished he had not written to her in this way. She was probably ten years older than him so why hadn't he picked on someone else? Someone younger and unattached. The ship was full of pretty young women, all eager for romance. It was written on their bright faces and the provocative way they tossed their hair and glanced beguilingly from beneath their little hats. By comparison, Hester felt quite dowdy. So what was Mr Barnes playing at?

She smoothed the rumpled note and read it again, trying to imagine what had been in his mind while he was writing it. Was it some kind of joke? Maybe his friend had dared him to do it. Or they might have made a bet on whether or not she was the kind of woman who would be flattered into accepting an invitation from a stranger.

Throwing down her table napkin in frustration, Hester stood up and hurried from the dining room, looking neither left nor right for fear that someone might be watching for her reaction. Unable to face Edith while her mind was in turmoil, she went out on deck and stood with some other passengers at the rail, staring blankly at the busy scene. Soon after eleven she knew they would weigh anchor and leave Ireland and head out into the Atlantic for a four or five day crossing.

What would happen, she wondered, if she failed to turn up at the Verandah Café? He might take offence and ignore her in future, making sure that she would see him being charming to another woman. But suppose she *did* go there and he stayed away. Was it just a test of some kind? Coming straight from the dining room, Hester was wearing no coat or jacket and the wind was cold. She wrapped her arms round herself, shivering inside as well as outside. If she was honest, she *wanted* to meet Mr Barnes, but common sense warned her against it.

But I like him, she thought. He was like no one she had ever met before. Breezy and seemingly uncomplicated, he was everything that Hester was not – but would like to be. And so unlike Alexander who took her for granted and rarely paid her a compliment – except the one of sheltering her from the hardships of life. She owed so much to Alexander, she thought with a resigned sigh. Had she, after all, made a mistake in allowing him to snatch her from the slippery path on which she was about to embark when they met?

The moment was engraved on her memory. Expelled from the house that had been her home and employment for three years, she walked away with tears in her eyes, the bitter accusations still ringing in her ears. Her last glimpse of the family had been little Davina's frightened face, pressed against the window of the front room. Amelia Cartwright had refused to believe that Hester had not encouraged her husband, and Clive himself had denied that he intended any impropriety. Only Clive and Hester knew how badly he had behaved towards her, invading her room, night after night, until in desperation Hester had asked his wife for a key. That had been a mistake because it had aroused Amelia's suspicions.

'I want you out of this house,' she had cried, her face white with anger and contempt. 'To think I trusted you. To think I allowed you to be with my daughter. I thought you were a respectable woman, but Clive tells me how you flaunted yourself. Oh, you disgust me. You can pack your bags and go . . . and don't you dare ask me for a reference! You call yourself a nanny, but you are no more than a . . .'

She choked on the words and turned away, tears rolling
down her face.

What exactly had Clive told her? Hester would never
know because he had kept well away until she had left the
house. Disgraced and with no reference, Hester had found
herself homeless and without the means to support herself.
She worked for a month as an assistant in a sweet shop,
but the wages had been insufficient to pay for her miserable lodgings and she had been forced to pawn some of
her clothes to make up the difference.

One dark winter evening, Hester had been spotted by
Alexander as she made her way along a street frequented
by fallen women. She had never admitted to herself her
reason for being there, but she had thought she might be
accosted by a passing gentleman. Stumbling on the cobbles,
however, she was thrown headlong and her inelegant fall
was seen by a gentleman passing the spot in a hansom cab.
Alexander had stopped, helped her to her feet and had given
her a sixpence to buy herself 'a hot pie'. As she stood at
the stall enjoying the luxury, he had returned. Apparently
impressed by what little dignity she retained, Alexander had
been attracted to her and the chance meeting led to a second
meeting and then to a relationship. When he suggested
renting a small flat where they could meet regularly, she
had gratefully accepted his offer.

Now she was facing another offer and she didn't know
what to do.

Three

The furious grey seas surprised many of the passengers as the ship left Ireland and headed into the Atlantic. The *Mauretania* began to react, pitching into the huge waves with a shock that sent tremors through the hull, or rolling from side to side, so that the passengers, both young and old, staggered drunkenly as they moved around the vast liner. At first people treated it as a joke and the children found it hilarious. As the hours wore on, however, the adults found it challenging, the older people grew wary of an accident and the children lost interest. Only the crew members moved easily round the ship, enjoying their superiority while handing out soothing comments.

'Don't worry, sir. You'll soon adjust,' or 'It's a matter of time, madam. By tomorrow you'll have your sea legs.' Neither was true. Most of the passengers would become queasy and lose their appetites while an unfortunate few would be seriously seasick and confined to their cabins.

To Hester's surprise, by lunchtime she was still feeling reasonably well and went into the dining room with Edith who, although slightly off-colour, refused to be cheated of a delicious meal which was included in the overall price of the trip. As they settled themselves at the unoccupied table, the old lady smiled triumphantly.

'Hah! Not up to it! I might have known.' She regarded the empty seats with satisfaction.

'Good afternoon, ladies.' The waiter smiled. 'How can we tempt you today?'

Edith picked up the menu and studied it without much interest.

Hester asked, 'It all looks wonderful. Can you recommend anything?'

He leaned over confidentially. 'The lentil soup is very good for lining the stomach, miss. Afterwards perhaps the lemon sole – that's very light – and, if you're still hungry, an ice cream is easily digested.'

'That's what I shall have then. Thank you.'

Edith was frowning. 'I'll have just the soup with some thin bread and butter. Brown bread, of course.'

He wrote busily. 'No main course?'

'I said "just the soup"!'

As soon as he had brought the soup, Edith toyed with it, apparently unwilling to eat it. She nibbled a triangle of brown bread and looked rather unhappy.

Feeling sorry for her, and to take her employer's mind off the ship's movement, Hester brought up the subject of the three dresses she was supposed to be altering.

'I had no idea you expected me to do some sewing,' she told her. 'I had to give up that line of work when my eyesight began to deteriorate. The problem—'

'Don't bother me with that now!' Edith took a spoonful of soup and swallowed it nervously.

'I just wanted you to understand. I'll do the best I—'

'What did I say?' Edith glared at her. 'I've other things on my mind.' She laid down her spoon and stood up. 'I don't feel too steady. You can help me back to my cabin.'

On the way out they were intercepted by the waiter and Hester informed him that she would be back shortly to finish her meal.

'I shall sit in my chair,' Edith informed her when they were back in her cabin. 'Put a glass of water beside me on the table and leave me to my own devices. I hate fuss. As long as I know you are next door, I shall be quite all right.'

Hester promised to return as soon as she had eaten and hurried back to the dining room. The twelve-year-old girl had now taken her place at the table and without her mother's presence, proved surprisingly talkative.

'Everyone calls me Elly or Nora which is nearly as bad,' she told Hester between mouthfuls. 'And I hate them both so please call me Eleanora – unless you want to call me Monique, which is a name I really like, only don't let my parents hear you or they'll blame me because it's French and they think it's silly because I'm not French. Could you pass the salt, please?'

Puzzled, Hester did so. The girl poured some on to the table, took up a pinch and tossed it over her shoulder.

'Isn't your mother hungry?'

'No. She's been sick and the stewardess brought her a tablet to take and I know she won't take it because she says tablets aren't natural and we should let our bodies deal with it naturally because it's not an illness, it is only because of the ship's motion. If I get sick, I shall take a tablet. They're made of dimenhydrinate in case you need one. And I can spell that, in case you're wondering.' She took a gulp of air and studied the menu.

'Thank you, er . . . Monique. I'll remember that.'

'I shall have the duck pate –' the girl glanced up at the waiter – 'and the roast beef and then the meringues – are they those white crunchy things?'

'Meringue, miss, is a crunchy mix of egg white and—'

'Egg white? Really? Ugh! I'll have apple pie instead.'

Hester's lemon sole arrived and she thanked the waiter. The girl's food arrived and the meal passed amicably. Hester was beginning to relax. Monique alias Eleanor amused her even though her presence reminded her of the fact that she would probably never have children of her own. Alexander, childless, had once talked about the family he had wanted, but lately, as Hester grew older and Marcia lingered on, the subject had been avoided. A shame, because she thought Alexander Waring would make a good father.

After lunch, she let herself in to check on Edith and found her asleep on the bed. Obviously she had agreed to take a tablet. Knowing that she might be needed any time, Hester bought herself a magazine and settled in her own cabin to read it. Try as she would, however, she could not concentrate, but allowed her thoughts to stray to the crumpled note in her purse. She had decided not to accept the invitation, but was regretting her decision more and more as time passed. Around five o'clock, Mrs Pontings knocked on the door to check on Mrs Carradine.

'I gave her a seasickness pill and I expect she's sleeping, but when she wakes she should drink a glass of water as her mouth might feel a bit dry.'

'I understand she's travelled before so she should know what to expect, but thank you for the advice.'

'They do rather knock you out, those tablets, but anything is better than feeling queasy all the time. She might need another to get her through the night, we'll see.'

'Are we expecting a rough night then?'

Mrs Pontings rolled her eyes. 'Oh, yes, dear! Very rough, I'm afraid. The Atlantic is hardly ever calm and rarely so in winter. But we're in good hands. We've got a good captain and that's the main thing.'

As soon as she had gone, Hester took the note from her purse and reread it. Suddenly she pressed it to her lips. More than anything she wanted to be at the Verandah Café to meet Charles Barnes. Just thinking about it made her feel younger than her years. A charming, fine-looking man was eager for her company, and that made her feel alive for the first time in years. She had made up her mind not to go, but she couldn't resist imagining how the meeting might go if she had decided to accept. She wondered what she would have worn. And who else would be there? Other crew members? Young married couples, perhaps. Or honeymooners. Older men travelling to New York on business, dallying in the bar late at night, hoping to 'pick up' an unaccompanied woman. Single women hoping to be picked up. She had heard that high-class courtesans used to travel on the liners in search of rich patrons. It all sounded wonderfully romantic and risqué and exciting . . . and she would not be there. She sighed as she imagined herself standing close to her escort, or sitting at a table, heads close as they chatted intimately.

'Oh, Alexander!' she groaned. He was her conscience and in a way she was grateful. Without him she knew she would be hurrying to the Verandah Café bar as soon as the big hand of her small travel clock showed eleven o'clock. Instead, she would probably be fast asleep by then for she had made up her mind to go to bed at ten. Charles Barnes would no doubt be annoyed to be 'jilted' in front of his friends, but he would quickly find another woman to take her place.

As though a voice had called her, Hester awoke later that night, sat up and peered at the clock. Twenty past eleven! Without a second's hesitation she scrambled desperately from the bed, splashed cold water on to her face and washed her hands. She ran a comb through her hair, pulled on her best skirt and prettiest blouse, slipped her feet into some shoes, snatched up her purse and let herself out of the cabin. Her heart was pounding. She would be too late. He would not wait. He would never speak to her again and it was her own fault.

'You coward!' she said out loud.

Turning a corner she almost collided with a stout gentleman who recoiled with a muttered, ''Pon my soul!'

The passageways were eerily quiet as she made her way with difficulty, lurching from side to side with the roll of the ship.

Wait for me, she thought. I'm coming!

What a fool she had been, too timid by far. Where was the wrong in meeting a friend for a late-night drink? What harm could she come to? Charles Barnes was a member of the crew. He was hardly going to molest her and disappear into the darkness, never to be found again. He had a job to do. He was not going to risk his career in any way by bad behaviour for fear she report him to his superiors.

She stopped suddenly and looked around her. Where was she? Surely she should be there by now – or had she taken a wrong turn?

'Please,' she asked nobody in particular. What on earth was the time? His friends would tease him, but she was on her way. A stewardess appeared carrying a pile of towels and Hester asked for directions.

'You're on the wrong level,' said the stewardess. 'Go left and then right, then up one level in the elevator. Turn right and you're there.' As Hester thanked her and turned to retrace her steps, she added, 'Don't worry. He'll wait. They always do!'

Hester was in the elevator when it struck her. Suppose she rushed in and . . . and he had grown tired of waiting and . . . and she found him with someone else. He wouldn't find it difficult. Leaning back against the panelled wall of the elevator, she took several deep breaths.

Don't even think it, she told herself. Calm down or else you will look desperate and people will pity you. Think of an excuse for your late arrival. Or pretend you did not notice the time . . . Say you were finishing a letter . . . or delayed by your companion.

Five minutes later she saw the words Verandah Café and almost cried with relief. Slowing down, she managed to fix what she hoped was a casual smile on her face and stepped inside. Despite the ship's movement, the room was packed with happy people, some sitting round the small tables, others standing along the bar. Some were even leaning on it for support! Whenever the ship rolled further than usual there was a concerted shriek followed by laughter. Hester envied them. So young and so carefree. They seemed like people from another planet. The lights were low and a small group of musicians played popular ballads. Searching among the crowd, she caught sight of Chalky White, who was with a group of young men and women. One look told her that they had already had a little too much to drink. There was no sign of Charles Barnes and her hopes began to fade.

'Over here!' It was Chalky who had spotted her. At least he seemed friendly enough, she thought, as she threaded her way between the tables and swaying crowds with murmured apologies. He had his arm through that of a young blue-eyed woman with a tumble of fair curls whom he introduced as Nurse Dulcie Anson. She was looking up at him adoringly, but when Hester reached him, he put an arm round her as well and gave her a brief hug. Despite her recently made plans, she found herself stammering excuses for her lateness. He shook his head.

'He thought you weren't coming, that's all. He was a bit cut up.'

'Cut up?'

'Yes. He's taken a real shine to you. Poor old Charlie! He's not used to being "stood up". Dented his pride, if you see what I mean.'

'Stood up? Oh, no! I didn't mean to . . . I was delayed by Mrs Carradine . . .' She couldn't quite manage to finish the lie. Had he actually been upset by her absence?

Freddy, the barman, leaned across. 'You Miss Shaw by any chance?'

Hester nodded.

Chalky said, 'Better late than never! A cracker, isn't she, our Miss Shaw?'

The young women regarded her critically as if assessing the truth of this. Hester felt her cheeks burn. Envying the peachy complexions and bright eyes around her, Hester realized she must be at least ten years older than most of them, if not more. Mortified, she hoped she wasn't old enough to be anyone's mother!

'I'm Freddy to my friends,' the barman told her with a broad wink. 'Charlie said, if you *did* turn up, to give you a cocktail of your choice – from him!' He grinned. 'What's it to be?'

Egged on by Chalky and his friends, Hester settled on a Manhattan. She sipped it dutifully but couldn't enjoy it. Nor could she join in the light-hearted banter of the crowd. They seemed so carefree that she felt old by comparison. Old and dull. When the music became romantic, one or two couples began to dance, and she made her excuses and left.

Finally finding her cabin again she let herself in and sank down on to the bed. Never again, she vowed silently. You are not one of them. You can't expect to be accepted. You will never fit in. She pulled off her clothes and tossed them on to the chair, neglecting to fold them, regardless of how they would look in the morning. They would be talking about her, she thought, and laughing at her behind her back. Or worse, they would already have forgotten her existence. What would Chalky say about her when he next saw Charlie? That she looked like a fish out of water.

Stick to what you do best, she urged herself as she lay

in bed and stared at the ceiling. You're a travelling companion . . . and a kept woman. The mistress of a middle-aged man with a wife who is going to live for ever. She got out of bed again and cleaned her teeth and climbed back into bed. *Forget tonight. Forget Mr Barnes. Count your blessings.* She laughed aloud. How many times had her mother told her that . . . But she did count them. She had her health. She had Alexander. She had enough to eat and a roof over her head. She was crossing in style on the *Mauretania* and soon she would be in New York where anything might happen. She closed her eyes and waited for sleep to claim her.

The crew's quarters were a far cry from those of the first-class passengers or even the cheapest accommodation favoured by the emigrants, but the food in the dining room was reasonable and plentiful and the hundreds of hungry young men and women who made up the staff, ate well most of the time. The seasoned crew were never seasick, but the newcomers took time to become accustomed to the rolling of the ship. At breakfast the next day, as most of the *Mauretania*'s crew were seasoned by virtue of duty on previous vessels, the behaviour of the seas did nothing to dampen their spirits, and the conversation was lively.

It was a vast room, the lights already lit because of the dark November sky outside, but steam rising from the tea urns gave the place a cosy, contained feeling and enticing cooking smells added to its cheerful atmosphere. On this particular Monday morning, the weather was growing worse as strong winds and gigantic seas battered the *Mauretania*, but few people took any notice of the forecast. It was time for breakfast, a time to 'stoke up' for the gruelling day ahead. Chalky White, short on sleep, but still cheerful, tucked into his egg and bacon, mopped up the juices and then wiped the plate with a thick slice of buttered bread. He grinned when his friend sat down next to him with his own breakfast.

'Cheer up, Charlie! It might never happen.'

'Stow it!' Charlie reached for salt and pepper. His usual

sunny expression was missing and he glanced at his friend irritably. 'Don't say it,' he warned.

All around them, the benches were filling up. There was a choice of menu and some were eating kippers. The noise was tremendous as voices rose above the clatter of knives and forks.

'Don't say what?'

'That you warned me. That you were right.'

The man opposite asked, 'What's up with heem?' He was Italian.

'Mind your own business, Stefano.' Charlie glared at him across the table.

Chalky reached for a fourth slice of bread and butter and took a large bite out of it. 'What's it worth . . .?' he began, 'for some good news? Ten bob?'

'Ten bob? You're mad!' Charlie began to eat.

'All right then, five bob? Two?'

'Sod off, you silly devil!'

'Good news . . . about Miss Shaw.' He grinned.

Charlie gulped down a half chewed mouthful and almost choked. 'What about her?' He looked round as though expecting to see Miss Shaw hovering somewhere.

Chalky beamed. 'She turned up looking for you but you . . .'

'She turned up?' His eyes brightened at once. 'You're not having me on? Miss Shaw turned up?'

'Yep. All dollied up, smelling of roses – or violets or whatever women smell of these days. Not a patch on my little nurse, mind you, but she looked very pretty.' He launched into the details.

Charlie's appetite suddenly returned and he began to enjoy his breakfast. 'I knew she'd turn up!'

'That's not what you said last night when you left in a sulk.'

'Me sulk? I was tired, that's all!'

'Tired my eye. You were as sick as a parrot. I swear there were tears in your eyes.'

'You need your eyes tested, chum.' A broad smile lit up Charlie's face. 'What? You thought I didn't think she was

coming? Course I did. I left her that drink with Freddy,
didn't I? I knew she was interested.'

'You were fed up to the teeth because she didn't show.
Admit it.'

'Please yourself. So why was she so late? Did she say?
Did she look sorry that I wasn't there? Did she give you a
message for me?' He gulped down steaming tea and gasped.
'Christ! That's hot!'

'Comes from a hot place and . . . No, she didn't leave
you a message. But she chose a Manhattan. Forced it
down like it was poison, but tried to make out she liked
it. The truth is she was like a fish out of water. We were
all nice to her, but she was nervous. On edge. She's a
funny one.'

Charlie beamed. 'Nothing funny about Miss Shaw, Chalky.
She's just a cut above the rest. You wouldn't appreciate a
woman like that.' He was rapidly recovering his confidence.
Miss Shaw had accepted his invitation. Miss Shaw was interested in him. 'She has class, Chalky. Class.'

'I thought you said she was a travelling companion. A
paid companion. What's classy about that?'

Charlie paused to consider. 'Probably down on her luck.
Rich Daddy went broke and shot himself and she's forced
to work for a living. You know how it is.'

Stefano showed some interest. 'Who ees shot heemself?'

'Who's talking to you?' Charlie blew on his tea and sipped
it cautiously.

Chalky stood up. 'I'm off. Word from above is that the
weather's getting worse. It's going to be a tough day for
the pampered darlings! All being "icky" and little piles of
sawdust everywhere. They pay all that money just to be
thrown around and lose their appetites.'

Stefano laughed. 'Tell us something we didn't know!'

Charlie simply smiled. His day was going to be brilliant,
he thought. The world was a wonderful place. Miss Shaw
was interested.

When Hester went into the next cabin around nine thirty, she
found Mrs Carradine nibbling a small chicken sandwich. She

was sitting up in bed wearing an expensive crocheted bed-jacket and seemed reasonably restored.

'Mrs Bunting brought it,' she told Hester, indicating the sandwich. 'She says it's the very best thing when one is recovering from any sickness. Because it's bland, you see, and light, and easily digested. Sit down and tell me that we are going to have better weather today.'

Hester obeyed. 'I can't agree about the weather,' she said. 'I haven't been along to reception and haven't heard the forecast. But you look much better. Perhaps you've got your sea legs.'

'Mrs Bunting – oh, no, it's Pontings – says if the weather doesn't improve I shouldn't venture far for fear of a fall. Her brother says it's not uncommon for elderly people to break an arm or a leg because we have such brittle bones. So I shan't be going far. I take it you've had your breakfast.'

'I did, but I shared the table with the girl. No one else appeared. Now, how can I be of help this morning?' She crossed her fingers and hoped her employer had forgotten the dress alterations.

Mrs Carradine seemed to be in a better mood. 'I fancy a little conversation – or would you care to read to me from the Bible. I used to read from the Good Book for my husband when he was ill. In his latter years he suffered with his eyes and reading small print tired him.'

Hester chose conversation. 'I visited the Verandah Café,' she confessed, leaving out the lateness of the hour. 'I thought you might enjoy it, but in fact it was a disappointment. It was entirely inhabited by bright young things and rather noisy.'

'Did you stay long?'

'No. I had a glass of orange juice and then left. I don't think you'd enjoy it.'

'Was there music?'

'Yes, a few people danced.'

'Danced? What time was this?'

'Early evening.' Hester was now wishing she had never mentioned the Verandah Café. She waited for the next question which would no doubt inspire another lie, but her employer had grown tired of the subject.

'Tell me something about yourself,' she suggested. 'My nephew was terribly vague. How did you two meet?'

The shock sent a shiver up Hester's spine. She must be very careful. Edith Carradine might be elderly, but she was certainly not slow-witted, and Hester could imagine her pouncing on any slip. She wondered desperately what Alexander had told her.

'Cat got your tongue?'

'No . . . that is . . . I don't quite know where to start.'

'Start with your parents, then.' Edith settled back comfortably. 'What did your father do? What sort of education have you had?'

This was safer, Hester thought. She could tell the truth.

'My father was in shipping – exports and imports. The company owned four ships. He was away quite often, travelling as part of his job – in Greece mostly.'

'Ah! Then presumably there was money for your education.'

'Yes. I was sent to boarding school in Sussex when I was nine.' She didn't explain how unhappy she had been.

Edith frowned. 'Then why did you become a dressmaker? I would have expected you to make a good marriage.' Seeing that Hester hesitated, she pressed her. 'Did something go wrong? Was that it?'

'Yes.' At least she could tell this part of her background. 'It was embezzlement. One of the directors went to prison for his part in the scandal. My father was not involved and was cleared of any part in the deception, but he never recovered from the blow. My mother says it was the shock that killed him. A heart attack when he was forty-five.'

She could still hear the tick of the clock as she waited outside her parents' bedroom where his body lay in the open coffin. She had to lean into it to kiss the cold hand and whisper a 'goodbye'. She could smell the burning candle wax from the four black candles in their tall brass candlesticks, one of which stood at each corner of the elaborate coffin. She was thirteen years old.

'My dear, how positively frightful!'

Edith's voice jerked Hester back to the present.

'My mother married again – a farmer in Hertfordshire. Life was very different after that.' The only good to come out of the second marriage, she reflected, was that she had been taken away from the hated boarding school.

She recalled her mother's face as she'd left her nine-year-old daughter in the care of one of the prefects on her first day at boarding school.

'If you aren't happy, Hester darling, you must write and tell us and we'll take you away.'

Hester had written countless letters, but later her mother insisted that the school had never forwarded them. Hester had felt utterly betrayed.

'Well! That is interesting.' Edith was regarding her with astonishment. 'How are the mighty fallen!' she said tactlessly. 'Was the second marriage fruitful?'

'No. I'm an only child.'

'So, who taught you to sew?'

'I suppose I picked it up as I went along.'

Edith was startled. 'You picked it up? My dear, dressmaking is an *art*. Not something you "pick up"! My last dressmaker was wonderfully talented. Show her a picture and she could copy the garment perfectly. She would take my measurements, draw out a paper pattern, cut the material and make it up! She had been properly trained.'

Hester hurried to correct the slip. 'I daresay I am more a seamstress, but . . . but I have cut out and made dresses. My mother didn't want me to be away from home because she was very lonely and anxious after Papa died, before she got married again. She helped me at first, but then I gradually taught myself.' More lies. When she returned to Alexander, she decided, she might well throttle him! 'I wouldn't compare myself to your last dressmaker.'

'I should hope not,' Edith huffed. 'And that's how you met my nephew, Alexander?'

Hester took a chance. 'We've never actually met – at least, he may have been among the company, but I don't recall ever being introduced. I think he probably heard of

me through a friend's wife.' Don't ask me her name, she
begged silently. 'I did some sewing for her. I cut up a ball
gown to make dresses for her twin girls.'

If the old lady queried this, she would pretend that
Alexander had been confused. Holding her breath, she
wondered how she could change the direction in which this
conversation was going. Perhaps she should suggest a walk
– but the ship was rolling heavily so that was hardly an
enticing prospect. In desperation she said, 'Shall I read to
you now? I always feel the psalms are very soothing.'

But Edith was not listening. Her mind had taken her in
a different direction. 'So you haven't met my nephew – my
sister Imogen's boy. You'd like him, I think. He's a
gentleman.' She sighed. 'He married a poor little thing.
Marcia Harcourt she was then. Not poor financially, but
poor in spirit and entirely lacking in energy of any kind.
She seems to dream her way through life, imagining that
she is ill. Her mind seems to drift at times, as though her
thoughts are elsewhere. I think she'd *like* to be ill, if the
truth were known. She loves to lie about on the chaise
longue and have people wait on her hand and foot.' She
shook her head. 'Poor Alexander. She must be a great trial
to him, but he never complains. That's what I mean by a
gentleman . . . If you think you have something wrong,
demand to see a specialist, I told her. That's what I do.
That's what I'm doing now, isn't it?'

'Indeed you are. We must pray he can help you.'

'Well, naturally he can help me. I'm told Mr Stafford is
an excellent heart man and his techniques and treatments
are far advanced compared with those in England. So, that's
where I'm going. Alexander suggests his wife should seek
a second opinion, abroad if necessary, no expense spared.
But she refuses.'

'But if she really is ill . . . she might die. That would
be—'

'Die? Of course she won't die. She's not even ill. She's
a malingerer! Poor Alexander.'

This was not at all what Hester had wanted to hear.
Alexander was promising to marry her when Marcia died,

but from what she was now hearing, she could expect a long wait. All her doubts resurfaced. Would he then prefer someone much younger who could give him a family? If she were to have a child with Alexander, their marriage would have to be sooner rather than later. Dare she raise the question with him on her return? She desperately needed to know but dreaded his answer. Suppose he said honestly that he had no immediate expectations of being a widower. What would she do? Leave him? Would he be prepared for her to go? Did he *want* it to happen that way so that he would not have to end the relationship himself?

With an effort Hester abandoned that line of thinking. Daringly, she asked, 'What is he like, your nephew? Apart from being a gentleman.' It would be interesting, she thought, to hear his aunt's opinion.

'Alexander is quite charming, very good-looking, due quite shortly for another promotion – and is very devoted to his foolish wife. A lesser man would have given up on her, but he is patience personified.' She smiled suddenly. 'As a boy he always loved his Aunt Edith. I used to take him to feed the ducks in Regent's Park and to run around with his hoop. I have a photograph of him somewhere in his little sailor suit. He was sweet natured, never a bully. He always abhorred cruelty and injustice.' She paused in thought. 'He once came home from school with a bruised eye and his parents were shocked to discover he'd been fighting the school bully! Defending a weaker boy. That about sums him up.'

'He sounds a nephew to be proud of.'

So Alexander was due another promotion, thought Hester. He had kept that to himself . . . and he was devoted to Marcia! She was beginning to doubt that she knew him at all.

'Indeed he is. He's the only one I approve of. My younger sister Imogen has another son, Bartholomew, but he is a bit of a wastrel, and they have sent him abroad to friends in South Africa to work. Always a sickly child, they were always too soft with poor Barty!' She shrugged. 'Not like Alexander. As he grew up he made up his mind to enter the police force, much against his parents' wishes. I encouraged him though. He wanted to do some good in the world. He's very high-minded and he's worked his way up by sheer hard work and a determination to succeed. Promotion is hard to come by in the police force. Too many men chasing too few opportunities.'

Hester was regretting that she had pried into Alexander's life. Depressed, she decided she had heard more than enough. 'Shall I read to you now?'

When Edith agreed and reached for her Bible, Hester didn't know whether to be pleased or sorry but at least she need not tell any more lies.

Four

It was after two in the afternoon when Charlie found Miss
Shaw. She was in the reading room, surrounded by elderly
ladies and ruddy-faced men with thinning white hair. The
women were reading, but most of the men were enjoying
the sight of Miss Shaw – and who wouldn't be. Charlie's
heart thumped as he crossed the room towards her. She was
wearing a soft tweed suit in grey, and a white collar showed
at the neckline. Slim and elegant, he thought.

He bent over and whispered, 'May I speak with you
outside, Miss Shaw?'

Startled, she nodded and he fancied he saw a faint blush
illuminate her face. She marked the page and left the book
on the small sofa where she had been sitting. As soon as
they were outside Charlie closed the door behind them and,
checking that no one else was around, pulled her close and
kissed her before she had time to know what he intended.

For a moment, she stared at him, shocked and embarrassed.

He said, 'If I've offended you, I expect you'll slap my
face! And I'll deserve it.' He had expected her to return the
kiss with fervour – he had hoped the young woman would
be thrilled and excited – but the expression on her face set
alarm bells ringing. 'I apologize, Miss Shaw,' he told her
desperately. 'Will you forgive me?'

It occurred to him that he had misinterpreted the situation, but if she didn't want to be kissed, why on earth had
she turned up at the Verandah Café? And suppose she was
really offended and reported him to one of the ship's officers. Fear was almost unknown to Charlie, but he felt a
prickle along his spine. 'I thought, Miss Shaw . . . that is,

I think I've made a mistake,' he stammered as his stomach churned.

Watching closely, he saw the shock fade to be replaced by confusion.

'No, Mr Barnes. It's I who should apologize.' Her voice shook slightly. 'I didn't mean to meet you last night – it didn't seem prudent – but then . . .' She shrugged. 'Somehow I changed my mind at the last minute and I knew that I wanted to see you after all. I rushed along and got lost and then, when I found the café, you weren't there and the barman said you'd paid for a drink so I couldn't not drink it without offending you, and . . . Oh, Charlie! I shouldn't have . . . have led you on.'

'But I wanted you to!' Hope flared suddenly. She had called him Charlie! He knew it was a mistake on her part – a slip of the tongue – but it thrilled him, anyway. 'I mean, I shouldn't have sent the note,' he told her. 'I should have asked you properly.'

But the reason he had not done so was in case she refused to his face. He wasn't used to rejection. He went on earnestly. 'I just can't stop thinking about you and wishing . . .'

Her eyes were large and intense and he struggled not to kiss her again.

'Mr Barnes, I – I don't think I'm at all suitable. For you, I mean – or anyone else for that matter. My situation is . . . complicated but there are plenty of other young women. I don't think it should be me because . . . I have attachments – of a kind. There is someone at home.'

'You're not married. You aren't wearing a wedding ring! Are you secretly engaged? Is that it?' Suddenly he realized just how much he wanted the answer to be negative.

'Not exactly, but . . . You really mustn't ask all these questions, Mr Barnes. You're embarrassing me.'

'Please call me Charlie.'

'Oh, no, I couldn't!'

The more she protested, the more he longed to throw his arms around her, but he fought off the urge and tried to remain reasonable. Women never held him at arm's length for long but this one . . . He was becoming worried, but before he could rustle up a more convincing reason why she should forget whoever was in England, the library door opened inwards and she almost fell into the arms of a plump bearded gentleman.

He cried, 'Whoa there, madam! You'll be sending up my blood pressure.' Laughing, he waved away her apologies and winked at Charlie before lurching his way along the passageway. Charlie had Miss Shaw to himself once more. But now they were both laughing at the incident and the earlier coolness seemed to have vanished. She looked beautiful when she smiled, he thought, his heart contracting a little.

'Could we start again?' he asked.

'Why not?' Her smile broadened. 'Good afternoon, Mr Barnes. What is the weather forecast for the rest of the day?'

'Not promising, Miss Shaw. The gale's getting worse. Some waves are breaking right over the ship and a few windows have been broken on the upper decks.'

'Really?' Her smile faded. 'Are we in any danger, Mr Barnes?'

He put a hand over his heart. 'If we are, then I will be at your service. If the ship sinks I shall rescue you.'

'Can you swim then, Mr Barnes?'

'Swim? Certainly not, miss! But I'm a very quick learner.' He closed his eyes in case his intensity frightened her away. With his eyes still closed, he said, 'I have a confession to make.' Opening them, he said, 'I'm not sorry I kissed you. I've been imagining it ever since I first saw you, but I *am* sorry you didn't kiss me back. Will you ever, do you think?'

He could almost hear the struggle going on within her mind. At last she said softly, 'I should hate to think I might not.'

The seas continued to become increasingly rough, with waves up to sixty feet high, and, like most of the elderly passengers, Edith Carradine refused to leave her cabin for fear of a fall.

'I could break a leg, the way this ship is behaving,' she

told Hester. 'Mrs Pontings says there has already been one accident. An elderly man lost his balance and has hurt his elbow. They say the ship's photographer has given up in despair because his clients can't stand still long enough for him to take the photograph.' She paused for breath and went on. 'Mrs Pontings's brother told her the galley is in a mess – everything that isn't nailed down has fallen over. And even a few crew members are sick.'

Despite these proofs of the roughness of the sea, Hester was sent on various errands. The third of these was to fetch the doctor because Edith complained of her heart, saying she was feeling dizzy and that her pulse was erratic. Hester was on her way up the main stairs when the ship's bow dropped into a steeper than usual trough and a man, coming down the stairs, lost his footing. With a cry of alarm he tumbled down on top of her. She was crushed against the woodwork and struck her head . . .

Twenty minutes later the doctor looked at the prone figure in the bed and tutted irritably.

'Why don't people behave in a sensible manner?' he asked. 'Isn't it obvious that it's not a good idea to go wandering around the ship in weather like this?'

The young nurse nodded earnestly, her blue eyes wide, her fair curls confined by her nurse's headdress. This was her first step into the real world since completing her medical training, but what she lacked in experience, she made up in enthusiasm. 'Will she come round, do you think? I mean, she isn't . . .?' The word 'coma' buzzed in her brain as did the phrase 'vegetative state'.

The doctor rolled his eyes. 'No, she isn't. Nothing dramatic, so don't get excited. A bit of concussion and a nasty bruise. That's all. She might be a bit delirious or disoriented, but she'll be up and about before long. If she says anything intelligible, make a note of it.' He took out his watch and frowned at it. 'I'll notify the captain, and then I'll be in my office writing up my log. When I get back you can find her cabin and see if she has anyone travelling with her who'll be wondering where she is.'

Left alone with her patient, Dulcie Anson busied herself smoothing the sheets around her patient and gently plumping the pillow.

'Nothing to worry about,' she said to her sleeping patient. 'You're in good hands.' There was something familiar about the woman, she must have seen her somewhere.

It was a pity in a way, that it wasn't worse, she reflected. They might have hit the newspaper headlines in New York. DISASTER ON NEW LINER'S MAIDEN VOYAGE. There might have been a mention of the devoted doctor and nurse pulling the patient through. Not that the ship would want headlines like that. They would obviously have to avoid anything which suggested that RMS *Mauretania* was not a stable ship. No bad publicity for Cunard. She understood that.

She tried to concentrate on the job in hand. The patient might wake up and vomit. She hurried to fetch a suitable bowl. Then she found a notebook and pencil and sat down next to her patient. Staring at the pale face, closed eyes and slack unresponsive mouth, she wondered if perhaps she was some-one famous, although she hadn't been wearing expensive clothes when she was carried in, barely conscious. Now she wore a hospital gown. She frowned. Where had she seen her? It came to her suddenly.

Of course! This was Charlie Barnes's lady friend – the one who stood him up!

Half an hour later, Dulcie was tapping on the door of the cabin occupied by a Mrs Carradine.

The door opened and a cross-looking woman glared at her. 'I didn't ask for a nurse,' she said sharply. 'I asked for the doctor, but that was nearly an hour ago.'

'Mrs Carradine?'

'Yes, but they are not fobbing me off with a nurse. I have a heart problem and am on my way to New York to see a specialist.'

'It's about your travelling companion, Miss Shaw. I'm afraid . . .'

The door opened wider. ' You'd better come in, I suppose. What has she done?'

Dulcie stepped into the cabin, hiding her astonishment at the luxurious fittings and furnishings which compared so favourably with her own cramped quarters. 'I'm afraid she was knocked down by a fellow passenger who fell against her, but—'

'Drunk, was he?'

'Oh, no! He simply lost his balance. Fortunately he escaped serious injury, but poor Miss Shaw was sent flying and hurt her head. She's in the ship's hospital under observation.'

'In the hospital?' The old lady sat down heavily. 'She is supposed to be taking care of me, not being knocked down! I sent her to ask the doctor to come here.' She put a hand to her heart.

The nursing training came to the fore and Dulcie spoke soothingly. 'The doctor assures me it is only a mild concussion and she may be released from the hospital later today or first thing tomorrow morning.'

'So is the doctor coming to me or isn't he? I sent my companion to summon him almost an hour ago. I could be dead by now!'

'I'm afraid he didn't receive the message because of your companion's injury. She was in no state to deliver messages to anyone. We had a job trying to find out her name. I'll let Doctor Dunn know your anxiety.'

'Ask Miss Shaw to explain it to him.'

Dulcie counted silently to ten. What an impossible old lady. Miss Shaw was probably better off in the peace and quiet of the hospital room. She tried again. 'Miss Shaw hasn't been able to say anything very coherent yet. She's still unconscious – although she has called once or twice for her husband.'

The old lady snapped, 'Aren't you listening? She is a Miss Shaw. *Miss* Shaw. She isn't married and doesn't have a husband.'

'So who is Alexander?' Taken aback, Nurse Anson frowned. 'She keeps muttering his name. I thought she said, "I'm sorry, Alexander." I thought quite naturally . . . Oh, dear, how silly of me. Perhaps it's her brother or her fiancé.'

'She doesn't have a brother or a fiancé.' She was staring at the nurse. 'Or if she has, it's the first I've heard of it. Are you sure it was Alexander? Maybe it was Alec.'

'I don't think so because once she called him Alexander.'

'Not Mr Waring?'

'Waring? No.'

'What else did she say? Think, girl!'

Dulcie objected to being referred to as a girl, but knew better than to say so. She tried to concentrate. What else had she written in her notebook? 'She said something about Chalker Street. "Being safely back at Chalker Street." Something like that.' She looked hopefully at the old lady.

'Did she now! Chalker Street . . . Chalker Street, London?'

'I don't know, ma'am. I don't know London. I come from Sutton in Surrey.'

'Hmm? This is very odd. I'm beginning to wonder—' She covered her mouth with her hand as though to prevent her thoughts escaping into speech.

For a moment neither spoke. Dulcie was brightening. Perhaps, after all, there was a mystery here. Was the patient using a false name? Travelling incognito, the way they did in novels? Was she running from her husband to her lover in New York? An heiress, maybe? NURSE UNRAVELS PLOT ON BOARD LINER!

This interesting line of thought was interrupted at this point by a new sensation which gradually distracted them from their conversation. For a moment or two they regarded each other in surprise, waiting to have their suspicions confirmed. Instinctively they both turned towards the port-hole through which the clouds now seemed to be moving in a different direction. The sound of the ship's engine had also changed. Mrs Carradine was first to break the silence.

'Am I imagining things or are we changing course?'

'We're slowing down!'

They looked at each other in alarm. Altering course mid-ocean sounded most unlikely.

* * *

On deck, dozens of the crew had been called out to fight a very real danger. The violent movements of the ship had caused a spare anchor to break free from the moorings on its cradle and this enormous piece of ironwork was sliding around the deck creating a serious threat to the superstructure as well as to the men who were desperately trying to secure it. It weighed nearly ten tons and its erratic shifts of position were difficult to anticipate and deal with. Adding to their problems were the giant waves which crashed over the deck and threatened to sweep the unwary overboard. To lessen the impact of the waves, the captain had decided to change the ship's course so that she would not strike the mountainous seas head-on and would thus provide a somewhat safer environment for the men whose hazardous work it was to return the anchor to its cradle and lash it down.

Meanwhile, Hester lay in bed unaware of the crisis on deck. She had dimly recognized the nurse's uniform and knew she must be ill or injured, but had no recollection of the accident on the stairway. At some stage, she had had flashes of memory and fancied that she had fallen and hit her head, but how, why or where escaped her. When she moved her head an ache began behind her eyes so she kept them closed most of the time and kept her head still. She had glimpsed the small room with its white cupboards and tables, each stocked with stainless-steel dishes and utensils – and she also recognized the antiseptic smell. Slowly her memory was returning. She finally remembered that she was on board the *Mauretania* . . . and then she recalled Mrs Carradine.

'Oh!' she groaned as more memories emerged from the corners of her confused mind. She put a hand to her head and felt a large lump on the right side above her ear. At that moment the door opened. She opened her eyes, as a man in a white coat appeared and introduced himself as Doctor Dunn. He was portly and his manner was brisk. He explained briefly what had happened to her, in a voice that suggested she had somehow brought it all down on her own head by careless, ill-advised wanderings. Finally he enquired how she felt.

'My head aches and I feel rather dizzy, but I'm probably well enough to go back to my cabin. My employer will be worrying about me.'

'She knows the situation. We found your room number on the key in your purse – I hope you'll forgive the intrusion – and then went through the passenger list. Nurse Dulcie Anson is with your employer as we speak. Mrs Carradine will expect you later this evening if you feel well enough. If not we will keep you under observation overnight. We shall see.' He held up a hand when she began to protest. 'We can't take any chances, Miss Shaw. We have the matter of insurance to consider. We can't have you wandering around the ship half-dazed, can we?' He gave her a humourless smile, made his excuses and hurried out.

With a resigned sigh, Hester settled herself for a long wait. She didn't mind being kept from Mrs Carradine for an hour or two. It would give her time to think about the pressing matter of Charlie Barnes. Did she dare see him again? She was almost certain she would manage it somehow.

By evening, despite the continued bad weather, a small number of hardy souls had managed to reach the bar where Chalky and Charlie were on duty. One of the women, pressing a handkerchief to her mouth, looked apprehensive, as though at any moment she would stagger back to her cabin. The men looked uncomfortable to a lesser degree and appeared determined not to be done out of their evening tipple. The atmosphere was subdued and the barman, with little to do, was wiping the bar counter to remove the spills due to the ship's erratic motion.

Since everyone had been served, the two stewards were able to stand together while keeping their eyes on the clients, ready to rush forward when anyone raised a languid hand or made eye contact.

Charlie said, 'Is Lizzie sure it was her? Miss Shaw doesn't look the type to go falling down stairs.'

'I told you!' Chalky rolled his eyes in mock frustration. 'Dulcie had to go and talk to the old lady and tell her what had happened. Anyway, she didn't fall down the stairs, this man fell down on top of her and knocked her over.'

'I'll send her some flowers then!'

'A florin says you won't!'

'And a get-well card!'

'What will the old dragon think?'

'Ah! Good point . . . I'll say they're from the crew, but I'll wink at her – Miss Shaw that is, not the dragon.'

Chalky looked at him. 'You're not going soft on this one, are you? She sounds a bit out of your league, if you ask me.'

The smile faded. 'I'm not asking you and what if I am soft on her? So what? I'm not married or anything.'

'What about Annie Whatnot back home? I thought you said if you ever tied the knot it would be to her.' He caught someone's eye and hurried away to collect the order, then over to the bar to load his tray with a sherry and a double whisky with ice, then back to the man and woman who had ordered the drinks.

And then he came back to his friend.

'Annie . . . yes,' Charlie said. 'I did think she might be the one, but I never said that to her, and I didn't say I would marry her. You can ask her. She'll tell you. But now I've met Miss Shaw, I realize Annie wasn't the one. I'll have to tell her.'

'A letter? After, what is it, three years? Poor Annie!'

'Two years not three. No, I couldn't do that to her. I'll tell her myself, face to face. I'll tell her the moment I get ashore.'

Chalky grinned. 'You don't know yet whether Miss Shaw will have you! She might turn you down. You don't know much about her. Then you won't have either of them.'

To his surprise this argument stopped Charlie in his tracks. He said, 'Turn me down? Oh God! She wouldn't, would she?' He regarded his friend with dismay. 'I'm not fooling, Chalky. It has to be Miss Shaw. I just know it. If she turns me down I'll . . . I don't know what I'd do! I just feel for her – in my heart! And don't laugh. I mean it. Didn't you know it when you met your wife?'

'No. Nothing of the sort.' He raised his eyebrows. 'She

told me she was expecting a baby, mine, and said her ma
would throw her out into the street and her pa would come
after me and beat me up. So I asked her to marry me and
she said, "Yes." And we get along fine.' He shrugged.
'Women are all the same.'

'Not what you'd call romantic!' Charlie shook his head.

'It doesn't have to be romantic.' Chalky tapped his forehead meaningfully. 'You're taking it too seriously. Believe
me, marriage is not romantic. My wife's a good sort. Could
have done a lot worse.'

'Well, it's not like that for me. I've fooled around a lot,
I admit, but this is different.'

I want to protect her, he thought. Chalky would never
understand. I want to be everything in the world to her –
but I can't tell him that. He swallowed hard, taken aback
by the strength of his feelings for Miss Shaw. He must stop
calling her that. He must find out her Christian name
. . . and he would send her some flowers. Better still, he
would take them to her. He was suddenly overwhelmed by
a need to see her, hear her voice and see her smile. He
would find the little nurse and ask for Miss Shaw's room
number. They would be in New York in a few days' time
and he might never see her again. A cold shiver ran through
him.

'I'm going to marry her,' he said doggedly. 'Whatever it
takes.'

'She might be a widow with five children!' Chalky was
determined to torment him.

'Miss Shaw.' Charlie reminded him. 'The old lady called
her *Miss* Shaw.'

'Have it your own way, then.'

'I'm going to ask her and she's going to say, "Yes."
Nothing and nobody is going to stop me. I'll do whatever
it takes.'

Early the following morning, Hester was deemed fit to return
to her cabin. There had been no sickness and the headache
had cleared.

'Go carefully,' the doctor warned. 'The seas are lessening

a little, but are still high. We're not going to make a record run, I'm afraid, after that business with the anchor, but we might make it up on the return trip. That means a few bumps.'

Hester thanked him for the information. It certainly didn't inspire her to walk too far.

'There'll be a fee.' The doctor turned away. 'I'll send an invoice along later.'

Hester hoped it wouldn't be an excessive amount. She might have to ask Mrs Carradine to lend her some money. She made her way back to her own cabin and sat there for ten minutes, collecting her thoughts. Then she went next door. Her employer's first words were not encouraging.

'So, there you are! About time. I have a bone to pick with you. Sit down.'

Hester's heart sank. 'It wasn't entirely my fault,' she began. 'A man fell and knocked me down the stairs . . .'

'I'm not talking about your accident. You look well enough now. I want to know why you were calling for Alexander while you were delirious. Is that who I think it is? If so, I believe you have some explaining to do.' Mrs Carradine folded her arms and glared at Hester accusingly.

Hester's mind went blank with shock as she stared at Edith Carradine. Had she called for Alexander before she regained consciousness? She supposed it was possible. Her mind spun frantically. Would she be able to lie her way out of this or would it be better to confess?

Nervously she looked at her employer who sat on the chair, her back like a ramrod, her eyes fixed, hawk-like, on Hester's face. With an effort she forced her mind into action. How much did she know? And, more to the point, how much had she guessed?

Edith continued. 'I may be elderly but I am not stupid and you have, I suspect, been pulling the wool over my eyes. I think I am entitled to an explanation.'

Still Hester hesitated. This was Alexander's fault, she knew, but would Mrs Carradine accept that her favourite nephew had chosen to deceive her? Gathering her courage, she decided to tell the whole truth.

She said, 'Alex and I are lovers. He pays for my flat in Chalker Street and has done for several years. Naturally he didn't want the family to know. He doesn't want to hurt Marcia.' She saw the triumphant gleam in the other woman's eyes.

'I thought as much! Well, I confess he had me fooled. I could have sworn to his integrity, but –' she threw out her hands despairingly – 'my nephew has had a mistress for Lord knows how many years and I knew nothing about it! I trusted that boy. I always have had the highest regard for him. How well do we ever know anyone?'

Hester saw that despite the brave words, the old lady was shaken. 'We have been very discreet,' she began.

'Discreet? You would *have* to be! Certain standards have to be maintained for his career. Has it occurred to you that you might be jeopardizing his hopes of promotion?'

Hester felt a flash of anger. 'Has it occurred to *you*, Mrs Carradine, that our relationship involves two people? For your information, the original idea was your nephew's and I took some convincing. I could see that by living with him in secret I was ruining my own chances of marriage. My being here with you was not my idea either. Alexander insisted. He wouldn't hear any arguments. As for being his mistress . . . I am hardly in an envious position.'

'Indeed? How exactly are you suffering, Miss Shaw?' The tone was colder now.

'I am thirty-one and have always wanted a home, a husband and children. In my present situation I can have none of these and my prospects are poor.'

'You have a home!'

'No. I have a roof over my head. Alexander has *two* homes and I live in one of them. I do not work because he wants me to be available at all times of the day or night – whenever he can steal time from work or home.' She swallowed as the words tumbled out and she realized just how resentful they sounded. 'We cannot go out together in case we are seen. I have few friends.' She became aware that for some time she had tried not to see her situation as a form of house arrest, but suddenly it was becoming horribly clear.

She had willingly entered into this relationship without proper regard for the consequences and had been reluctant to face the truth.

Mrs Carradine drew herself up. 'There is no need to take that tone with me, Miss Shaw. You have stayed with him and presumably you were not locked in. Not held prisoner against your will.'

Hester cried, 'I am nothing but a glorified whore!' As she heard the words she had uttered, she was appalled. Not at the utterance, but at the truth behind them. Mistress or whore? Her throat tightened.

Mrs Carradine gave no answer, but turned sharply away. The minutes passed. Hester's headache threatened to return. She felt exhausted from the recent concussion and resentful of her employer's condemnation although she knew it to be deserved. This really was not the best time to have this particular conversation, she thought, putting a shaking hand to her head.

'Have you eaten today, Miss Shaw?'

Hester shook her head. She was starting to feel sorry for herself and was afraid of breaking down. Tears, she was sure, would only incense her employer. Edith Carradine would not tolerate weakness.

With an effort she said, 'Alexander told me that your daughters were both unable to accompany you and that you were having trouble finding someone suitable.

'He seemed to think I would take good care of you. He obviously didn't want you to know that . . . that Marcia wasn't the only woman in his life. I didn't fancy the journey so late in the year, but he was insistent and I agreed to please him. It was his idea to pretend I was a dressmaker.'

'Not easy for you, I imagine.'

'No. It's been worrying me.'

'I'm revising my opinion of Alexander.' The old lady pressed her lips together. 'I have always found him perfect in every way and it's almost a relief to know that he does have failings.' To Hester's surprise Mrs Carradine's tone had softened. 'He is human, after all, and as fallible as other men. Well, well! He has a mistress. Wonders will never cease.'

Hester said nothing, hiding her surprise at the change in the old lady's attitude. She seemed on the point of saying something when, quite abruptly, she rang for the stewardess. When she arrived, Edith ordered a pot of tea for two and a round of chicken sandwiches for Hester. 'You must eat,' she said. 'I need you to be fit again. I certainly don't want to be looking after you! As for Alexander, I shall talk to him about this situation. I intend to leave him all my money and he needs an heir before I do. Marcia will never have a child, so he needs to give the problem some serious consideration before it is too late. Perhaps it should be you.'

'Me? But we are hardly in a position to . . .'

'Then, when Marcia dies, Alexander can legalize your position and that of the child.'

Despite the headache, Hester's head jerked up in astonishment. 'Have a child out of wedlock? You can't mean that.'

'I can and I do. It happens all the time.'

Hester hesitated. 'I think you should save this conversation for your nephew, Mrs Carradine.' The threatening press of tears had receded and she made an effort to compose herself. 'I dislike the feeling that I'm being interrogated. I may have done wrong—'

'You certainly have!'

'But Alexander is also to blame for betraying his wife.' Hester spoke defiantly. Out of the blue, her world was turning upside-down. The secret of their liaison was out and she had no idea what would happen next. She would never agree to have a child out of wedlock. No son or daughter of hers would go through life burdened with such a terrible stigma. It was unlikely Marcia would die while she, Hester, was still young enough to have a baby. Maybe when he knew his secret was out, Alexander would end the affair and start looking for someone younger, secure in the knowledge that his wealthy aunt would eventually approve. Her head throbbed relentlessly now and she wished herself back in the quiet of the hospital room.

A knock at the door brought the tea and sandwiches and

they busied themselves with food and drink. Hester found to her surprise that she was both hungry and thirsty.

Her employer was obviously considering every angle of the situation. Her lips were pursed and her brow was furrowed. The lengthening silence was abruptly broken by another knock on the door. Edith indicated that Hester should answer it and she rose carefully to her feet. To her consternation she found Charlie Barnes outside with a small bouquet of flowers.

'Oh, Mr Barnes!'

Edith said, 'Who is it?'

He winked at Hester and said loudly, 'A small token from the crew of *Mauretania*, miss. Our regrets at your accident and our best wishes for your recovery.'

Hester's throat was dry with shock and her heart was racing. Charlie turning up like this completely unnerved her and she was thankful that her back was towards her employer.

'That's . . . I mean, this is so . . . so kind. I didn't expect . . .'

She stared at the red rosebuds, at once thrilled and terrified. Not for one moment did she believe that the flowers were from the ship's crew. They were from Charlie Barnes and she wondered whether Mrs Carradine would sense that.

Apparently she did not. She said, 'It's the very least they can do. Thank him, Miss Shaw, and close the door.'

Hester studied the flowers, praying that there would be no telltale message. She looked imploringly at Charlie and chanced a quick smile.

'Thank you, er . . .'

'Charlie Barnes, miss. Glad to be of service. I'm afraid the weather is not likely to improve much so do take care as you move around the ship. Good day to you, ladies.' He gave her an intensely appraising look, turned sharply on his heel, and walked away.

She watched him until he turned the corner and was then filled with a strange sense of loneliness. Shaken, Hester closed the door and tried to calm herself. She felt flushed and excited by the unexpected meeting, but told herself she was being ridiculous. Praying that her face would give nothing away, she turned back from the door.

'Flowers at sea are so inconvenient!' Mrs Carradine tutted irritably. 'You'd better ring for Mrs Pontings and ask her to put them in a vase for you. You'll have to keep them in your own cabin, and you'll have to anchor them in some way. Such a nuisance especially when the ship is being tossed about like a cork!'

To Hester's relief, she showed no interest in the eight roses. *Eight*. Would the old lady read anything into that?

'I'll ring for her from my own cabin,' she said. Then made her exit before Edith could protest.

Eight red roses! One for each letter of 'I love you'! Back in her own cabin she allowed herself a smile. Charlie Barnes was a cool customer, she thought, amused and thrilled by his audacity. No one had ever sent her flowers before. She rang for the stewardess and sat on the edge of the bed to wait for her. Pressing the flowers to her chest, she was overwhelmed by a rush of happiness and, closing her eyes, gave herself up to the pleasure of the moment.

Five

Back in Liverpool, a day later, Maisie Barnes was summoned to the front door by the bell and opened it reluctantly. It was nearly seven in the evening and she was not feeling her best and had only just returned from work at the nearby laundry. Her plump face was still red from the steam, her hair was lank and her back ached from hours bent over tubs full of boiling clothes. It irked her that Ginnie Wenn was still working there. Ginnie had been threatening to leave for weeks now and Maisie had been promised her job in the ironing room which would mean a little more money and better working conditions. It would be a step up in the world and waiting for it filled her with frustration.

She found Annie Green on the doorstep and regarded her without enthusiasm. Charlie's pretty lady friends always made her feel inferior.

'What's up?' She was used to her brother's friends popping in hoping for news of his whereabouts and the dates for his shore leave. Annie, she guessed, would be no different although she had lasted a little longer than most. Blocking the doorway, she tried to convey the idea that she was busy.

Annie said, 'Hello, Maisie. Any news of Charlie? I need to talk to him.'

Maisie held back a sarcastic comment. Annie knew that news from Charlie was impossible, but her interest was aroused. Annie needed to talk to him – or so she claimed. Intriguing. Reluctantly Maisie opened the door to let her in.

'He's halfway to New York!' she reminded her visitor. 'How can I have any news? Unless he's sent a message by carrier pigeon and if so the bird got lost.' She led the way into the kitchen where the stove had gone out during the morning and she had only just relit it. There was a chill in the air, but the small tin kettle, perched above it, was making encouraging noises and a one-eared tabby, by the name of Moggie, had curled hopefully on the rag rug in front of the stove. 'Cuppa?'

'Please.' Annie's glance held the familiar hint of envy before she turned away and began fussing over the cat.

The envy was for Maisie's position as Charlie's brother. No one, Maisie knew, envied her for her youth or beauty – she had no delusions about that. An unkind quirk of fate had decided that Charlie should be the handsome one with a sunny disposition and an easy charm. The same fate had given his sister mousy hair that refused to curl, brown button eyes and a tendency to worry. She was now a shapeless woman of thirty-five with no husband and very little money to spend on herself. This morning, a large, coarse apron was tied round her non-existent waist and the word 'unlovely' fitted her to a T – but Charlie was her baby brother and, as always, that brightened her world enormously.

Annie envied her that, if nothing else, because Annie longed for a similar closeness, but she was simply one of many young women who had come and gone in Charlie's short life.

Annie leaned forward. 'Has he said anything more about . . . you know? Wanting to settle down.'

'Getting wed, you mean?' Maisie shook her head. 'No, not to me. But who knows how my brother's mind works.' She fussed with the teapot then glanced up sharply. 'You haven't lent him any more money, I hope, 'cos I can't help you. You know what I told you last time! Say no!'

'It was only a shilling.'

'Only!'

Annie sucked in her breath with a disapproving hiss. 'You never did! You're mad!'

'I know, but . . . Maisie, there's something else. It's about . . . you know. Me and Charlie have been . . . I mean it's hard to say "No" and he . . . I think I'm . . .' A telling blush was making her prettier than ever.

Maisie's stomach lurched and she clapped a hand to her mouth. 'Don't tell me you're up the spout! I don't want to hear it! Oh Lord! You're not, are you?'

Annie nodded wordlessly and Maisie stared at her in dismay.

'I thought you could talk to him for me.'

Maisie rolled her eyes. Charlie and his women! She had no children and no experience of married life, but they seemed to consider her some kind of expert just because she was his brother. But this particular problem had never cropped up before and she wondered what Charlie would say when he knew.

'Are you quite sure?' she asked. 'You can miss a month without it meaning anything.'

Would Charlie be pleased if there was a child on the way, she wondered. Maybe it would settle him down – if he wanted to settle down. Knowing her brother, it would take a really special person to get him up the aisle! Was that person Annie Green?

'It's two months,' Annie confessed. 'Not one. I tried to tell him the other night when he turned up, but I couldn't find the right moment. You know what he's like.'

Out of her depth, Maisie shrugged and changed the subject. 'I hope he gave you back that shilling!'

Annie shook her head. 'He borrowed some more but . . .'

'You idiot! What did I tell you?'

'He'll pay it back some time.'

'Like when?' She poured the tea.

'When he has a winning streak – and he's going to take me to Blackpool.'

'Gordon Bennett! That makes it all right then, does it?'

'He can't help it. He'll pay me back out of his wages soon as he gets back.'

Maisie folded her arms. 'But is he going to *wed* you? That's a mite more important than swings and roundabouts and bright lights in Blackpool.'

She regarded Annie moodily. In a way she had been dreading the day when her brother would set up home else-where. Not only for his share of the money which helped pay the rent, but for the company. She had never lived alone. When her widowed mother died, twenty-one-year-old Maisie had taken over the tenancy of the flat because Charlie was still at school. Later he had helped keep a roof over their heads. Charlie was fun and he was always cheerful. The men Maisie took a shine to never even noticed her and she was resigned to the fact that she would probably always be single. She lived for Charlie's shore leave and missed him while he was at sea. When he finally moved out she would be forced to take in a lodger, but the prospect held no real appeal.

Maisie said slowly, 'Suppose he won't marry you, then what?'

Annie's face sagged. 'He wouldn't say that, would he? Oh, Maisie, don't say that!'

'Well, how do I know what he'll do? I'm his sister, not his mother!'

'But you wouldn't advise him against me, would you? If he asks for your advice? I mean, wouldn't you like to be an auntie? It would be fun, wouldn't it? I mean, it's going to happen sometime, isn't it, and we could get married before anyone knew? My pa will kill Charlie if he leaves me in the lurch!'

'What about your ma?'

'She's long gone. Left us when I was seven.'

'So why don't you live at home with your pa?'

'Because he's a miserable old devil at the best of times, he's mostly drunk, he hates the sight of me because I'm so like my ma! Is that enough reasons?'

Maisie fought against a frisson of compassion. 'You could always . . . You know. There are people . . . doctors . . .'

Annie shuddered, covering her ears with her hands. 'Don't even say the words!'

Maisie hesitated. 'They say that if you jump off a table or something it doesn't hurt that much and . . . Or there's something you can drink, but I don't know what.'

Annie uncovered her ears. 'Go to one of those so-called doctors? How could you even think it? How could you tell me to get rid of your own brother's baby?'

Maisie stiffened. 'I didn't say you *should* go to one of them. You were the one who said about your pa killing him if he found out and if you don't get wed. If the worst came to the worst you'd have to think about it. You wouldn't be the first or the last . . . but I'm not saying do it.' She stared at Annie with growing dislike. The truth was that she had wanted to give Annie a bit of a fright because Annie had given *her* one – turning up with such news and wanting to take Charlie away. 'So don't you go telling Charlie that I said you *should* do it because I didn't mean it like that and you know I didn't and if you *do* tell him that I shall say you're a liar!' She sat back breathlessly, all her kindly feelings gone. Annie should have been more careful. So should Charlie, but he was her flesh and blood and if she had to take sides it would be with her brother. Did she want this Annie woman for a sister-in-law?

Slowly Annie rose to her feet. 'You haven't even asked me how I feel,' she said, her feelings hurt. 'You don't care, do you?'

'How do you feel? Being sick?'

'No.'

'Then perhaps you aren't. Let's hope not.'

'I am! Not everybody gets to be sick. You an expert all of a sudden?'

Maisie also rose to her feet. She had to be careful, she realized. If Charlie married Annie – and she was beginning to hope he wouldn't – she would want to be a part of it so she shouldn't really antagonize her. In a softer tone, she said, 'Well, let me know how things go. I won't say anything to Charlie when he gets back. I'll let you break the news.' She led the way to the front door. 'And take care of yourself.'

She watched Annie go with a heavy heart. Yesterday everything had been more or less fine. Not wonderful but good enough. She had felt in control. Now everything was spoiled. She closed the door. Back in the kitchen she glared at the cat.

'I hate change, Moggie,' she told her.

* * *

Two days later, on the twenty-second of November, the RMS *Mauretania* reached Sandy Hook and her maiden voyage to North America was all but over. The triumphal entry into New York Harbour was impossible due to thick fog and Captain Pritchard insisted that they delay entry on to the berth. The ship waited outside Quarantine until the fog began to disperse, and then made her way cautiously towards the 14th Street pier. Edith was delighted to be in New York, but for Hester it was a heartfelt wrench. In spite of Charlie's insistence that he would see her when they made their return trip, she felt hopelessly bereft. She finally admitted to herself that she had fallen in love with Charles Barnes and had promised to marry him. Their whirlwind romance had left her reeling with shock and dizzy with joy and every moment without him was an agony.

New York was a fascinating and bewildering city, but in the days that followed, Hester was unable to appreciate it. Edith rushed them from pillar to post in the first four days before her appointment with Mr Stafford, the heart specialist whose reputation was solely responsible for their stay in New York. She and Edith Carradine turned up at his lavishly furnished consulting rooms on the fourteenth floor of a skyscraper. Ushered into the waiting room, Edith took one glimpse of the city from the window and sat down hurriedly.

'This is ridiculous,' she told Hester. 'America is a very large country. I see no need to put up buildings at such a height.' She glanced upward. 'How many more floors are there?'

'I believe there are forty in all.'

Hester wished she were with Charlie. Admiring the view together would make sightseeing perfect. She was hoping that Mr Stafford would quickly assess Edith's problem and decide on the best treatment. The sooner the better, in her opinion. The *Mauretania* would make another round trip before Christmas and she was praying they would be on the return voyage. She longed to see Charlie again, every minute was an hour and the intervening hours and days stretched ahead interminably. She hoped the old lady had not noticed her restlessness, but she couldn't be sure. She had said nothing about the promises she and Charlie had made to each other.

First she had to return to Alexander and tell him that she was leaving. It would be hard, but in a strange way she welcomed the challenge. There was nothing she wouldn't do for Charles Barnes. She trusted him utterly. He so obviously adored her and in an intense way, and Hester found this profoundly moving. Once they were together she was determined to make him the happiest man in the world. *The happiest man in the world.* How unoriginal you are, she thought, amused.

'Do sit down, Miss Shaw!' Edith waited, her hands folded neatly in her lap. Raising her voice, she continued. 'He's late! Would you believe that? I come halfway round the world to see him and he's late! It really is unpardonable.'

Hearing this, as she was meant to do, the glamorous receptionist smiled apologetically. 'I'm so sorry, Mrs Garradine. Can I fetch you some refresh—'

'No, no!' Edith fussed with her fur collar. 'And it's Carradine with a "C".'

The receptionist gave a polite nod by way of apology. 'I'm afraid his last patient was ten minutes late, Mrs Carradine. It's hard for Mr Stafford to catch up once that happens. Have you come far?'

'Only from England!'

'Oh!' She was at once interested. 'On the *Mauretania*? How wonderful.'

Edith tossed her head. 'On the contrary. It was a dreadful trip. Ghastly weather and the ship's spare anchor broke free from its moorings and—' She stopped as a tall thin man with silvery hair appeared from another room and beckoned the receptionist. After a whispered conversation, he disappeared again to be followed seconds later by a matronly looking nurse in an immaculate white uniform.

She smiled at Edith. 'Mrs Carradine? Mr Stafford will see you now.'

Edith stood up and turned to Hester. 'I may be some time. Wait for me here.'

Hester watched her go with relief. Now she was free to

think about her future. Take as long as you like, Mr Stafford, she told him silently. She reached for a nearby magazine and opened it at random. Staring at a page of garden plants with unfocussed eyes, she thought about Charlie. He was so very different from any man she had ever met or expected to meet. He spoke with an accent she had never heard before and with a freedom she had never known. Words tumbled straight from his heart, warming her with their passion, and instantly brushing away her initial doubts.

Standing at the ship's rail together, at half past eleven on their last night, Charlie's proposal had taken her completely by surprise.

'You do realize . . .' he had begun nervously. 'I mean, we do have to . . . I mean, there's no way you can turn me down. You wouldn't, would you?'

'Turn you down?' She stared at him.

'If I . . . when I ask you to marry me.' His expression was hard to see in the light from the nearby companionway, but Hester detected a note of desperation in his voice. It was very different from his usual light-hearted tone, and his body, normally so relaxed, seemed stiff with an unfamiliar tension. Had she heard him correctly? The silence was fraught with uncertainty.

'When you ask me to marry you?'

'Yes, because I will. I am. That's what I'm doing. Asking you . . . You may not have noticed that you love me. It's early days. But we have to stay together. I have to know now because you're going away and . . .'

'Oh, Charlie!' Her voice shook. 'I have noticed that I love you, but isn't this all too fast? Are we sure?'

'I'm sure. I'm sure enough for both of us because you can't go back to him and we could marry in New York. At least we might be able to . . .'

'No!' She shook her head. 'I can't do that to him. I have to end it properly. Decently.' She hesitated. 'Do you have anyone to tell, Charlie?'

'No, at least . . . yes. I suppose so. It was nothing. I hadn't promised her anything. But . . . Are you saying yes?'

Hester held her breath. This was so sudden. It might be

a terrible mistake. *Did she love him? Could she bear never to see him again?*

'Yes, Charlie. I am. I will marry you. I can't think of anything I'd rather do!' She laughed shakily as he pulled her towards him and hugged her passionately.

They had remained on deck for another hour and Charlie had made her see that there was another way to live and that her life as Alexander's mistress had been entirely devoid of genuine affection. Through Charlie's eyes, she saw that her relationship with Alexander had been composed of gratitude on her part and convenience on his. She had settled for security in the present with a man who could promise nothing definite for the future except a long wait for the death of his wife – and even then nothing was certain. A younger woman might replace her, leaving her stranded and alone.

Charlie promised her a loving heart, a home and a family. They would never be rich, he warned, but they could be happy and contented.

'My sister Maisie will love you,' he had told her, his eyes shining with anticipation. 'I can't wait to see her face when I take you home. She's certain I'm never going to settle down. You'll get along. She's been more like a mother to me than a sister. We'll get a place nearby so she won't think we've abandoned her – and so she can see her nephews and nieces. They'll be more like her grandchildren because she's older than me – thirty-five or six. Something like that.'

'Not much older than me.' Hester was glad to have the chance to spell it out for him. 'I'm thirty-one.'

He grinned. 'My very favourite age for a woman. Promise me you'll never get any younger!'

'I'll get older.'

'We'll get older together, how's that?'

Now, turning the page of the magazine, Hester smiled at the memory. Charlie was unflappable. In his eyes she was wonderful in every way. He was already planning a wedding and a list of friends who must be there to share the occasion. His delight in her made her feel more lovable and her confidence was growing.

The receptionist leaned forward and coughed to attract Hester's attention. 'Would you like some coffee or tea, Miss Shaw? Mr Stafford may be doing some tests and you may have quite a long wait.'

'Thank you. I would like a cup of tea.'

The tea appeared within minutes, in a small pot with a matching jug full of hot milk. There were three small biscuits on a plate and a dish of brown sugar. As she sipped the tea and nibbled the biscuits, she thought about the best way to break the news to Alexander. She wanted to spare him any pain he might feel at her disloyalty. He had been good to her in many ways, but she didn't think he would try very hard to make her stay with him. Plenty more pebbles on the beach! Younger pebbles, she thought with a smile. But should she tell him face to face or do what Charlie suggested?

'Pack and leave, with a letter propped on the mantel-piece,' he had advised. 'That's what I'd prefer if I was him. I wouldn't want to have to listen to you explaining why you were going off with another man. That'd be hurtful. But make a clean break. It's kinder.'

Was it kinder? Hester wasn't entirely convinced, but she didn't relish the thought of a confrontation either. If Alexander were upset by her betrayal, she would feel guilty and if he were angry she might be frightened of him. He was a proud man and powerful in his sphere of work and used to getting his own way. What would he do? Not that he would do her any physical harm – at least she didn't think so – but he hated to be thwarted. She remembered Drummond and wondered what had happened to him, if anything.

'I don't think I could just vanish,' she told Charlie. 'He might come after me and make a scene. I couldn't bear that. I'd prefer to get it over with in private. Just the two of us. I owe him that much. And there are my clothes ...'

His eyes narrowed. 'Don't bring anything he has given you. He might accuse you of stealing. You said he was a policeman. He'd know how to make it stick.'

She regarded him helplessly, then shrugged. 'Why am I fooling myself that he'll care? He'll probably breathe a sigh

of relief that he's rid of me. He may have found someone
else already.'

Recalling Charlie's immediate rejection of this scenario,
Hester smiled and turned another page: *A nourishing family
stew. Serves four or five* . . . Was she really going to be part
of a family, cooking and washing for four or five?

'Please God, yes!' she mouthed.

Wash and scrape your carrots, she read, *and cut into neat
cubes. Repeat with the potatoes and parsnips and add to
the pan.*

Hester felt a moment of panic. Could she cook? She had
never had to try. Alexander had always insisted on eating
at home with Marcia or at his club and, before that, when
she was a nanny, there had been a part-time cook to prepare
the meals. But it couldn't be that difficult, surely. Her glance
fell on another recipe – for a lemon tart –which involved
making pastry. That looked slightly more daunting, but she
would learn. She would learn to sew and mend and cook
and plant vegetables and whatever Charlie needed her to
learn. Slowly she ate the last biscuit.

As the last biscuit crumb vanished, the door opened and
Mrs Carradine reappeared with a face like thunder. She
glared at Hester. 'We're leaving and we're not coming back.
I never heard such nonsense in all my life.' The receptionist
half rose to her feet, looking anxious, but Edith snapped,
'Sit down, woman. I have to write a cheque – apparently
I have to pay for Mr Stafford wasting my time!'

Opening her purse, she drew out a cheque book, snatched
a pen from the inkstand on the receptionist's desk and filled
in the cheque with impatient jerks of the pen and angry
snorts of breath. She tore it out and handed it over.

'Mr Stafford hasn't earned a penny of it,' she told the
receptionist. 'It's highway robbery and I told him so. All
this way to be told there is nothing wrong with my heart.
Telling me it is all in my imagination. He's a disgrace to
his profession.'

The young receptionist, embarrassed, was lost for words
and Hester thought it was probably for the best. Any concil-
iatory remarks, efforts to apologize or attempts to support

her employer would simply add fuel to the fire of the old lady's wrath.

In the taxi on the way back to the hotel, Edith enlarged on her comments.

'He had the audacity to tell me he could reassure me that there was nothing wrong. *Reassure me?* If I believed that I would never have come to New York. You're a charlatan, I told him, or else you are an incompetent fool. I need to know what is wrong with my heart and I want you to bring about treatment and a cure. But, no, the man tells me to be thankful he could find nothing wrong.'

Hester searched for something appropriate and hopefully safe to say. She decided on, 'Oh, dear! How disappointing!'

Edith fanned herself with a fierce hand. 'Disappointing is an understatement. Disgusting is nearer the truth. He ought to be crossed off the medical register. I shall write to the medical profession.'

A sudden thought brought a hastily hidden smile to Hester's face. Presumably this meant that they would be returning to England sooner than expected and *that* meant she would soon be reunited with her future husband.

Six

Monday, November 25th, 1907 – What a wicked waste of time and money Mr Stafford has proved to be. After various tests he declared that there was nothing wrong with me and I should stop worrying about my health. The man's a fool and I told him so. He actually had the cheek to say I was 'as strong as a horse' and would outlive him. Well, I certainly hope I do. I shall hope to dance at his funeral! As soon as I get home I shall search out a new specialist – someone with something between his ears apart from American fluff!

As for Miss Shaw, I am still wondering what to make of her. I have to confess that, in spite of all that I have learned recently about her duplicity, I rather like the woman. She is efficient and mostly dutiful and has a pleasant manner. I tried to discover how she and Alexander met, but she was discreet without being evasive so I thought it better not to pry for fear she tells my nephew and he takes it badly. Will I ever see her again, I wonder, when she is no longer my travelling companion. I have decided we shall travel back on the Mauretania *as soon as possible.*

I shall make enquiries as to her next sailing.

Ten days later, on Thursday the fifth of December, while Hester and her employer were still travelling back from New York, the telephone rang in an upper office at Scotland Yard and the call was passed to Alexander.

He listened, frowning, while his housekeeper, Mrs Rice, gabbled incoherently about Mrs Waring and the hospital.

'Stop crying, for God's sake,' he told her. 'Start again and don't mumble!'

'It's Mrs Waring, your wife, Mr Waring. She didn't wake up when I went in with her breakfast and, you know how heavily she sleeps, I shook her and then screamed because, you know, I thought she was dead, Mr Waring, and . . .'

As she continued piecemeal with her hysterical account, Alexander extracted the basic facts. His wife was still alive. Relieved, he rolled his eyes.

'So what you're saying is that Marcia was taken ill and is now in hospital. Give me the telephone number and—'

'The number? Oh, no! I mean, I don't know because I called her doctor and he called the police and they arranged everything, that is to say I was in no state to . . . Well, it was such a shock, Mr Waring, and I was on my own, and it's not every day you find a dead body which was what I thought . . .' She began to cry again. 'I feel all of a bother.'

'For heaven's sake, pull yourself together, Mrs Rice. She's not dead so why are you crying? Get on with your work and I'll get in touch with the doctor and I'll take a taxi to the hospital as soon as I can rearrange my appointments. Make yourself a cup of tea and carry on as usual. She might be sent home later and she won't want to find the house in a mess.'

Forty-five minutes later he was sitting by his wife's bed. Marcia was unconscious and the young doctor was explaining the position.

'She was unconscious when they brought her in and has remained so ever since. When Mr Barrac comes in, we'll have a better idea of what happened. We've just . . .'

'Mr Barrac being the consultant, I assume?' The man looked too young to be a doctor, Alexander thought, surprised. But perhaps that was a sign that he was getting old. His thoughts reverted to his wife's condition. Thinking rationally, it would almost be a mercy if Marcia were to die – she had no real life and would never recover from whatever ailed her.

'Yes. A very senior consultant,' the doctor agreed. 'He's

due in ten minutes for his rounds, but he does have another private practice and is sometimes late. Can you tell me what medication your wife has been taking – for our notes?' He tapped his notebook with his pencil and tried to look experienced. 'Your wife's pupils are dilated and—'

'I'm afraid not. I don't understand it. I leave it to her doctor to prescribe what she needs. When I left for work she seemed to be sleeping normally and I always try not to wake her. Didn't you ask her doctor for these details?'

'Ah!' He looked somewhat discomfited. 'The truth is there was a bit of a muddle at the time. We had a patient back from theatre and another elderly patient who came in vomiting blood and with one nurse absent . . . in the confusion . . .' Leaving the rest to Alexander's imagination, he shrugged apologetically.

Alexander nodded, his mind elsewhere. If Marcia died he would keep her death from Hester for as long as possible. She would be back in England shortly and he wanted time to decide what to do about her. If he were free to marry again, he must make a sensible judgement and not choose Hester from a sense of misguided loyalty. She might soon be too old to have a child and he needed a family. On the other hand, she had been good for him and he bore her no ill-will. Perhaps he should settle a small sum of money on her so that she could survive until she found another man to take care of her. Perhaps he could find her a job as a housekeeper. He could write her a reference. That would please her . . .

But he would miss her. And suppose she found another protector – someone better off who could do better by her than he had done? The thought of Hester in another man's bed hurt him more than he expected.

She might compare him with the next man. Might even *discuss* him with the next man! That thought really did trouble him. Damnation. There must be a way out of the situation. If Marcia were going to die, he would have to give it some serious thought. And quickly.

He took out his watch and frowned. Interrupting the young doctor, he said, 'I have an important meeting shortly.

Regretfully I shall have to return to my office. But I'll keep in touch and hopefully be back later in the day.'

There was no point in hanging about at the bedside of an unconscious wife who may or may not recover.

In his absence another secretary had entered his office brandishing *The Times*.

'Have you seen this?' she asked.

The two secretaries bent their heads over the short news item on the front page although it was not the main headline.

> *Scotland Yard officers have arrested a senior figure in the Home Office and he has been detained while further enquiries are made. Mr Francis J. Drummond has been accused of obtaining information by illegal methods. It is understood that an anonymous phone call precipitated the arrest.*

That same evening, after midnight, Hester and Charlie sat together in her cabin, making plans. They were also sharing a bottle of wine and some biscuits which he had brought with him.

'So it's all settled, then,' he asked hopefully. 'You will find the right time to tell your chap that you are leaving him to get married. I'll find a vicar to call the banns and get a licence. I'll break it to Maisie and Annie.'

'Who's Annie?' Hester asked drowsily, her head against his shoulder.

'Annie? Oh, she's just a woman I know. Got to tell her I'm spoken for, haven't I? Like you and your bloke, I'll tell her to her face.'

'Was she someone special?' Hester sat up. 'Will she mind? How special is she?'

'Special that I've known her some time, but not so special I ever wanted to marry her! Don't worry, Hes. She'll be fine. She knew it would happen some day.' He slipped an arm round her shoulder by way of reassurance. 'So then, you'll get in touch – you've got our address – and you'll come up. Maybe by Christmas. Then we'll get ourselves down to the church. And don't bring anything with you that *he* bought you. I'll send you a bit of cash from my next wages to tide you over.'

Hester relaxed again. 'And we'll find somewhere to live,' she prompted, smiling.

'Chalky knows a place that might do us nicely. And we'll buy furniture.'

Hester sighed with contentment. 'I can hardly believe this is happening,' she told him. 'Tell me nothing will go wrong. I won't wake up, will I, and find it's all a dream?'

'Course you won't. What could go wrong? It is a dream, but it's a dream coming true. Trust Charlie Barnes.' He hugged her so hard she cried out in protest. 'Sorry, I just love you so much! I can't wait to show you off to all my mates back home. They'll be so jealous. Sick as parrots.' He laughed.

'Ssh! Remember Mrs Carradine's next door,' Hester reminded him, pointing at the wall which separated the two cabins.

'Sorry again!'

Hester said, 'I'll have my wages from this trip. I'll buy myself some clothes. And I'll always love the *Mauretania* for bringing us together. Oh, Charlie! Whenever I dared to wonder about my future it was never as wonderful as you and me!'

Charlie kissed her. 'The same goes for me with knobs on! I do love you. You're stuck with me, you know, because whatever happens, I'll never leave you.'

Early snowflakes were falling on Saturday as Alexander hurried up the steps to the front entrance of the hospital and made his way to the ward where he would find his wife. Once there he received his first shock. Marcia's bed was empty and he glanced round. Perhaps they had had to operate on her. Maybe, God forbid, she had been felled by a stroke or a heart attack – or maybe she had recovered and they had moved her to another ward to make way for more urgent cases. If she had had a stroke, it would mean months of home nursing with a live-in nurse and the house smelling of antiseptics and disinfectants. Ugh! An appalling thought. Frowning, he went in search of the ward sister.

The sister's expression changed when she recognized Alexander. Without a word she drew him aside where they could not be overheard. 'Mr Waring, I'm so sorry to give you sad news, but your wife . . .'

His stomach churned with apprehension. 'She's not . . . Oh, no!'

'I'm afraid so. She slipped away quite painlessly. One minute she was breathing and the next . . . We were actually standing beside her bed at the moment she died. It may be a mercy in one way.' She eyed him anxiously. 'She may have remained in a coma for weeks or months and then died. It happens quite often and that's terrible for the relatives. I'm so sorry, Mr Waring. I can assure you . . .'

Alexander had stopped listening, overcome with feelings of guilt that overwhelmed any sense of loss. That would come later. He had been plotting her demise, he thought, and had somehow spoiled her chances of recovery. And he should have stayed longer yesterday, to talk to Barrac about Marcia's condition. Forgive me, Marcia, he begged silently. You were a good wife. She had supported him through the difficult times and was always . . .

The sister interrupted his thoughts. 'There will be a few official things to attend to and the Lady Almoner will be happy to advise you.'

He felt dazed by the speed of Marcia's departure. He had not had time to fully consider his future. Nodding, he tried to gather his thoughts. Hester would be home before long and it might look odd if she wasn't informed.

'Would you like to see your wife's body? To say goodbye. I can arrange that for you.'

A young nurse was hovering close by. Bright red curls were held back by the white headdress and he noticed that her eyes were a dark green. Possibly Irish. But did he want to see Marcia's body?

'I'm not sure. Maybe I should remember her as she was yesterday. Sleeping peacefully in the bed.'

The sister looked surprised so maybe he had said the

wrong thing. He began to feel pressurized. He was used to being in control and this situation was unfamiliar and put him at a disadvantage.

The nurse said, 'Most people like to say something to the dear departed.' She gave him a gentle smile.

The sister nodded. 'Let Nurse take you down. You may regret it if you don't.'

Alexander found himself glancing down at the nurse's left hand. No ring. He at once felt ashamed of himself for the interest and hoped neither woman had noticed the glance. What on earth was happening to him? He closed his eyes. *Pull yourself together. It will only take a moment.* In his position, at this time in his career, he should behave with the utmost propriety. Opening his eyes he said, 'Thank you, Nurse. I'd like to see my wife.'

He followed her from the ward and they walked side by side along the corridor and down the stairs. She spoke once or twice, the usual platitudes that people feel are suitable for the newly bereaved. She had a pleasant voice and as he stole a sideways glance at the trim young figure beside him, he was startled to see that she was smiling up at him in a way that spoke volumes about the living, and nothing about the dead. Presumably she was unmarried, he thought, and available. In the present circumstances Alexander was afraid to return her obvious interest, but he thought he might remember it for future use. Her figure beneath the uniform was nicely rounded. Perhaps he would send her some flowers to thank her for her care of his wife prior to her death. He must find out her name . . .

As soon as the doorbell rang, Maisie smiled. Quarter to eight in the morning meant Charlie had left the ship at the earliest possible moment. He loved his home. But as she hurried to the door, the smile faded. She always looked forward to his shore leave, but this time was different. This time she would have to tell him about the baby Annie was carrying and that meant he would marry her and everything would change. Still, she mustn't greet him with a gloomy face. She would wait for the right moment to tell him the

news. Restoring a smile to her face, she hurried to the front
door. Charlie refused to take the front-door key with him
when he was at sea because he loved to stand on the
doorstep, waiting to be let in. He was funny that way.

She opened the door, but, before she could greet him, he
grabbed her round the waist and lifted her up, crying, 'Wait
'til I tell you my news, Mais! You're going to love it.' He
kissed her, released her and charged past her into the kitchen.

Wait until you hear *mine*, she thought, closing the door
and following him along the narrow passage. You might
not be so thrilled.

He looked radiant, she thought, puzzled, so the news
must be great. 'You've been promoted!' she cried. If so she
would send him out to bring back a large chicken and she
would stuff it with slices of lemon and cook it with bacon
and tiny sausages. They would celebrate. Hands on hips,
she waited, watching him with affection as he prowled
around the small kitchen, his face one big smile, his eyes
gleaming with excitement.

'I'm going to be married!' he told her. 'You will have a
sister-in-law and then you will have some nephews and
nieces to fuss over. What do you think of that?'

Maisie froze. He knew. He had come home on leave and
had gone straight round to Annie. Why? She was hurt by
his disloyalty. He *always* came home to her first. Always
had done, saying that home was the most important place
in the world. The home she had created for him all those
years ago. 'You went round to Annie's!' she said dully.
'Why?'

That meant that Annie had told him about the baby so
at least she was spared that dubious task.

He stared at her. 'What are you talking about? I'm getting
married! I've met this wonderful girl – at least she's not a
girl. She's a bit older than me so I suppose you'd call her
a woman. Hester Shaw.' Her name brought another smile
to his face. 'She was on the ship. The one I told you about
in my letter.'

Maisie sat down under the weight of this revelation. 'The
one in the Verandah Café? That woman?'

'Yes!'

'But you've only known her a few weeks!'

Maisie's criticism washed over him like water off a duck's back. If anything, his smile broadened and he continued to prowl around the kitchen, opening the larder door for no reason and admiring the new teapot that stood upturned on the draining board. 'Wait 'til you meet her, Mais. Honestly, you'll love her. You'll love each other! She'll be coming up to Liverpool as soon as she's sorted things out in London. She's . . . . Well, she's living with this man and he's married.' He snatched a glance at her face.

'Oh, Charlie! Do please sit down,' she implored. 'You're making me dizzy. I need to think.'

'What about? Aren't you pleased? I thought you'd be excited for me.' Now it was his turn to look hurt. 'Don't you want me to be happy? We're going to have a proper wedding – she's that sort of person. We're—'

'Wait a minute!' She held up her hand. 'I thought you said she was living with a married man? Where's his wife living? I can't make head or tail of all this.' She was stalling, giving herself time to decide whether or not she should tell him about Annie's child.

His smile faded. 'He lives with his wife who's dying of something or other but he pays for a flat where they spend time together. She's not happy with him. He sounds a real bully and . . .'

'So he's rich, this man?'

'I suppose so. He's some sort of policeman, but high up. A detective superintendent maybe. Or an inspector. I forget. I don't want to think about him. I just want Hester to tell him about us and get out of there. She can stay here, can't she, until we find a place of our own? I can kip on the floor with some cushions. We're going to live very near you so . . .' He stopped, disappointment written large over his face. 'What is it, Mais? I never expected you to be like this. Such a wet blanket. Don't you see? I *love* her. I've never felt like this before. Never.'

'Not even for Annie?' Annie was the better bet, Maisie decided suddenly. Annie was one of them and she and Maisie got along. Sort of. This posh woman from London was much more of a threat. Maisie began to prejudge her with what little she knew. 'Has this Hester woman said she'll marry you? Do you trust her?'

He stared at her, astonished. 'Do I trust her? What a ridiculous question! Course I trust her – with my life! She'd never do anything to hurt me.'

'I think Annie trusts you.' She held her breath.

Charlie threw out his hands in a gesture of helplessness. 'Trusts me to do what? I never promised her anything. You ask her. We never talked about getting married. Nothing like that. She'll tell you herself. We had fun, that's all. Now it's over.'

He sat down, watching for her reaction.

'She might have hoped to marry you.'

He shrugged. 'The word never came up. She knows what I am. A girl in every port.' He tried to laugh, but it was more of a grimace.

'Until now?'

He nodded. 'I'm not good with words, Mais, you know that. I can't tell you how much I love Hester, but if I don't wed her, I won't wed anyone.'

Maisie hesitated, her stomach churning with anxiety. Whatever happened, she mustn't turn him against her. If he married this awful Hester woman, they might move away. They might go back to London! The woman might turn Charlie against his own sister. 'If this married man's wife is dying,' she said slowly, 'he might want to marry Hester.'

Charlie snorted. 'Fat chance. She's in love with me. Honestly, Mais, she adores me and I can't live without her.' His expression darkened and his voice changed. 'If I thought I couldn't marry her I'd . . . I'd do something terrible! I just couldn't bear it. I'll go mad if anything comes between us.'

'Don't talk like that!' Maisie was frightened. She had never seen her brother in this state of mind and it set alarm bells ringing. Would he really do something terrible? 'Do something terrible? Such as . . .?' she asked, dreading his answer.

His face showed his anguish. 'Chuck myself overboard,' he whispered hoarsely.

That was the moment when Maisie knew she could *not* tell him about Annie. Whatever happened, she couldn't be the one to break the news. She had never seen him so taken with a woman so perhaps this *was* the one. There was no way she could ruin his chance of happiness – but Annie could definitely put a large dent in it!

With an effort she thrust Annie to the back of her mind. For the moment she and Charlie must be happy together. He must never think that she was less than enthusiastic about Hester.

'Right then, Charlie!' she cried, forcing a bright smile. 'Today it's going to be your favourite – a big fat chicken and all the trimmings! Get along to the butcher's while I start on the rest of the meal.'

To her relief, his mood brightened. Jumping up he hugged her so that she cried out, kissed her hard on the cheek and obediently rushed off on his errand. Please, she thought, don't let Maisie turn up with her news. Not today of all days. Today must be a celebration. If Hester *was* the apple of Charlie's eye, she would play along. She would make herself love the woman. If Charlie loves her, I'll love her, she vowed. Annie Green was a wild card, however, and she and Charlie must work it out between them, although Maisie couldn't see how it could be done. Sighing deeply, she crossed her fingers. She was used to being important in Charlie's life and prided herself on having guided him through various crises when he was younger, but events, she now realized, were spiralling out of her control. Charlie's future seemed to hang in the balance and for once she had no idea what would happen next.

Marcia's funeral took place on the twelfth of December in pouring rain. Refreshments for the mourners were offered at Hilsomer House, but nobody lingered too long after they had eaten. As the last mourners had left, only Edith remained. She had endured the funeral, not because Marcia had been a favourite of hers, but because she needed to talk to her nephew alone. She had found it hard to mourn the dead woman, and trying to project an air of grief had been a struggle. In her eyes, Marcia had been a weak woman and had not deserved Alexander. Her only asset had been the money and fortunately that now belonged to her nephew.

He gave her a tired smile as he sat back in the armchair with his legs sprawled in front of him. 'I'm glad that's over,' he told her. 'At least she went peacefully and didn't suffer.'

Sitting upright on a hard chair, Edith narrowed her eyes. She would not beat about the bush, she decided. 'I think you should now make an honest woman of Hester Shaw!' She watched with satisfaction as his mouth fell open with shock. That would teach him to make a fool of her. 'Did you really think I wouldn't find out? You must take me for a fool.'

'But how . . .' he gasped, too shocked to hide his discomfiture. 'Did she tell you?'

' "She" being the cat's mother!' she snapped. '*Miss Shaw* did not tell me because obviously you had instructed her to keep your nasty little secret! I'm surprised at you, Alexander. Leading a double life is not what I expected from you.' She explained briefly how the truth had come to light. 'You can hardly blame the poor woman for rambling when she was concussed. You are the deceiver, Alexander, not Miss Shaw. All my sympathies are with her, if you must know. You have treated her very shabbily.'

He was struggling to regain the high ground, she thought. It served him right. It irked her that she had been deceived for so long.

'I suppose you kept her locked away in a cupboard somewhere!'

'It was a neat little flat!'

'Ah, yes. Chalker Street. And you never took her out anywhere. How could you if you were constantly afraid you would be seen together? Not much of a life for an intelligent and attractive woman.'

'She didn't have to stay,' he protested, flushing with annoyance. 'She could have walked out at any time.' He sat up and drew in his legs.

Edith relished his difficulties. Recovering from the shock, he had obviously resigned himself to the discovery, but he had no real idea what pressure his aunt could bring to bear. He knew he had always been the favourite, but he would be wondering if she was about to disown him. Poor Alexander. Edith held back a smile. She was enjoying herself.

Leaning forward, he tried to justify the past. 'You don't know the state she was in when we met. She was walking along the pavement in Euston Road. Yes, *Euston Road!* You know what that means. She was hoping to find a client. Do I need to spell it out for you? She was at her wits' end. Thrown out of her position as a nanny because the husband wanted to share her bed! Did she tell you that?'

'No. I didn't press her. The past is the past.' She would not allow him to see that she was shocked. So Miss Shaw had a shady past.

'She wasn't a prost—' He bit off the word. 'She wasn't a fallen woman, but she was hovering on the brink.'

'And you rescued her. How very noble of you.' She spoke with a touch of sarcasm in her voice, but she did admire him for rescuing Miss Shaw. However, what had Alexander been doing in Euston Road? She preferred not to dwell on that aspect.

'I took pity on her – she looked so out of place and it was raining hard. She was bedraggled and miserable. When I stopped the cab to speak to her she nearly died of fright, but I would have been the first of many. She said that had been her plan. Eventually she would have fallen very low. You might say I found her in the nick of time. Ask her. She'll tell you that's how it happened.'

Edith's curiosity was aroused. She found it impossible to imagine Miss Shaw tramping the streets around Euston Station, competing with an assortment of street women, who were all in search of wayward men who were looking for . . . for what Edith could only call 'gratification'.

'Did she take you back to her room?' she asked, intrigued. This was a side of life that had never interested her before.

'Back to her room? For heaven's sake, Aunt Edith! How

could she? She didn't have a room! Hester had no room, no money, nothing and nowhere. I took her to a cheap hotel where I thought I would go unrecognized. There she burst into tears and I felt sorry for her. She was desperate,' he protested, 'and I've been good to her. If she pretends otherwise, she's lying – and I don't think she would lie.'

'Unless you tell her to! She's been sharing your lie for weeks. Friend of a friend cum travelling companion cum dressmaker! Hah!'

A spiky silence lengthened uncomfortably. Edith hesitated. She had to ask a very personal question and it might be that she had gone too far. Alexander might tell her to mind her own business and he would have a right to do so. She took a deep breath. It was harder than she expected.

'You could marry her and have a family, couldn't you? She's not too old, surely.'

'Presumably.' He stood up and crossed to the window.

'She's a good woman. I like her. She has spirit and you know her well enough. She owes you a great deal. That's my suggestion. You may have other ideas.'

'I have thought about it,' he said slowly, 'and I know she'd agree but . . .' He turned to her. 'Maybe I need a younger wife.'

Edith shook her head. 'Young women are scatter-brained and cannot be trusted. A younger wife would not have Miss Shaw's presence. Can you imagine attending an important function with a young and foolish girl clinging to your arm? I fear for today's young women – they have no idea of how to behave in a formal setting, and would be of no use to you as a responsible adult. I fear that the modern generation is restless and unreliable. You would regret it, Alexander. Mark my words.' She thought he looked disappointed.

'You're being a little harsh,' he said, resuming his seat. He eased his shoulders with a small groan. 'I feel so tense. I ache all over.'

'It's been a trying time for you, these last few days. Try to snatch some rest. Let Miss Shaw look after you.'

'I shan't move her in at home just yet – that's if I decide to marry her,' he amended hastily. 'I think a few months would be discreet, don't you?'

'Certainly.' She was suddenly hopeful. He seemed to have agreed with her. A few words from her from time to time would probably convince him. 'But you should marry her before she moves in and not after. There must be nothing at which people can point the finger. I want to hear no whispers. Nor do I want to see any sly glances. We have never had a scandal in the family and I don't want one now. You must make an honest woman of her. I imagine that that's what you promised her.'

'I dare say.' *Had he said any such thing?* It was possible, he supposed.

'Good. It must all be above board from now on. Remember you have a career and a reputation to think about.' She frowned. 'That fellow that's been arrested. Drummond, isn't it? Isn't he one of your colleagues? I read about it yesterday. Monkey business of some kind, wasn't it?'

'I knew him, yes. Odd fellow. I never did like him. Something not quite right there.'

'Avoid him like the plague. He could contaminate you.' Edith stood up, having neatly changed the subject. She had said enough about Miss Shaw, she told herself. Let the advice simmer in his brain. He had almost certainly understood the unspoken message. She wanted him to marry Hester. If he did, Edith's money would follow.

Alexander sat for a long time after his aunt had left. Their conversation had left a sour taste in his mouth. It was clear what Edith Carradine wanted, and she was rarely refused. So much for easing out Hester and trying his luck with the young nurse at the hospital. She was a perfect example of the modern young woman his aunt had been describing. He had thought about her a great deal and recognized that she had signalled her interest in him. She was pretty and flirtatious and young – and very desirable, but his aunt had pointed out a flaw. She would find it difficult to move into

his middle-aged way of life – and she might even leave
him at some stage for a younger man. The point his aunt
had made about his professional life was also valid. Would
Della know how to behave at a formal dinner? Would she
be able to give a dinner party for business associates and
their sensible wives? In other words, would she embarrass
him and spoil his chances of promotion? The police force
did not suffer fools gladly. Damn.

He glanced up as the housekeeper knocked and entered.

'The washing-up is done, Mr Waring, and I've sent Rosie
home. I said not to bother you right now, but said you'd
give her the money next week.'

'Thank you.'

'And I know this might not be the right time, Mr Waring,
but are you keeping on all the staff now that your wife . . .
that is, Mrs Waring has gone to a better place? God rest her
soul.'

He nodded. 'I doubt I'll be making any changes for a
while, if ever. Is Cook still here?'

'No sir. She slipped away as soon as the refreshments
were served because she came in two hours early because
of the funeral and with her bad leg. But she left you some
of yesterday's mutton pie and I'll put the vegetables on
before I go. Will seven o'clock be all right with you?'

He nodded.

'And I'm to say how sorry we are about poor Mrs Waring.
You'll miss her.'

Alexander watched her retreat and wondered if he would
miss Marcia. He knew he ought to, but that was another
matter. Rousing himself, he went upstairs and into the
bedroom where his wife had slept beside him for so many
years. The room smelled of her perfumes and face powders
and when he looked into her wardrobe the racks of clothes
seemed to reproach him for the fact that they would never
be worn again. Perhaps he could give some to Hester, he
thought. She could have them altered to fit. Waste not, want
not. Marcia had been a spendthrift in her younger days and
had enjoyed shopping in Bond Street and frequent visits to
the dressmakers. On second thoughts he would give the

clothes away. Even on Hester, they would remind him of his wife and he would rather forget her.

Marcia had not been the ideal wife and had failed to give him children. Her doctor had considered her too frail to risk her health. He recalled his aunt's words about Hester. Would she give him children – and did he still want a family?

'Hell and damnation!' he cried and turning on his heel, strode out of the bedroom and slammed the door. He could not face a night on his own while his mind struggled with so many problems. He needed sympathy and understanding, he thought in a rare moment of self-pity. He would eat his mutton pie and vegetables and then spend the night with Hester. And this time he would stay until morning.

Seven

Hester had not seen Alexander since her return. A note from him about Marcia's death and the coming funeral had taken her by surprise. Her first reaction had been guilt that for so long she and Alexander had been deceiving the poor woman. Then curiosity filled her and she wondered whether she dare attend the funeral. Discarding that idea – Mrs Carradine would spot her – she had tried to concentrate on the words she would use to convince Alexander that he would be better off without her. Unfortunately she had wasted time by luxuriating in thoughts about Charlie Barnes and the prepared speech she needed had not materialized.

This evening she was hoping Alexander would not come to her because she was still not ready to break the news. More importantly, she was determined not to allow him into her bed and had decided to complain of a sore throat and aching joints. She would say she had contracted something on the ship. Alexander hated ill health and would not want to risk catching anything infectious. Trying to think of kind ways to break the news, she had tried to convince herself that he would be relieved at their parting of the ways. Without her tugging at his conscience, Alexander would be free to choose a younger wife and make a fresh start, but Hester suspected that he would prefer to be the one who ended the relationship. How, though, to arrange that?

Hester had received some money from Edith – her wages for her duties as travelling companion – and had secretly bought herself a simple tweed skirt and jacket and a warm blouse to wear on her journey to Liverpool. She still needed to find some stout shoes, but planned to go shopping again tomorrow. Her hopes were that she and Alexander would part on reasonable terms and she clung to that idea as he turned the key in the lock and called out a greeting.

'How did the funeral go?' she asked as she helped him off with his wet coat and hung it on the hall stand. She assumed Edith had told him that she knew of their relationship.

'Well enough,' he replied. 'There was quite a crowd in the church, but don't ask me who they were. Friends of Marcia's, I suppose. I didn't know she still had any. She's been ill so long and they soon lose interest. You could have come, actually.'

'But why should I? I've never set eyes on her. What excuse could there be for my attendance?' She gave a slight cough and grimaced, putting a hand to her throat, but he seemed not to notice.

'The vicar spoke well, but the hymns went on and on.' He threw himself down on the chaise longue and yawned.

'Who chose the hymns?'

'I left that to the vicar. What does it matter? Poor Marcia wasn't going to hear them.'

'Sometimes people write down the hymns they want for their funeral.'

'Well, if she did, I didn't find the list. Don't I get a kiss?'

'I have a sore throat. I was keeping my distance.'

'Oh, God! You sound just like Marcia!' He stretched out his legs and surveyed his shoes. 'I had to wear these old things. The others were ruined by the wet grass. I do hate rain-sodden funerals.'

Hester poured him a glass of brandy.

He sipped it gratefully. 'I shall see the lawyer on Tuesday next.' He held out his hand. 'Come and sit with me. I have to tell you that something odd happened afterwards. It will make you smile. Don't look like that! I won't bite you.' As she settled beside him, he put an arm round her shoulder.

'Someone has recommended you as a replacement for Marcia!'

'Oh, no!' Unguarded, the words slipped out.

'Oh, yes. You'll never guess who it was?'

'Not Mrs Carradine.'

'The same!'

'But why should she? How can she think me at all suitable?'

'She obviously does.' He grinned suddenly. 'Why didn't you warn me that she knew about us? It gave me a terrific shock. Why didn't you tell me she'd discovered our secret?'

'I haven't seen you since I arrived back. You were busy with the funeral arrangements. I would have told you tonight. I'm sorry, Alex. I was going to tell you.' His attitude confused her.

'She thinks I should make an honest woman of you!' He actually laughed. 'I thought you'd be surprised. My stuffy, prim old aunt is urging me to marry my mistress, settle down and raise a family! Wonders will never cease.'

For a moment or two Hester was seized by panic. She went hot and cold with shock. His arm around her shoulder made her feel disloyal towards Charlie so she coughed again to remind him that she was infectious.

Ignoring the cough, he turned to look at her. 'Nothing to say, Hester? I thought you'd be pleased to have a champion. She seems to have formed a very favourable opinion of you.'

'But she doesn't know about . . . I mean, she doesn't know the full story.'

'Yes, she does. That's what is so amazing. She insisted on knowing how we met and why we set up home together. She was taken aback, but quickly recovered, and still thinks you're the woman for me! You're fortunate that she and Marcia never did get along. Almost any woman would be preferable to Marcia according to my aunt.'

Hester looked at him. Was that meant to be a compliment? If so it was somewhat dubious. She tried to concentrate. The conversation was leading in the wrong direction and she didn't know how to deal with it. The fates seemed to be conspiring to make it difficult for her to tell Alexander that she was leaving him for another man. Did she dare tell him now, she wondered, before he actually proposed to her? How ironic that Edith Carradine had decided that she liked Hester enough to push her name to the top of any list of suitable future Mrs Warings. Ironic and a little dangerous because Hester had no wish to humiliate Alexander. There was no need to make an enemy of him. Far better to pre-empt a proposal which she would have to refuse. She would tell him immediately, she decided, and took a deep breath.

She said instead, 'Have you had some supper?'

Coward! What was the matter with her? He wasn't going to bite her! And she had promised Charlie that she would tell her lover what was happening.

'Yes, thanks.' Alexander stretched and rubbed his eyes. 'What about you?'

'I'm not hungry . . . My throat's rather sore,' she repeated. 'I feel full of aches today.'

'A sore throat?' At last it registered and he leaned away from her.

She tried again. 'Alex, there's something I must tell you . . .'

'I got Drummond, by the way.' His eyes shone. 'He's under investigation. He won't thwart me again. It even made the front page!'

Distracted, she asked, 'What happened to him? What did he do?'

'You mean what did *I* do!' He grinned.

Suddenly she did not want to know. She took another deep breath. 'There's something I have to tell you. It's about you and me.' She felt his arm stiffen around her shoulder and rushed on before she lost her nerve. 'I do think we've been happy together and I'm glad you're free to marry again but . . . I don't think it should be me.'

He drew back and turned so that he could face her and she saw the surprise in his eyes. Tell him now, she told herself, while you still can. 'It's not that I'm not very fond of you or that I don't appreciate what you're offering but . . .'

He raised his eyebrows. 'What do you think I'm offering?'

'I thought you were suggesting that we marry. Am I wrong?' Hope flared. How stupid it would be to tell him about Charlie if Alexander were not intending to propose. Flustered she hesitated.

'I'm thinking about it.' His expression was enigmatic.

'Ah! Well, so am I and . . .' She had a flash of inspiration. 'And you will want a family and I am probably too old.' She felt weak with relief. Of course, she could persuade him that she would be a disappointment. That way Alexander could reject her without losing face.

'You're not too old, Hester.' He kissed her lightly. 'I have it on the best authority. Aunt Edith tells me so!'

'She can't know how I feel. It's not simply *having* the children, I would have to care for them for years and I'll be forty-one in ten years' time.'

Please, she prayed, be swayed by this argument and then you need never know about Charlie Barnes. You can get rid of me and not face any criticism.

He shook his head. 'You're not getting cold feet, are you? You will have help, Hester. A nanny, a children's nurse – whoever you need. You can choose them yourself.'

Hester closed her eyes and conceded defeat. They were going round in circles and he was going to propose. She had promised Charlie she would tell him and then leave. Come what may, she would have to tell Alexander.

'There's someone else,' she said. 'It's only fair to tell you. If you want me to go I'll . . .'

He stood up abruptly and stared down at her in disbelief. Hester thought of the address she had in her purse. If he threw her out she would make no protest. She had enough money for the fare and she would go north on the next train and find Charlie's house. The idea frightened her, but she would do it.

The silence lengthened as Alexander towered over her, a strange expression on his face. An expression she could not read.

She said, 'I'm sorry if it upsets you.'

Deliberately Alexander sat down opposite her and leaned forward. He seemed very calm and that worried her.

'Someone else?' He shook his head. 'What on earth are you talking about? It's settled between us, Hester. We've had an understanding for a long time. You and I will be married and . . .'

'I can't marry you! Please listen to me, Alexander. I have promised to marry someone else.'

He laughed. 'I don't believe you! You don't *know* anyone else.'

'A man I met recently. We met on the ship. He asked me and I said "Yes." '

'Nonsense! That's impossible. You were travelling with Aunt Edith. She would know if . . .'

'We kept it from her. She was indisposed most of the time. It all happened very quickly and it took us both by surprise.' She could see by his eyes that perhaps he was starting to believe her. 'I'm truly sorry if you're . . . distressed in any way, but I have never promised to marry you because you have never asked me.'

'Now you listen to *me*, Hester.' He sat back in the chair, eyeing her steadily, and she felt a shiver of fear run through her. 'You are going to marry me because I say so. There will be no discussion about any other man so don't speak of him again. We had an understanding which you are trying to ignore. Marcia is dead and buried. You will marry me.' He gave a thin laugh. 'We can't disappoint Aunt Edith, can we?'

Secretly annoyed by Hester's refusal, Alexander collected his coat and without another word, slammed out of the flat before his temper got the better of him. How dare she find someone else!

'Cheap little whore!' he muttered, striding rapidly through the dark streets, dodging the puddles. He turned up the collar of his overcoat and tried to think calmly. Who the hell was this 'other man'? And why hadn't his aunt kept an eye on Hester? Perhaps with hindsight it had been a mistake to send Hester along on the trip, but it had seemed perfectly reasonable at the time. He could hardly have guessed this would happen. It was enough to try the patience of a saint – and he was no saint. He thought of Drummond and his eyes narrowed.

'You got what you deserved!' he told his absent colleague.

The London streets were eerie at night and heavy cloud made this particular night gloomier than usual, but

Alexander strode purposely ahead, his walking stick striking the pavement sharply with every second step. He passed few people – a drunken man weaving his way along the middle of the road and a woman slumped in a doorway. Destitute, sick or drunk?

'This is the twentieth century, for God's sake!' he said aloud. 'This country is going to the dogs!' He glared around the empty street. 'Where the hell are the constables?' Tomorrow he would write a sharply worded memo.

He walked on towards his home, but abruptly, as he reached a corner, he changed direction. Talk to Aunt Edith, he advised himself. She never went to bed until midnight. His aunt would help him find out more about this wretched man who had so impressed Hester. How old was he? Was he a passenger or a member of the crew? An officer, maybe? His breath came rapidly and his heart rate had quickened. Where did he live? What sort of man had Hester fallen in love with? God, what a fool she was.

Unless he was wealthier, younger and better-looking than he was. For a moment his self-confidence wavered, but he quickly straightened his back. Whoever and whatever the man was, Hester was going to remain with him, Alexander – the man who had protected her for years. He would see to it that she regretted her disloyalty and he would eventually convince her of her stupidity. Hester was his property and he was keeping her.

Ten minutes later he was sitting opposite his aunt, perched on the edge of the chair with a glass of malt whisky in his hand. Edith was wearing a voluminous plaid wrap over a pink flannelette nightgown and her thinning hair was hidden beneath an old-fashioned mob-cap made of frilled cotton. If she found it embarrassing to be found in her bizarre nightwear, she gave no sign but gave her nephew all her attention, listening in a disbelieving silence to his revelation. Now it was her turn to be shocked, he reflected grimly.

Edith tossed her head. 'Miss Shaw with an admirer? I can assure you that was quite impossible. I would have known. Really, Alexander, you must think me very dense to have allowed a romance to blossom under my very nose!'

'So, you didn't know.' He forced himself to sip his drink, trying to hide his agitation, aware of his aunt's beady eyes watching his every move.

'There was nothing to know! Perhaps she is pretending.'

'Lying you mean? Why should she lie about such a thing? I'm offering her marriage. Surely that is what she's been waiting for.' He made a determined effort to slow down his rapid breathing. 'I don't think she was making it up. She seemed very nervous, but she was convincing.'

Alexander suddenly hoped she *had* invented this man, but if so, why? Was she trying to make him jealous, perhaps? Women could be devious creatures, in his experience. He recalled the occasion when he had discovered a much younger Marcia burning a letter which she claimed came from a male acquaintance, but which she later confessed she had written to herself to try and reawaken his interest. Contrite, feeling partly to blame, he had forgiven her, uncomfortably aware that he would never be able to discover the truth of it.

If Hester was also inventing an admirer she would soon admit it. Yes, that was it. She was trying to make him jealous.

'You may be right.' He grasped at the idea with relief, relaxed a little and leaned back in the chair. 'Really, Hester is a little old for those girlish tricks!'

Edith was frowning. 'There was one thing . . . I do remember one thing that happened which seemed a trifle odd. After she had fallen down the stairs – or been knocked down, whatever it was – the crew sent some flowers. They said it was by way of an apology or some such. A nice gesture, I thought, but the young man was positively beaming at her and I remember thinking about it later and wondering if it were some kind of joke they were playing on her. Or a way of sweetening her, in case she was considering making a claim for compensation for the accident. Something other than a genuine goodwill gesture.'

'What sort of flowers?' he asked slowly.

'They were roses. Red roses.' Her eyes widened as she replayed the scene in her mind. 'You don't think it was . . .

Oh, no! Not *eight* red roses! Do you?' Appalled, she stared at him.

'Eight? I don't see the significance of eight.'

'I didn't count them, obviously, because she at once took them back to her own cabin – to send for Mrs Pontings, the stewardess. They always have suitable vases.'

'But eight?'

'One for each letter of "I love you"!' She stared at her nephew. 'He would never dare! Would he?'

'It depends what sort of man he is. How did Hester react?'

'I don't know. I daresay she was pleased. Flattered. She mostly had her back to me. I hardly saw the young man because Hester was between us, facing the cabin door.'

'You said "young man" so presumably you saw him.'

'Not really unless – maybe just a glimpse. He had a young voice and a young way of speaking. You know what I mean.' She let out a long sigh and drew her shoulders together, hunching into her plaid wrap.

He said, 'If it's true, all our plans are flying out of the window!'

Alexander felt unable to blame his aunt to her face, although he did hold her responsible for the situation. But he needed her on his side. There was no way he could alienate her without suffering the financial consequences. Somehow he must find out the man's identity. How he hated to be put on the defensive. The wretched girl had made him look a fool.

Finishing his drink in one large gulp, he studied the empty glass until his aunt took the hint and offered to refill it.

'I have an idea,' he told her.

Hours later, in Garth Street in Liverpool, Maisie and her brother ate their boiled bacon and onion and mopped up the juices with slices of thick brown bread. The atmosphere was tense. Charlie was tetchy and saying very little, while Maisie watched him with a stony expression. When at last he sat back in his chair, Maisie braced herself.

'So when are you going to tell Annie?' she demanded. 'I don't want her turning up here when you're at sea so that I'm the one that has to tell her. It's not fair, Charlie. If you're set on this other girl you have to tell Annie – and the sooner the better. Especially if your girl is coming up here.'

He looked at her unhappily. 'Couldn't you break it to her, Mais? You're good at . . .'

Her voice rose. 'No I couldn't! I mean I could, but I won't. You've got yourself into this mess, so you can jolly well get yourself out! She won't take it well and you can see why. She must have thought you would settle down with her or she wouldn't keep lending you money.'

He brightened. 'That reminds me, I'll be late tonight. There's a game at Mick's place and they've counted me in. I'm feeling lucky today!' He gave her the boyish grin that always touched her sisterly heart, but she was not about to be distracted from her line of argument.

'Don't talk to me about poker,' she said crossly. 'I'd like a penny for every time you've felt lucky. I'd be a million-aire by now.'

His face fell. 'Look, Mais, I must get a bit of cash together. I've got responsibilities. I've heard of a flat, but it'll most likely be a month's rent in advance.'

'You've been out looking for a place to live? You never said! That's not like you.'

'Chalky told me about it.'

Her eyes widened as a new thought struck her. 'Suppose Annie gets to hear about it – the flat – and you making enquiries at the church and everything. She'll think it's for you and her!'

'Jesus wept!' Charlie was shocked.

He looked, Maisie thought, the way he had looked when he was caught scrumping apples in someone's back garden when he was ten years old. She had to resist the urge to hug him. At the time she had pleaded with the constable who led him home by one ear, persuading him to give Charlie another chance. Now she could do nothing to help him. He was on his own.

The front-door bell made them jump.

'That'll be her!' cried Maisie, jumping to her feet. 'I bet

it'll be Annie! If it is I'm off to do some shopping.' She rushed into the passage and struggled into her coat.

'Don't go!' cried Charlie. 'Mais, please!'

He doesn't know what's coming to him, thought Maisie, determined not to be dragged into the coming row. Ignoring her brother, she snatched up her shopping basket and purse and headed for the front door. As expected Annie waited on the step, her expression a mixture of hope and apprehension.

'Hello, Annie!' Maisie said loudly. 'I'm just off shopping, but Charlie'll give you a cuppa.' She flashed her a smile and hurried out, leaving the door ajar so that Annie could let herself in.

Annie called after her. 'Did you tell him?' Maisie pretended not to hear.

'Hester Shaw!' Maisie grumbled as she distanced herself from the inevitable conflict. 'I'd like to ring your blinking neck!'

Charlie stumbled to his feet as Annie came into the kitchen and in doing so, jerked the table and the milk jug shook enough to spill some of its contents. He was mopping it up with a tea towel when Annie threw her arms round his neck in a clumsy embrace.

'Hang on!' he told her gruffly.

She at once drew back, eyeing him nervously. 'So you're home, Charlie.'

'Looks like it!' He forced a smile. 'I suppose you've come for your money. Well, there's a poker game . . .'

'No I haven't, Charlie. I've just come to see you – because you didn't come to see me and you always do. First thing when you get your shore leave.'

He cursed his sister for rushing off. She should have stayed to help him. Telling Annie about Hester was going to be very tricky. 'Sit down, Annie. Cup of tea?'

'No, thanks – I mean, yes, please.' She sat down on the chair Maisie had recently vacated and folded her hands over her stomach.

She was giving him a funny look, he thought, but she

couldn't have heard. He'd made Maisie a promise – he would tell Annie face to face. He took a deep breath. He would brazen it out. Make it clear that marriage between him and her had never entered his head. He would say, 'Wish me luck, Annie. I'm getting married.' Annie was a good sort. She'd understand.

He said cheerfully, 'Well, how's things?'

'I'm not sure,' she said. 'It's up to you.'

Wrong question and wrong answer. He shook his head as if to clear it.

'Thought you was giving me a cup of tea,' she prompted.

'Sorry. Yes.' He busied himself with tea and milk and handed a cup to her. 'Annie, I've got some great news!' That sounded OK, he thought. 'Yes. Exciting news. I'm . . .'

'So have I.'

'What?' The interruption distracted him and he frowned. 'Seems I'm getting married!' He closed his eyes, unable to bear the look on her face.

'Oh, Charlie. Maisie told you. Oh, so you are pleased? I mean. I did wonder but . . . You know.'

Whatever was she talking about? He opened his eyes and saw that she was beaming at him over the tea cup.

'I thought I'd never get round to it,' he said. 'I said I wouldn't – I never expected to feel like this but . . . I just know it's the right thing to do. As soon as I set eyes on her, I couldn't think of anything else. Like a bolt from the blue!'

Poor Annie. She looked totally confused. He wasn't doing this very well. He frowned. 'Mais told me what?'

'About . . .' Annie frowned. 'Set eyes on who? What are you on about, Charlie? What bolt from the blue? Have you been drinking? You're talking in riddles.'

She lowered the cup and settled it in the saucer and he noticed that she was no longer beaming at him.

'Set eyes on who?' she repeated.

'Hester.' His mind refused to work, but as she continued to stare at him a few of her words came back to him. 'What am I supposed to be pleased about?'

'The baby, of course. Didn't Maisie tell you?'

'Hester Shaw,' he said, determined not to stop now that

he had made a start. 'I met her on the ship. We're going to be married.'

As they each grasped the significance of what the other had been saying, shock settled heavily on Charlie's shoulders. He slumped in his chair. A baby. She was telling *him* so it must be his child. A trickle of fear ran down his back and his throat felt dry. He said again, 'I'm going to marry her. I asked her already and she said "Yes".' Did that create some prior claim, he wondered desperately. 'A few weeks ago. I met her on the ship.'

'You've said that already.'

She swallowed hard and he saw the misery in her eyes.

'Look, I'm sorry,' he muttered, feeling his face grow hot. 'I didn't know about . . . you having a baby.'

'*Us* having a baby,' she corrected him. 'It's yours as well. I was hoping you'd be pleased. That we could . . .'

'No! I'm marrying Hester. It's already been arranged. She's coming up here any day now.' Annie must understand, he thought, that there was no way he was going to give up Hester. 'You'd like her.'

'No, Charlie, I won't like her. I'll hate her – because you ought by rights to be marrying me.' Her fear and shock were turning into anger – he could hear it by the tone of her voice.

'Annie, I'm truly sorry,' he told her. 'If I'd known earlier . . .'

He left the rest unsaid because it wasn't true. Nothing would have stopped him. Or would it? Could he have fallen in love with Hester if he had known Annie was carrying his child? Probably not, because by then he'd have been set to marry Annie and he would never have gone back on his promise. He'd have married Annie and mourned the loss of Hester for the rest of his life.

Annie said, 'I wonder what she'll say when you tell her about me and the baby.'

'She doesn't have to know. I won't tell her.'

'Maisie might. Maisie knew, but she must have been too scared to tell you. She said I had to do it – so I have.' She slid from the stool and faced him, her face pale. 'So you're going to abandon me, is that it? Me and your baby? That's definite?'

'Yes.' He could hardly speak, his throat was so dry.

'Just like that! You're not even going to think about it? Not even for a minute or two?'

'No. At least, I'll help you with the money. I promise.'

'What – with the money you win at poker? You already owe *me* money. Thanks very much!'

'I'll provide what I can, Annie.'

'You don't understand, do you?' she accused him. 'It's not just about the money. It's about us being a family and the baby having a father.'

He felt breathless, paralysed. Couldn't think of any words that would lessen the blow. What would Hester think of him? Would Maisie tell her? Maybe Maisie and Annie would gang up on him. Try to make him do the decent thing by Annie and the baby. How much time had he got before the child would be born, he wondered.

'When's it due?' he asked.

Her eyes brightened. 'July. A summer baby. They say they're the best because of the warm weather and you can put the pram outside in the fresh air.' She was suddenly hopeful and he cursed his stupidity.

'Want to change your mind, Charlie? It might be a little boy. You can play footie with him. It'd be fun.'

He shook his head. If he said any more he would only make it worse. Better to keep quiet. He tried to imagine himself showing a toddler how to kick a ball. Yes, it would be fun, but he would give Hester a child.

Annie put a hand out to him, but he ignored it.

She said, 'Don't you love me any more? You did love me. You said so.'

'I never said I wanted to marry you, Annie.' His heart was heavy and he wanted to cry for Annie's grief. 'I never wanted to marry anyone. You know that. Look, I'm truly sorry but . . . It's impossible, Annie. You wouldn't want to marry me, would you, knowing I'm in love with Hester? We'd end up hating each other. I'd hate you because you made me give up Hester and you'd hate me because I couldn't love you . . . Oh, Annie, please. I can't!' He put his head in his hands. 'I don't want to hurt you, I never wanted that, but what am I to do?'

'It's really what am *I* to do!' she snapped. 'Your own child and you don't care tuppence about it! You're a selfish pig, Charlie. What happens when I'm out with your kid and I pass you and her with your other kids? How are you going to feel then? How am *I* going to feel – or the kid when it's old enough to understand? How's it going to feel, eh? So much for the great Charlie Barnes!'

Her voice had risen and she was suddenly furiously, wordlessly at the mercy of her emotions. With a cry, she leaned over the table and swept everything on to the floor. 'Damn you, Charlie! You and your blooming Hester!'

Turning in search of something else to throw, Annie snatched up the teapot and hurled it at him. He ducked and she burst into tears as it smashed against the window and fell into the sink. A large crack spread across the window as she ran sobbing from the house, Charlie bent his head, clutching at his chest, as though a similar crack had opened in his heart.

Eight

Two days passed while Hester waited anxiously in London, waiting for the letter from Charlie, wondering whether to go or stay. This was not because she had any doubts about Charlie, but because Alexander and Edith Carradine were making it so difficult for her. Alexander had pointed out that it was almost Christmas and that Edith was spending Christmas with him and wanted Hester to be there to share it. That, Edith had told Hester, would give her time to be certain in her own mind that she was doing the right thing by throwing away a secure and happy future with a wealthy God-fearing man for someone she hardly knew. Edith had added her own particular line of reasoning, saying that with Marcia gone to her eternal rest, Alexander would face a lonely and miserable Christmas if Hester and Edith did not keep him company.

'Surely you owe him that much,' she said. 'You can leave when the Christmas period is over. A few more days cannot make that much difference if you are going to spend the rest of your life with Mr Barnes. I cannot believe you would be so selfish, Miss Shaw.'

When Hester tried to argue, Edith spoke more sharply. 'I think Alexander and I have behaved very well towards you, considering the way you have treated us. I have interceded with my nephew on your behalf and he has forgiven you for your deceit. The least you can do is spare him a few more days.'

Hester's protests that she and Charlie wanted to spend Christmas together fell on deaf ears. There always seemed to be one or other of them present in the flat and Hester wondered uneasily if this was deliberate. She presumed she was free to leave at any moment, but a new nagging doubt had taken hold of her. There had been no letter from either Charlie or his sister. He had promised to write, trusting her to leave London and travel to Liverpool when she felt the time was right – so why was there no letter, she asked herself desperately. Perhaps his sister had talked him out of it, had convinced him that he had a duty towards Annie. Hester would not believe that Charlie had willingly changed his mind. She knew he loved her and she had no doubts about her feelings for him. Was he ill, perhaps? Would anyone let her know if he were sick? Or had his sister been taken ill?

She forced herself to consider what she would do if Charlie had changed his mind – or had it changed for him by Annie or Maisie. Could she go on living with Alexander? No. That would be impossible, but she had nightmares about travelling to Liverpool only to discover that Charlie had been forced into an alternative relationship.

Edith did her best, whenever the chance arose, to undermine Hester's faith in Charlie.

'You really know nothing about him, Miss Shaw. Compared with Alexander he is an unknown quantity. What do you know about him except what he has told you? He might be a practised liar or . . . or a fantasist who believes what he says. He might have a prison record!' She rolled her eyes.

'He would hardly tell you if he had,' she went on. 'Oh, I know you don't want to consider these possibilities but you should at least listen to me and think carefully before you throw yourself into his world. Marriage to Mr Barnes may not be at all what you expect.'

Her other frequent argument was the wonderful picture she drew of her nephew. 'Alexander is a thoroughly upright man and he has been good to you. I can assure you, life with Alexander would suit you very well, my dear. I can honestly say that my nephew has never had an unkind thought in his life. He is highly respected in the force and will no doubt rise to even higher office in time. Marcia never did appreciate him. One should never speak ill of the dead, I know, but the truth is she was a silly, shallow woman.'

Wednesday morning brought yet another visit from Edith Carradine who breezed in with an armful of holly and a determinedly cheerful smile.

'I don't think Christmas begins until the holly is up!' she told Hester. 'Alexander thinks me an old fool – oh, yes he does! But I don't take any notice of him. I want his house to be wonderfully festive for the first time for years. The three of us will have a happy time – he deserves it. I've watched him over the past five years as his wife went steadily downhill. Christmas was only a shadow of what it should be. She was useless, you see. Poor Marcia.'

'But she was ill, wasn't she?' Hester said. She was beginning to feel sorry for the much maligned Marcia.

Edith tossed her head. 'She wanted to be ill,' she said. 'It gave her an excuse to show no interest in anything. That woman lived from day to day in a world of her own, and nothing I could say would inspire her. I nagged her, flattered her, coaxed her – nothing made any difference. Alexander spent one Christmas Day at his club because she had given the cook the day off! Would you credit such a thing? I was always with my daughters so I could do nothing to help him.'

'That must have been rather sad for him,' Hester agreed. 'I was always alone over the Christmas period so I know exactly how that feels. Alexander never felt it was right to leave his wife Marcia alone at such a time, but he always had a special meal sent round to me from Harrods.'

'Did he? That was very thoughtful of him.' She brightened. 'Well, now, put on your coat. The taxi is waiting outside.'

Hester stared at her. 'Where are we going?'

'To Alexander's home, of course. Hilsomer House. You and I will decorate it and he'll get a big surprise when he gets back from the office. From now on, things are going to change, Miss Shaw – or may I call you Hester?'

The question took Hester by surprise and she hesitated.

Somehow she knew that once they were on first names the situation would be subtly changed.

Without answering the question, she asked, 'Should I be seen in Alexander's home? So soon after the funeral it might appear rather . . . inappropriate.'

'Nonsense. If anyone asks you are my travelling companion whom I have befriended. Do hurry, dear.'

The 'dear' was obviously going to replace the first name, thought Hester, but, not knowing how to deal with it without seeming rude, she allowed it to slip past. Minutes later they were in the taxi, on their way to Hilsomer House.

Alexander's home was a gracious, three-storey house – one of a row of expensive houses in a desirable street in Chelsea. The front door was reached by steps which meant there was a basement where she supposed the kitchen would be found. The area below ground level was neatly swept and boasted two large pots, each containing a small but well-clipped bay tree which stood each side of a dark green door.

The woman who answered the bell to the door at the top of the steps was a Mrs Rice and she greeted them with enthusiasm. Hester was introduced as Miss Hester Shaw and then Edith swept past the housekeeper saying, 'Ask the taxi driver to bring in the holly, please, Mrs Rice. He can leave it in the hall. And give him this.' She pressed a coin into the housekeeper's hand and hurried along the wide passage towards the rear of the house.

'Do come along, dear,' she urged Hester. 'I'll show you the garden and then we'll have a quick tour of the house. The garden is quite remarkable. As you probably know Alexander hates gardening, but a man comes in twice a week and Alexander does have an eye for colour and design.'

She had not exaggerated, thought Hester, impressed. A smooth lawn curved between neat flowerbeds and small shrubs. She was aware that Edith was watching for her reaction.

'It's lovely,' she agreed politely. This was their plan then, she thought. They would make her see just how much she would be giving up if she turned down Alexander's proposal. It was all rather obvious, but she tried not to be flattered. No amount of grandeur, she told herself, would persuade her to give up her life with Charlie. She knew she was being reckless, but she didn't care. For the first time in many years she felt totally alive and in spite of any doubts, she was eager to start her new life.

Upstairs, the house was spacious and elegantly furnished. She looked at the double bed and found it strange to imagine Alexander sleeping there with his unfortunate wife. No, she thought, firmly, I could never live here. Everywhere they went there were reminders of Marcia – her portrait on the wall, a scarf tossed over a chair, delicate satin slippers still beside the bed.

Edith turned suddenly. 'My nephew has bought you a very special present. I'm not supposed to say anything, but imagine how disappointed he will be if you are not here on Christmas Day! I hope you will bear that in mind.'

To avoid answering, Hester said, 'What beautiful curtains! Marcia obviously had very good taste.'

Edith shrugged. 'She did her best, I daresay, before she gave in to this stupid illness.'

It seemed there were four servants. There was a gardener; the cook; Mrs Rice, the housekeeper, who lived in; and Rosie, a young housemaid who came in most days and worked extra hours from time to time when required.

'Marcia had all the help she needed,' Edith informed Hester. 'She wanted for nothing. Although, I say it myself, Alexander is a very good provider.'

'I'm sure he is.' Charlie will be, too, she reminded herself.

Edith sat down suddenly and indicated that Hester should do the same. They were in a large reception room where the December sunshine filtered in through delicate lace curtains.

'I want you to know that if you decide to marry Alexander, I shall settle some money on you myself.' Ignoring Hester's shocked expression, she continued. 'He will provide for you, as I've said already, but I do feel a wife should have some money of her own. I know nothing has been decided yet . . .'

'Oh, but it has! I thought I'd made that clear.' Agitated, Hester sat forward in her chair.

'But I thought you should know. Now I don't want to discuss it. We have work to do. If you look in the chest in the passage you will find some Christmas baubles and coloured ribbons. Christmas decorations take time if you intend to do it properly and I do.' Fitting actions to words, she hurried from the room and after a moment's uncertainty, Hester followed.

Saying nothing was safer than saying anything, she reflected. For the time being she would allow herself to be swept along in the Christmas atmosphere. Time to break the spell when Charlie's letter arrived.

Meanwhile a telephone was ringing in Bearsley Police Station. On the outskirts of the village on the edge of Dartmoor, the building was a single storey with a large shed to one side, which housed two stretchers in case of accidents, various boxes of equipment, much of it outdated, plus a lawnmower for use on the small square of grass which filled the space between the building and the stone wall which surrounded it.

Some of these items should have been inside an office in the building, but in a rush of belated enthusiasm some refurbishment was being undertaken and two local men were scraping paintwork and whistling loudly.

Police sergeant Jon Harrow, much to his annoyance, found himself banished to the small reception area with nothing but a chair, a card table and a telephone. Feeling thoroughly disgruntled, he snatched up the phone when it rang and barked, 'Bearsley Police Station.'

'Is that you, Harrow?'

The voice was familiar. Responding instinctively to the voice of a superior officer, Sergeant Harrow sat up a little straighter and fastened the top button of his tunic. 'Is that who I think it is? Is that Alexander Waring?'

'It is. How is life treating you?'

'I can't complain.' The sergeant spoke cautiously as the years rolled back along memory lane. He and Waring had been posted to the same nick in the wilds of Hampshire – it must have been nearly twenty years ago. He grinned at the memory. In those days he had been keen as mustard, eager to put away the villains and determined on promotion. Now he was more interested in keeping his nose clean, but at that time they were both sergeants – before Waring started moving up the ladder. He married the right woman and met the right people. Jon recalled the wedding – a very posh affair. Marcia! That was her name. Snooty name for a snooty woman, he'd said at the time – but not to Waring. Her old man had forked out for a big wedding reception.

Poor old Jon was left behind to rot and he'd given up hope of promotion years ago. He knew he had only himself to blame, but it didn't make him less bitter. He'd heard on the grapevine that Waring had been made a superintendent. No surprise there, then. Still, better watch his p's and q's, he thought.

'I have a little job for you – a couple of questions,' Waring told him.

'Ask away. Anything I can do!' He tried to sound eager. During his six years in Hampshire, Jon Harrow had well and truly blotted his copybook over a stupid bribe and Alexander Waring had saved him from suspension by lying on his behalf. Was this pay-back time? He felt a prickle of apprehension. 'Anything within reason,' he amended.

'I've had an enquiry,' Waring said. 'I'm working on something that needn't interest you, but I don't want to go through official channels until I'm sure of the facts. At present it's just a hunch – you know what I mean?'

Harrow tapped his nose. 'I know.'

'D'you recall the Seaforth case? I think it was '98 or '99. We sent a nasty thug down for three years. Battered a chap half to death while drunk! Can't remember his name, but I can see him clear as day. One eye was blue and one was brown.'

'Assault and battery? I remember. Bit of a bruiser, meaty hands. A bit dim, as I recall. Hadn't he been a boxer at some time? He was called . . .' He closed his eyes to help him concentrate. 'Something beginning with F. Short name. Fish or . . . Fitch, was it, or Finch? Tried to pin it on his mate, didn't he? Sang like a canary!'

'Fitch! That's him. Well done. Any idea where he is right now?'

'None at all. What's he done? Killed someone? Never did know his own strength, that man.'

'He hasn't done anything yet . . . At least, he's possibly implicated. Just a rumour at the moment. We need evidence and I need to find him. I'm putting feelers out. Can't say more than that, but I need to finger him and it's urgent. But you've no idea where he is?'

'Lord no! Might even be dead. His sort die young and he wasn't exactly popular!' The silence from Waring's end suggested that this was the wrong answer. Harrow said hastily, 'But I could do a bit of snooping if that's what's wanted. See what I can dig up. Can't promise anything, mind. These chaps have a habit of falling through the net. Could be anywhere. Six feet under if I had my way!'

'But you'd know if he was incarcerated somewhere?'

'I could try and find out, but if he's not on record it'll be like looking for a needle in the proverbial!'

'Do your best. You always had your ear to the ground as I recall. I'll ring tomorrow after lunch. Thanks.' The line went dead.

Sergeant Harrow stared at the silent telephone. 'Tomorrow after lunch? Christ! Who does he think I am? Sherlock bloody Holmes!'

Wednesday, 18th December, 1907 – It seems that Alexander's little plan may be working. I don't know whether to be pleased or sorry. We are both keeping a close eye on Hester and trying to involve her in Christmas at Hilsomer House. She must surely fall in love with the place and see the possibilities of life as Alexander's wife. So far she has made no effort to leave her flat and I have promised to settle some money on her which surely must be a big inducement for her to stay. I suspect she is wavering about her feelings for this other man. Alexander believes that the longer she stays here, the more likely she is to come to her

senses and give up the idea of going to Liverpool. I
hope he is right.

I am prepared to overlook her foolish behaviour
while we were at sea – she was under the man's influ-
ence. The entanglement with this ridiculous Charlie
person can be considered just a silly fling. Sadly we
women are always vulnerable to the excitement of a
new admirer. I thank the Lord that I came to my senses
before I left Mr Carradine for charming Archie Spicer.
(He went on, years later, to be involved in a sordid
little fraud and earned himself some very unpleasant
publicity. That scandal would have crucified me.)

In retrospect the trip on the Mauretania *was unfor-*
tunate for both of us. I wasted time and money on that
fool Stafford and poor Hester fell under the spell of a
very smooth operator! I shall never refer to him again
if she comes to her senses and agrees to marry my
nephew.

My dearest wish is to see him wed again and to
someone who will be prepared to take my advice when
necessary. Hester is the one. I am never wrong on
these matters and I have taken a strong liking to her,
and I believe she is warming to me. She is mature,
looks the part and will give Alexander handsome chil-
dren. I will not be thwarted in this matter.

The following day Edith Carradine reappeared in Chalker
Street, this time to discuss the Christmas Day menus with
Hester, who was in the middle of writing to Charlie. Seizing
the opportunity, Hester tried to clarify the situation as she
saw it.

'Do sit down,' she said. 'I won't keep you more than a
minute or two. I'm writing to Charlie and I want to catch
the early post. Please excuse me.'

She returned to her small writing desk and searched for
the right words to finish the letter. She had tried to explain
to him how awkward the situation was becoming for her
and ask him to confirm that everything was in order in
Garth Street for her to move in with them temporarily.

My hope is that your sister is willing for me to live with you both for a short period and that the banns have been called. Once we are man and wife everyone, hopefully, will accept us and there will be no unpleasantness from any quarter. Mrs Carradine's pressure on me is mounting and Christmas is only a week away. Are you ready for me to travel up? I am longing to be free of my connections here.

I love you so much, Charlie, but your promised letter has so far not arrived which is beginning to alarm me.

All my love, dearest Charlie, from Hester

PS You can rest assured that there has been no physical contact between me and Alexander as he now knows about you.

Edith was watching her through narrowed eyes. As calmly as she could, Hester folded the letter and slid it into the envelope. She addressed it and added the stamp. 'It will only take me two minutes to the pillar box and back.'

Edith pursed her lips disapprovingly. 'Writing to Mr Barnes, I presume.'

Hester nodded. 'He'll get it when he comes ashore.'

'Have you told him you'll probably be spending Christmas here in London?'

'I've told him you've suggested it.'

'Does he know you are still accepting Alexander's hospitality?'

'He knows I have nowhere else to go – but he trusts me with regard to your nephew.'

The old lady tutted impatiently. 'And I suppose you trust him.'

'I certainly do!'

Annoyed by the direction of Edith's comments, Hester went into the hall and pulled on her coat. She threw a shawl over her head and round her shoulders, then hurried from the flat before the old lady could make further comment.

When she returned Edith was apparently busy with a list.

She glanced up and her manner had changed. The disapproving expression was gone.

'I need some help with the menus,' she told Hester. 'I'll read out what I have planned and you can give me your opinion.'

Hester steeled herself. If this was going to be a battle of wills, she would play her part. She sat down and folded her hands in her lap.

'That sounds fun,' she said lightly. 'Even if I am no longer in London I shall be able to think of you and Alexander enjoying good food and opening your Christmas presents.'

Edith ignored her comment and referred to her list. 'I'm catering for three, just in case, and for two days. I shall be with my daughter Dorcas on Christmas Eve. Evelyn may or may not join us. So we start with Christmas Day. A reasonably light breakfast, I thought, with scrambled eggs and smoked salmon with perhaps some melba toast. What do you think?'

'I think it sounds perfect.'

'For the main meal do you think we should have a goose? They are rather fatty, but the flavour is good and Alexander is fond of it. He likes all the trimmings.'

'I personally prefer duck, but I'm quite happy to compromise. When I was working as a nanny, my employer used to stuff duck with orange sections.'

'Did she?' Edith hesitated then wrote again. 'Goose, medium size,' she murmured. 'And a savoy cabbage. Dark green vegetables are very underrated in my opinion. Which vegetables do you like, dear?'

'Parsnips and peas.'

'Parsnips and peas,' she repeated carefully as she wrote them down. Then she glanced up. 'Just in case you may still be with us.'

By the look on her face, Hester knew something more important was coming.

'I've been thinking, dear,' Edith began, 'that the present circumstances must be very difficult for you. Living in Alexander's flat while you are in love . . . while you are *involved* with another man must make you feel rather uncomfortable. Taking but giving nothing in return, if you understand my meaning.'

'I do and you are right – except that Alexander isn't asking for anything in return. He quite rightly stays away from any form of closeness and sleeps at Hilsomer House.'

'Does he? I see. What I wanted to suggest . . .'

'I really don't think you are in any position to suggest anything,' Hester cried, her face colouring with annoyance. 'What happens between me and your nephew is—'

'Wait, wait!' Edith held up her hands. 'I'm only thinking of what's best for the two of you.'

'But we aren't a twosome, Mrs Carradine. I am in love with Charlie, not Alexander. Any day now I shall be leaving London for Liverpool and you will both be rid of me! I won't be causing either of you any anxiety at all.'

Edith shook her head resignedly. 'You young people are so quick to take offence,' she said. 'What I was going to suggest is that you might prefer to come and live with me for a few days, before you leave London. Then you need not feel you owe Alexander anything. My house is quite large and you would have your own room. I should enjoy the company. If you *are* still here over the Christmas period you could come to Dorcas with me on Christmas Eve and then we could travel to and from Hilsomer House together on Christmas Day and Boxing Day.'

Hester was completely taken aback. On the face of it, the suggestion appeared well-intentioned, even generous. 'Thank you, that's most kind. I can't . . . that is, I'll think about it – but I doubt very much I shall still be here.'

'If he answers the letter you've just posted, you mean.'

'Yes.' Hester was mortified. Edith had obviously realized just how desperately she wanted to hear from Charlie.

'Right, then we must return to the menus. I don't care for rich puddings so I usually have a light lemon custard on a pastry base. What do you think? Alexander always has a plum pudding – Cook made it weeks ago. Suet, dark sugar, dates, plums and all sorts of rich ingredients. I don't object to a small mince pie, but my digestion suffers if I am careless with my diet.' Waiting in vain for a comment from Hester, she changed the subject abruptly. 'You do know that Alexander is fond of you, don't you? I would go as far as to say he loves you. Most men find it difficult to speak about their finer feelings, but I can assure you that, if you stay with him, he will do his best to forget all this nonsense and make you happy.'

Hester nodded. 'I appreciate what you've said, but it would be so unkind for me to pretend. Charlie is—'

'Don't! I don't even want to hear the fellow's name. You deserve a decent life for your children when you have them. I hate to think of you scratching a living as the wife of a ship's steward.'

Hester's face was suddenly illuminated by a radiant smile. 'While I cannot wait to be Mrs Charlie Barnes!'

They regarded each other in silence and Hester felt that they had ruined the mood. Before she could think of something to say, Edith took a deep breath.

'I shall leave the choice of wines to Alexander. I am perfectly capable of selecting suitable wines, but Alexander imagines he can do it better. I will allow him that pleasure.'

Snow fell during the night and the people of Liverpool woke up to find two inches of snow transforming the landscape. Grimy houses towered over white streets, children ran wild, screeching with excitement, and the sound of the traffic was strangely muffled. Dogs chased each other up and down the street, cats perched moodily on snow-capped fences, and horses waited with less patience than usual for the comforting contents of their nosebags.

Maisie woke up and was immediately filled with guilt. She now regretted that she had not posted her brother's letter to Hester Shaw. If he ever found out – and the postmark would be a giveaway – he would be furious with her. For the first time she felt stirrings of anger towards Annie who had talked her into these delaying tactics. Faced with Annie's tears, she had agreed, in the hope they both shared, that Hester would think he had changed his mind about her and decide to stay with her rich lover.

But suppose Hester had grown tired of waiting. She might

take matters into her own hands and travel up without
waiting for the letter. She might appear suddenly at Maisie's
front door. What was Maisie supposed to do then?

'Blooming typical!' she grumbled, climbing out of bed
with the beginnings of a headache. She unwound her curling
rags and surveyed the result in the mirror, wondering if
Hester Shaw was really as beautiful as Charlie had claimed.
Just in case she turned up unexpectedly, Maisie wanted to
look presentable. She would iron her best blouse, she
decided, and give her shoes a polish. And she would bake
a few scones.

In the kitchen she made some tea and raked up the embers
in the stove. As she sipped her tea she thought of scathing
things to say to Annie while a growing curiosity about
Hester began to establish itself in her mind. True, she was
older than Charlie, but Maisie wouldn't let that influence
her. Thirty-one wasn't *that* old. And her brother must have
seen something in her that attracted him. Charlie, she knew,
was head-over-heels in love with her. In two days' time
Charlie would be back on shore leave and if Hester hadn't
arrived he would probably go to London and bring her back
with him. She refilled her cup and cut herself a thick slice
of bread which she smothered with honey and folded into
a rough sandwich.

Perhaps she would stop fighting and give in gracefully.
There was no way she wanted to fall foul of her brother.
Hester Shaw must not come between them.

'I will like her. I *will*,' she declared. 'Hester and I will
be friends!'

She realized that they would certainly not be friends if
Hester ever discovered that Maisie had deliberately delayed
her letter from Charlie. In it he had told her to come up
immediately so they could all be together over Christmas.
Now there were only five days to go and if she posted the
letter Hester might read it tomorrow and catch the train in
time.

'Right. First things first. Tidy through,' she told herself
and, swallowing the last of the honey sandwich, she jumped
to her feet and prepared to make a start.

An hour later Annie arrived with Charlie's Christmas present. As Maisie let her in, her heart sank.

Annie glanced at the mantelpiece and her face fell. 'You've posted it!' she cried. 'When? When will she get it?' She was clutching a parcel tied with thin red ribbon.

'Sit down,' Maisie suggested, setting an example by settling herself on the kitchen stool. 'Is that for Charlie?'

'Yes – but the letter. You promised!'

'I changed my mind this morning and dashed to the post box. She won't get it until tomorrow. What did you expect me to do with him coming home on Sunday? It's the first thing he'd see!'

'Not if you'd hidden it like I said! Suppose she turns up here – she'll ruin everything! I wanted Christmas to be wonderful – just the three of us. I've made a cake.' Her mouth trembled. 'You've ruined everything, Maisie!'

'There's not much to ruin, Annie, is there? If she doesn't come up, he'll go and fetch her. I don't want to get the blame for what happens. I wish to God I'd never let you talk me into it and that's the truth – and don't start with your tears, Annie! I've had about all I can stand.'

Annie glared at her. 'So, what about Christmas, then?' She tightened her grip on the parcel. 'I'm not leaving the waistcoat here. If I'm not invited he can come and get it. If he wants it, that is. Maybe she'll be giving him a waistcoat made of gold thread with real pearl buttons and mine won't be good enough! You're a selfish pig, Maisie!'

Maisie sighed. *Here we go again*, she thought. *I'm getting the blame, as usual.*

'You must do what you think best,' she said. 'As far as I can see, Hester Shaw will be here by Christmas. I can't sort out your life for you, Annie. I'm sorry, but you'll have to go. I'm busy.'

Annie stood up slowly, her face hardening. 'So now you're throwing me out. Well, thanks!' She stood up. 'I might as well get rid of the baby. And myself! No one is going to miss us, are they? Certainly not your brother!'

Maisie flushed angrily. 'Don't talk such rubbish, Annie.

Charlie's not the only man in the world. You'll find someone else. You're a very pretty girl.'

'A very pretty girl *with a baby*? No man's going to look at me!'

'It's happened before, to other girls. You'll sort something out.'

'Well, for your information, I won't! I daren't tell my family – you don't know them like I do! If Charlie won't do the right thing by me, I . . . I don't want to live. Tell him that from me.'

'Why didn't you tell him? You had the chance.'

'Because I didn't really believe he'd leave me in the lurch,' she snapped.

Maisie gazed at her. 'Well, I'm sorry, but it's not up to me.'

It was so unfair, she thought, that even when she was in a temper, Annie looked beautiful. You and Hester Shaw. And me as plain as a pikestaff!

'Can't you see how it is for me?' Maisie grumbled. 'Stuck between you and him and this Hester Shaw? I feel like a piggy in the middle! Hester could arrive at any minute even without the letter. If the man throws her out she has nowhere else to go.'

The bright curls clung round Annie's flushed face and her blue eyes shone with anger. Maisie could see what Charlie had seen in her. Why did life have to be so difficult? 'Hester Shaw might be on the train right now!' The thought frightened her. Suppose she was on the train and the house was still in a mess. She must find the spare sheets and give the windows a bit of a clean.

'I've got to get on, Annie.'

Annie regarded her with disgust. 'Thinking about yourself again! That's so like you, Maisie Barnes. No thought about me.'

'I didn't get you pregnant, Annie.'

The challenge hung between them, but before Maisie could wish her words unsaid, Annie seemed suddenly to run out of anger. Her eyes lost their hard glint and her mouth drooped. She said quietly, 'You'll be sorry when they find my body! Your brother won't care, but you will! I'll be on your conscience for the rest of your life.'

Maisie sighed resignedly. 'Don't threaten me, Annie. I've got enough on my plate already. Just go, please. Talk to your mother or your aunt or your cousin. You've got family. They'll help you.' As she spoke she was leading the way to the front door, thankful that Annie was following.

As she hesitated on the doorstep, Annie said, 'If he wants his present, tell him to come and get it!'

With a furious toss of her head, she turned and walked quickly away without a backward glance.

Maisie watched her for a moment and then slowly and quietly closed the door.

'Happy Christmas, Annie!' she said sadly and went back to her housework.

Nine

Alexander arrived at Hester's flat very early the next day and said he would like to talk to her. She was still wearing a dressing gown over her nightdress and, pleased that he had wrong-footed her, he refused her request to wait for her to wash and dress.

'I can't stay too long,' he told her. 'I have to be in the office in an hour for an important meeting, but I wanted to talk to you about my aunt's offer of accommodation.'

They both sat down and he thought she eyed him warily. *As well you might*, he thought grimly. *You have no idea, my dear, how much havoc I can create for you.*

She waited for him to speak, clutching her dressing gown round herself protectively as though suddenly reluctant to let him glimpse her nightwear.

'I think it might be a good idea,' he began, keeping his voice low and reasonable. 'This awkward period in our relationship is difficult to say the least. For both of us. Edith thinks that we should no longer be seen together here.'

'I'll be leaving any day now,' she protested.

'We don't know for certain, do we? I understand you are waiting for a letter before you leave London. Has it come yet?'

'No, but I'm sure it—'

'Nothing is sure in this world, Hester.' He checked his tone as her expression changed. He must not sound as though he were threatening or bullying her. She must assume his concern was genuine. 'If the letter doesn't come – for whatever reason – you should be seen to be quite separate from me in the eyes of my friends. It should appear, as Edith suggests, that you are *her* friend and that you and I are simply acquaintances of long standing who are then drawn to each other once I am a widower. Are we in agreement over this so far?'

Was he earning her trust, he wondered, watching her closely. Was his kindly approach working? If he was honest, he would admit that what he really wanted to do was slap her and give her a severe shaking, but he must play out his role as planned. He could wait for his moment of triumph.

Unhappily she said, 'I don't want you to think so far ahead, Alexander. You seem determined to believe that Charlie will desert me. He won't. I know he won't. He may not be rich or powerful, but he is a very decent man.'

She leaned forward, her expression earnest and if Alexander hadn't been so angry, he might have been amused. What an innocent she was, he thought.

She said, 'Alexander, I would like to leave you knowing that we both remember the happiness we once shared. You are a wealthy, attractive man – you will easily marry again and make a much better match. You'll find happiness again and you don't have to consider me any more because I shall be happy with Charlie.'

Not if I have anything to do with it, he thought. I think you can forget that glorious scenario.

Instead, he said, 'But I want you to stay with me, Hester. I owe it to you after all these years and Edith is confident that we will make each other happy. She also worries about you. She has become quite fond of you in fact. Her own daughters have been such a disappointment to her, but . . .'

Hester stood up abruptly and crossed to the window. Once there she turned.

'May I be brutally honest with you, Alexander?' she asked. He noticed that her voice was shaking. 'I don't love you any more, Alexander. I don't know how to convince you of that. Even before I met Charlie . . . I'm truly sorry, but my feelings were already changing. We can't choose who we love.'

He kept his face straight with an effort. Silly little fool. Did she think he had ever loved her? *Loved* her? Of course not. It had been convenient for both of them, that was all.

You are an attractive woman, he thought, and I had needs

which my wife could not or would not satisfy. That is all it was. If you chose to have romantic notions that is your problem . . .

But Alexander knew he had to handle this carefully. He had made arrangements to change Barnes's mind for him, but if scrutiny were ever brought to bear, it must appear that he, Alexander, had truly loved Hester.

He said heavily, 'Is that your last word?'

'Yes, it is. Please let me go, Alexander, without any bitterness.'

He covered his face with his hands and let a minute or two pass. She must think he was finally bowing to the inevitable. When he looked up, he tried to look crestfallen. 'Then I accept your decision, but with this proviso that if your letter doesn't come and Mr Barnes has let you down . . .'

'He won't let me down!' she cried.

'I am thinking of you, Hester. I – I can't let you go without a struggle. If you change your mind . . . There's still time.' She nodded and he shrugged. 'I shall talk with my aunt. Poor soul. She has set her heart on our marriage.'

Hester opened her mouth to speak, hesitated and changed her mind. She stayed silent, staring down at her hands.

Alexander watched her, fighting down the jealousy and humiliation. Hester actually preferred this cheap young steward who could give her so little, to Alexander Waring, a respected man of position and power. When she discovered her mistake it would be too late – and his aunt would have to make do with his young nurse. Della Telson. He had sent some roses with a note promising to meet as soon as it would be considered suitable. He liked to imagine her face when the flowers arrived. How thrilled she would be when they met. The old lady would come round in time, he assured himself.

He returned his attention to Hester. 'Would you like me to take you round to my aunt's house later?' he offered. 'I could collect you in a hansom cab at midday if you could have your things ready.'

She struggled to hide her shock at the abrupt plan for her departure.

'Thank you, Alexander, but is she expecting me?'

'She is. In the circumstances, we have agreed that this flat is not your home any more. I shall put it back on the market.'

In other words she was homeless, he thought, and relying on Edith Carradine for a roof over her head. The thought gave him great satisfaction.

He felt even more satisfied as, on his way downstairs, he patted his coat pocket and heard the rustle of the letter from Liverpool which he had intercepted from the postman on the doorstep when he arrived. His fourth early morning wait on the draughty steps below had been well rewarded.

It was Saturday the twenty-first – four days to go before Christmas. Fitch sat at the bar nursing a pint of ale, oblivious to the mistletoe hanging from the centre ceiling-fitting and the grubby red and gold ribbons draped over one or two pictures. Around him the lunchtime trade was trickling in. Deep in thought he didn't hear his name until it was repeated.

'Wake up, Fitch!'

Sam sat down beside him and Fitch ordered another pint for his friend. They were very different: Sam lean and wiry with thin features, Fitch stocky with a broken nose, short arms and fingers like sausages.

Sam regarded him quizzically. 'What's up with you, Fitch?'

'Me? Nothing. Why d'you ask?'

''Cos I know that look! You're up to something.' He appealed to the potman. 'Hasn't he got that look? Smug, I call it.'

The potman looked at him. 'Yeah. Smug!'

'Well, you're wrong,' Fitch bluffed. 'I'm not smug. Anyway, it's none of your business if I am.'

'That means you are.' Sam drank deeply, eyeing his friend. He and Fitch had been friends since before they shared a cell together at His Majesty's pleasure for burning down a warehouse for a friend – an insurance scam that went wrong. Sam grinned. 'Come into some money, have you? Rich old grandmother left you a fortune?' He and the potman laughed.

Fitch said, 'You'd be the last to know, mate, I tell you straight 'cos you'd be on the borrow!'

'You've got a fight lined up! That it?'

'No.' Fitch was not averse to the occasional illegal back-street fight. He could always use the extra money. 'Nothing like that.'

The potman lost interest and wandered to the other end of the bar where three roustabouts were getting noisy. Not that he cared but the governor would be coming downstairs before long and the old man prided himself on keeping an orderly house, much to the amusement of his punters who knew he'd failed long ago.

Sam lowered his voice. 'It's something shady.'

'Exactly.'

'But you're not telling?'

'Right again.'

Sam lowered his voice to a whisper. 'I know it's something.'

Finally Fitch could no longer resist. He tapped his nose. 'Interesting orders from above.'

'Above? What, you mean someone high up?'

'Exactly. Who says you're daft! A whisper from a friend of a friend. Starts with a W.'

'A W?' Sam frowned. 'Who the hell . . .?'

'Think, Sam. You know what I mean. A dark alley, a few minutes' work and . . .' He rubbed his fingers and thumbs together.

Sam's eyes opened. 'A good earner?'

'Not half!' He drained his glass. 'Drink up, Sam, while I'm still feeling generous.'

Sam frowned. 'Paid up front, was you?'

'Half now, half later.'

Sam held up a clenched fist and raised his eyebrows. Fitch nodded.

'Starts with a W. Friend of a friend. Anyone I know?'

'Maybe, maybe not.' Fitch shook his head. 'Enough said! Hush-hush.'

Sam's eyes opened wider. 'Not . . .!' He drew an imaginary line round his throat.

'No! Course not. Keep your voice down.' He glanced round nervously.

'A beating?' Sam's voice rose.

Fitch nodded. 'Keep it down, I said.'

'What is it? A debt?'

'No. Woman trouble. Don't ask.'

'Ah! Need any help?' Sam looked hopeful. 'I mean, two of us . . . You could slip me a bit of cash.'

'I can handle it.' As two fresh pints were placed in front of them, he said, 'It'll be just like old times.'

In London, Hester was finding it difficult. There had been no letter from Charlie, and Alexander had manoeuvred her from the flat she knew as home and had deposited her at the spacious and elegant flat in Tessingham Terrace where she lived in considerable comfort. The shock of finding herself dependent on Edith Carradine's hospitality had been more traumatic than Hester had expected. She had woken this morning in an unfamiliar bed to unfamiliar sounds as the butcher's boy arrived whistling on his bicycle and the housekeeper clattered cutlery in the dining room. Now she sat in nervous anticipation. Edith had decided that, since Hester might still be in London over Christmas, she should meet Dorcas where they would spend Christmas Eve. To this end, she had invited Dorcas to have some lunch with them the following day. Saturday arrived and Alexander dropped by to assure her, with apparent regret, that there had been no letter at the flat post-marked Liverpool.

There would not be another post until Monday. If it came Hester could still be in Liverpool by Christmas Eve and all the doubts and fears would be swept away, but if it didn't . . . In the meantime Hester had spent the empty hours tormented by the unthinkable idea that there never would be a letter. She had begun to suspect that there was an ulterior motive to the kindness Edith Carradine was showing her, as well as the reasonable manner Alexander had adopted towards her. Now that she had been eased out of her home, she found herself entirely vulnerable and this made the letter from Charlie even more desirable.

'Have you been crying, dear?' Edith demanded, peering across the room at her.

They were awaiting the arrival of Dorcas and Hester was beginning to feel hopelessly outnumbered. Had Dorcas also been primed to add her persuasions to Hester on the suitability of Alexander as a husband?

'Crying? No, at least, maybe just a few tears,' Hester admitted. 'I feel rather adrift and I'm not used to the feeling.' Was it her imagination or did she see a brief glint of triumph in Edith's eyes?

'I can understand that, in a way,' Edith told her, 'although I never allow myself to be overcome by emotion. It gets in the way of reasoned thought, and is also a great drain on the body's resources. You need to develop a thicker skin, dear. My mother used to drum it into us that circumstances can only defeat us if we allow them to. If we choose to remain unaffected by . . . Oh! There's the bell. This will be Dorcas.'

Hester stiffened, preparing for the worst. Don't lose your temper, Hester, she advised herself, and don't let either of them rile you.

'So, you're Hester Shaw!'

A middle-aged woman bustled into the room, her hand outstretched. The likeness to Edith was clear, thought Hester, but Dorcas was much heavier. She wore tweeds and heavy shoes and her thick hair had been carelessly arranged.

Hester shook the proffered hand and returned the smile as Edith introduced them.

'You're not quite how I imagined, Miss Shaw,' Dorcas told her, her voice less authoritative than her mother's. They both sat down, eyeing each other cautiously.

Edith remained standing. 'I'll have a word with the house-keeper about lunch. I shan't be long. I feel sure you two will get along splendidly.'

The two younger women regarded each other politely, barely hiding their curiosity.

As soon as Edith had left the room, Dorcas said, 'She doesn't think that at all. She has taken a liking to you, but has never liked me. Alexander has always been her "darling boy" and her own daughters have never been able to compete for her affection. I thought you should understand the position just in case you are foolish enough to remain in London.'

Shocked that Dorcas knew so much and had spoken so frankly, Hester wondered what to say.

Lowering her voice, Dorcas spoke urgently. 'You have a young man in Liverpool. You should go to him.' She glanced towards the door, listening for returning footsteps. 'I don't know what they're up to, but they've had their heads together for days. My mother has always been very manipulative and Evelyn and I had to struggle to free ourselves. We've learned to keep a safe distance.'

Hester thought this rather overdramatic. 'Your mother has offered me a few days here while—'

Dorcas leaned forward. 'Don't trust them, Miss Shaw. My cousin is a very powerful man and can make things happen. Believe me.'

'He's been very fair to me,' Hester protested. 'I do owe him a lot and . . . His wife's death has made matters rather complicated. I can understand how he feels.'

'No you can't! You have no idea how his mind works. Poor Marcia. She had a wretched time with him.' She crossed to the door, stepped into the hall and listened. Coming back, she sat down again. 'They are discussing the shopping. We have a few more minutes, I think.'

Hester felt a frisson of alarm at the turn of the conversation. 'Alexander would never do anything to harm me.'

'Don't count on it, Miss Shaw. Ask Evelyn. He's devious and I don't say that from jealousy. Even as a boy he was deceitful. We learned not to trust him as children and he hasn't changed. He's a bad loser. Always has been.'

Hester was becoming distinctly nervous, disturbed not only by these odd revelations but by the obvious sincerity with which Dorcas confided them.

'But now I hear that you have fallen in love,' Dorcas continued.

Hester stared at her. What else did she know, she wondered.

'Lucky you,' Dorcas went on. 'Don't let them spoil things for you. Mother says you owe it to Alexander to marry him, but that's because she feels she can control you. If he marries someone else, she may not be so fortunate. She . . . oh—' She put a finger to her lips and sat back in the chair.

As Edith entered, Dorcas said, 'I don't envy you the trip. Mother told us about the rough weather and the trouble with the spare anchor – and the man who knocked you unconscious.'

The housekeeper followed with a tray of tea and biscuits which she set down on a small table before withdrawing.

Hester pulled herself together. 'That was bad luck,' she agreed, 'but we did admire the ship. It was beautiful, wasn't it?' She turned to Edith who was pouring tea through the strainer into the cups.

'It was very attractive, dear,' said Edith, 'but I don't feel any desire to sail on her again. It was a wasted journey. That ridiculous Stafford. What a charlatan! What he knows about the heart could be written on the back of a postage stamp!'

Dorcas said, 'But at least Miss Shaw met a very charming young man which is wonderful, so it wasn't entirely wasted. She has just been telling me about him.' She smiled warmly at Hester. 'Soon you will be Mrs Charles Barnes. How exciting! I imagine it more than compensates for the bang on the head when that man fell on top of you.'

Hester quickly joined in Dorcas's laughter.

Edith gave her daughter a sharp look. 'Nothing in this world is ever certain, Dorcas. It may be that Hester will change her mind. Alexander is very fond of her. We shall see.' She handed Hester a cup of tea. 'I'm sorry to say that only Dorcas married well. Her sister made a wrong deci-sion and now regrets it.'

Dorcas said, 'By "married well" my mother means I married money.'

'You've been very happy, Dorcas. Ian is a good husband.'

'By that, Mother means "a good provider"!'

'He has given you two lovely children.'

'No, Mama, I gave *him* two lovely children.'

'Really, Dorcas, you are quite impossible. Whatever will Miss Shaw think of you?'

Hester took a biscuit from the plate Edith offered, not because she was hungry but because it gave her something to do. The conversation was unsettling and the prospect of spending Christmas Eve here set alarm bells ringing. She bit into a sultana biscuit and came to a sudden decision. She would not wait for Charlie's letter which presumably had gone astray in the post. He might at that very moment be wondering where she was. The *Mauretania* was expected to dock in Liverpool tomorrow. Drawing on reserves of courage she came to a decision. This was a turning point. As soon as an opportunity presented itself she would make her escape from the net which she now realized was closing inexorably around her.

Her chance came when Edith settled on her bed at three o'clock and prepared to take a nap. Dorcas was no longer with them. She wrote a hurried note.

> *Dear Mrs Carradine,*
>
> *Please forgive this hasty exit but I am becoming desperate to be with Mr Barnes and can wait no longer for his letter. Suppose he is ill? I have to go to him. I feel sure you will understand and forgive me. I hope so. Thank you for your past kindness.*
>
> *In haste, your friend, Hester Shaw.*
>
> *PS I shall write to Alexander shortly.*

She hailed a taxi and went straight to the station where she boarded the next train to Liverpool. It was very full and she had to stand but, heady with excitement and happy anticipation, she cared nothing for the discomfort. Soon she would see Charlie again and would start her new life. As the train gathered speed and rattled out of London and into the suburbs, Hester recalled her conversation with Dorcas. There was time to reflect on the surprising direction the conversation had taken and Hester searched her memory carefully to check whether it really had been as worrying as she had imagined. In retrospect the woman's warnings sounded melodramatic and slightly sinister and had certainly galvanized Hester into making her move. Was that the intention and if so, was there an ulterior motive? At the time, Dorcas had made Alexander and his aunt appear as conspirators, but that, Hester told herself, was surely ridiculous . . . although Dorcas's manner had seemed genuine and her advice had sounded heartfelt and kindly meant. Perhaps she was prejudiced against her own family – it certainly looked that way. Or did she actually believe that her mother and cousin were trying to control Hester?

She drew in a long breath and let it out slowly. A stout man squeezed past her as he made his way unsteadily along the narrow corridor and she wondered what the time was and how long it would be before she and Charlie were together again. Was he still at sea? If the ship had docked on time perhaps he was already on leave. How would he seem when they met? Would he still love her – and how would she feel about him? She told herself to calm down and think sensibly. With an effort she forced her thoughts away from the future and back to the present. Her back was beginning to ache from standing in the cramped conditions and she was thirsty. Perhaps, if the train paused somewhere, she would join the rush for some refreshment at the station buffet. She had no luggage with her except a small valise containing a nightdress and clean underwear for the next day.

Everyone else seemed to be heading home for a family reunion over the festive period and the excited chatter all around her, plus squeals and giggles from innumerable children, made it difficult to concentrate on her own problems. Better, perhaps, to think only about the future. She pushed the past few days from her mind and tried to focus on Charlie, but in her present emotional state, she was unable even to summon his cheerful image and her uneasiness deepened as the train clattered on, taking her closer and closer to an uncertain future.

On board the *Mauretania*, Charlie whistled cheerfully as he stuffed clothes into a carpet bag and prepared to disembark. He met up with Chalky as they headed for the gangway and terra firma. Chalky punched him playfully on the arm.

'So by the time we next meet you'll be a married man like me.'

'Can't wait,' Charlie told him. 'I've fixed the time at the church and I've found a flat. Not as nice as the one you mentioned, but it'll do until my luck changes. I've paid four weeks in advance.' He beamed at his friend. 'Know what? I feel married already.'

'So will she be waiting for you on the dockside?'

'Most likely. But your missus won't.'

'Nor will yours when she's got kids to look after! Mine will be in the kitchen knocking up some grub to welcome me back. A mutton pie most likely.' He patted his stomach.

As they went down the gangway, Charlie stared hopefully at the small crowd waiting to greet the crew members but there was no sign of Hester Shaw.

Disappointed, he shrugged. 'Probably still chatting with Maisie. Women have no idea of time – have you noticed that? No idea at all, bless them.' He was trying to sound nonchalant, but his heart was beating fast with excitement at the prospect of seeing Hester again.

At the end of the dock they separated. Charlie set off on his own, wending his way through the back streets, taking a well-known short cut. As he reached a corner and crossed the road, he was unaware that someone had moved out of the shadows and had begun to follow him. Someone who was keeping pace with him fifteen yards back. If he *had* been aware, Charlie would not have troubled himself. Born in the area, the narrow streets and hidden alleys were as familiar to him as the lines on the palms of his hands and there was nowhere in the world he felt safer.

Behind him Fitch moved warily, waiting for the right place to launch his attack. It had to be free of prying eyes, preferably in the shadows and somewhere where his running footsteps would not be noticed. Nothing he did must arouse the slightest suspicion in anyone he chanced to meet. He was relying on the element of surprise. *'Get in, do the business and get out!'* They were his orders. The beating was to be a warning, nothing more. He was to leave the victim on the ground after removing all forms of identification.

To the police, if they were involved, it should seem like a robbery. Watching the unsuspecting Barnes he refined his plan of action. He would empty the man's pockets and take the bag. That should do it. Once a safe distance from the crime, he would make his way to the room he had rented and see what he had in the bag. He had been told to burn whatever he took but who was to know? He would keep anything he fancied and sell the rest. He assumed the man had papers and he would burn them in the grate in his room. Tomorrow he would catch the first train out of Liverpool and make his way home.

In his pocket he had a small cosh, but he didn't expect to need it. He was handy with his fists and the man would be unprepared. A few quick blows and he'd be on the ground and a few kicks would be enough. They turned into a narrow alley and Fitch narrowed his eyes. There was no one else in sight and this might be the best chance he would get. Barnes was whistling, swaggering along, on top of the world. He, Fitch, would soon change all that! Fitch had no idea why he was being paid to attack the man and he didn't care. He liked the fact that his victim was in a cheerful mood, but that would not last much longer.

Glancing behind him, Fitch saw that the alley was still empty and decided this was the moment. Breaking into a run, he covered the space between them and had his hand raised before the man turned. Fitch's fist crashed into his victim's face and he dropped his bag and staggered back. Another blow sent him reeling against the wall and he began to fight back. Barnes managed to land two blows to Fitch's stomach which made him gasp with shock and gulp for air. Barnes was shouting now, yelling for help and Fitch knew it wouldn't be long before his shouts were heard and some busybody would be fetching the nearest copper. He took the cosh from his pocket and swung it at Barnes who dodged it and smashed a fist against Fitch's nose. With a cry of pain and rage Fitch retaliated with a stream of curses and another swipe to the side of Barnes's head. He felt it land and was aware of deep satisfaction. That would show the bastard!

With a groan, Barnes slid slowly to the floor and Fitch began to kick him.

'That's a warning,' he grunted. 'Whatever you done to upset his nibs, don't do it again! My boss don't like it, see!' He stood panting, watching his victim to make sure he was not going to get up again.

'You just lie there,' he said, dabbing at his nose which was bleeding profusely, 'and suffer! Christ! He's broke my bloody nose!' The pain made him angry and he landed a further flurry of kicks on his victim.

A shout from the end of the alley behind him alerted him to the presence of a woman who peered through the gloom. She started towards him. Damn. He had intended to retrace his footsteps.

'You,' she shouted. 'What you up to! Get off him!'

'Mind your own damn business!' he yelled but she had reminded him of his orders. *Get in and get out!* He rifled the man's pockets, snatched up the bag then turned and ran down the alley away from the direction of the woman who was hurrying forward towards the still figure on the cobbles. God help me if there's someone waiting for me at this end, he thought. This could get messy.

He'd hidden the money in his overnight lodgings. He'd put it in a small bag and hung it behind the wall mirror. There was no reason why the landlady would expect him to have that sort of money. At sixpence a night she didn't expect her lodgers to have plenty of cash.

Glancing back he saw that the woman had been joined by a man who now yelled, 'Stop, thief!' Doubling his efforts, Fitch put on a spurt and broke free from the alley where, to his dismay, he saw a constable running towards him from the right. Abruptly Fitch veered to the left and, ignoring the constable's whistle, ran faster than he had ever run in his life.

Three hours later, just after seven that evening, Maisie hurried to answer the front-door bell. She was smiling, expecting Charlie, but the smile faded when she found a strange woman on the doorstep.

'I'm Hester.'

She was beautiful, thought Maisie resignedly, but she was also obviously tired and anxious. She carried almost no luggage.

Maisie tried a welcoming smile. 'So you got the letter!'

Thank the Lord for that, she thought. Charlie would never know about the small attempted sabotage.

'No. I've heard nothing, but I . . . I couldn't wait any longer. They were trying to . . . they wanted me to stay for Christmas, but I just left everything and walked out. Is he here?' She glanced past Maisie with such a desperate expression that Maisie's guilt returned. She had said 'I will like her!' and here she was, keeping the poor woman on the doorstep. Opening the door, she said, 'Please come in. He's not back yet, but he will be soon. His ship just docked.'

As they settled in the front room she saw Hester glance at the decorations. A candle surrounded by holly and a scene of the nativity which had been carefully arranged on a small piece of green baize. It consisted of small wooden figures dressed in token robes, and rather shapeless animals made from clay.

Seeing them through fresh eyes, Maisie rushed to defend them. 'Pa made them for Charlie when he was a kid. He loved it. Called it his "Tivity"!' She smiled. 'It's years old, but he still won't part with it. He says it wouldn't be Christmas without it. I offered to redress the figures because their clothes have faded, but Charlie wouldn't hear of it.' She glanced round the room over which she had slaved earlier, busy with polish, dustpan and brush. 'I don't expect it's the sort of thing you're used to.'

'It's lovely! Truly!' There were tears in her eyes which she blinked back, but Maisie felt no need to offer sympathy. She felt shabby beside Charlie's bride-to-be. Although not richly dressed there was a whiff of London fashion in the cut of Hester's suit and she wore it with a certain poise. There was a long and awkward silence.

Hester broke the silence. 'Snow already,' she said, with forced enthusiasm. 'I think it's going to be a white Christmas. I do love snow, but I must buy some suitable shoes.'

'It gets cold up here,' said Maisie.

She's struggling, thought Maisie, with sudden and unwilling compassion. All she wants to do is be in Charlie's arms and she has to sit here making polite conversation with me, knowing that I think Charlie should marry Annie. Or maybe she doesn't know that. Does she know about the baby Annie's expecting? Maybe Charlie hasn't told her everything. She wished, not for the first time, that she had had the courage to steam open her brother's letter, but she had drawn the line there. In the past she had occasionally opened a letter *to* Charlie but never *from* him to someone else. In her role as 'mother' she had felt she had the right to know if his girlfriends were worthy of him and had actively discouraged two of his relationships. Now, instinctively she realized that this time she dare not meddle. Many young women had wanted Charlie, but this time it was different. Charlie wanted Hester.

'He won't be long,' she said. 'He'll come straight here. He says he doesn't feel he's really home until he sets foot in our hall! This is where he was born.'

'There's so much I don't know about him,' Hester said wistfully. 'I've almost forgotten what he looks like! It seems so long since I last saw him.' Her voice trembled.

Maisie jumped to her feet. 'I know. Let's celebrate. Let's have a glass of sherry while we're waiting for him. Then we'll all have another one when he arrives.' Seeing Hester hesitate, she said, 'It'll perk you up. All that travelling. I hate trains – not that I've ever been on one.' She laughed. 'While I get them, you take off your jacket and put a bit more coal on the fire. I can lend you a shawl if you want one.'

In the kitchen she found a bottle of cooking sherry and poured two glasses. She had made a currant cake and cut two thick slices. She wanted Charlie to see that she was looking after his beloved Hester. Hopefully he wouldn't ask about the letter she had posted. Hester, she admitted to herself, was not at all how she had imagined her. She was beautiful but not at all haughty. As the mistress of a wealthy man, she might, Maisie thought, have been rather snooty but she seemed normal enough. The London accent grated a bit but the poor woman couldn't be blamed for that. Born in London, it was to be expected. She longed to ask the question that had tormented her from the start – what was it like being a mistress? It sounded at once mysterious and exciting – but a little dubious. Not quite a lady but not quite a fallen woman either. Almost but not exactly. Intriguing. Maisie knew she would never have the courage to ask but, if she and Charlie's wife ever became good friends, Hester might confide in her.

She carried the refreshments on a small tray and bustled back into the front room. She had never expected to utter the following words, but she now took a deep breath and held up her glass. 'This is a private toast between the two of us. Here's to a long, happy marriage for you and Charlie!'

Ten

Detective Constable Blewitt stared across the table at Fitch and then down at the sheet of paper in front of him on the table that divided the two men. This was a statement given by the suspect but written down by the detective constable. He read it aloud.

> *I was walking through this alley, minding me own business, when a man in front of me turned and started into me, knocking me around something frightful. He broke my nose and then tried to stab me with a knife, but I was too quick for him and run off.*

'And this is it, is it?' he asked sarcastically. 'This is your version of what happened? A full account?'

'Exactly.'

'So how come he's in the hospital and you're not?'

'Picked on the wrong man, didn't he?' Fitch nodded. 'I never done nothing wrong. I'm innocent and he broke my nose. Second time, this is, my nose got broke.'

'So you didn't even know the man. You can't give me any reason why he should attack you.'

'Exactly. Never set eyes on him before.' That was almost true, he thought. 'He could have killed me!' He held up both forefingers. 'This long the knife was. Blooming carving knife.' He shook his head at the fictional near escape he had had.

'We found no knife at the scene, Mr Fitch, and you have no visible wounds except your nose which was punched. How do you explain that?'

'I fought him off, that's how! I can look after meself.'

He punched the air by way of demonstration, thinking hard. 'She probably picked up the knife – the old woman, I mean. Saw that it was a good one. It's probably in a pawn shop by now.'

'So why did he attack you, Mr Fitch? Why pick on you, particularly?'

'Dunno. Probably wanted to rob me.'

'Rob you? You look wealthy, do you?' He raised his eyebrows in disbelief.

Fitch had put on his oldest trousers, a frayed jacket and a skimpy muffler – an outfit he had thought would attract no unwanted attention. 'No-o,' he agreed reluctantly, 'but he might have been a bit, you know, touched in the head. It could have been anybody, but he picked on me. I might have been the first man he saw. My unlucky day, you might say.' He nodded. 'Yes, most likely touched in the head. Not making any sense really.'

The policeman sighed dramatically. 'And you're not making any sense either, Mr Fitch. According to the witness, Mrs Wragg, *you* were doing the attacking.'

'What does she know? Probably blind as a bat.' Fitch looked pained. 'He pinched me watch! Gold it was, an' all!'

'What make was it?'

'Dunno. It was just a watch.' He frowned unhappily. Perhaps the watch was a mistake. Fitch knew he had to be careful. These detectives were sometimes cleverer than they looked – and the blasted man was still scribbling down every blessed word he said.

'What did you do with the bag?'

'Nothing. What bag?'

'The witness, Mrs Wragg, saw you running off with a bag.'

'She's lying. There wasn't no bag.' He felt sweat break out on his skin. There would have to be a witness. Silly old cow. Just his luck.

'So if you were being attacked, why did you run away when help was at hand?' He leaned across the table. 'A constable tells me that you saw him coming towards you and you turned and ran the other way. Why would you do that? If you were the victim you'd surely have greeted him with open arms and reported the attack.'

'I was confused. Dazed by the hiding he'd given me.' It didn't sound convincing but it was the best he could do.

'Your statement doesn't tie in with what we know, Mr Fitch. Your victim is lying unconscious in the hospital, but he did recover for a few moments and he repeated something you said to him.'

Now Fitch's hands became clammy and he rubbed the palms on his trouser-legs. He didn't believe for a moment that the detective was telling the truth. It was a favourite trick and he was a bit old in the tooth to be fooled.

'Something I said? Oh, yes? What was that then?'

'So you accept he is the victim?' The detective smiled.

Damn! He'd walked right into that one. 'I didn't say that.'

'He quoted you as saying . . .' He produced a notebook and flipped through it. 'Let's see . . . Ah, yes! According to the victim you said to him, "Whatever you done to upset his nibs, don't do it again. My boss don't like it, see!" So who is "his nibs" and what doesn't he like? I can assure you, you *will* tell me, so why not be smart and get it over with? Prove that you're not as stupid as you look.'

Fitch's stomach clenched with shock. He had never said anything so stupid – had he? 'He's lying,' he declared. 'All lies. I never said that. Why should I? *He* was having a go at *me*, as I recall. So why . . .?' He sank back in the chair and rubbed the back of his neck. He'd lost track of the argument. It was all unravelling. He should have kept his mouth shut. He'd been told not to say a word, but in the excitement . . . Perhaps he could still bluff it out. 'If he said that, *if* he did, then he's a liar and he's trying to set me up.'

The detective said, 'Listen carefully, Mr Fitch. The man you attacked in the alley is in a critical condition and if he dies you will be up on a murder charge. You'll hang, Mr Fitch. I hope you understand your position.'

Murder? Coldness swept through Fitch. 'Hanged. Gawd! Don't even say such a thing!'

'If someone put you up to this, you'd better tell us his

name – unless you want him to get off scot-free while you dangle on the end of a rope.'

Fitch drew in a long, quivering breath and tried to pull himself together while he considered his options. There was no way Barnes was going to die – they were trying to frighten him.

'Murder, Mr Fitch! Think about it.'

Fitch shivered. He recalled the final kick to the head. How hard was that, he wondered uneasily. If only he'd run back past the old woman. He could have pushed past her easily. And turning left at the end of the alley had been a mistake because he had quickly run into a second constable. It had all gone horribly wrong.

He said, 'Gimme a chance to think, can't you?'

If he could bluff his way out while Barnes was still alive, he could scarper up to London, collect the rest of his money and disappear. In the circumstances, he might even get a bit more from the boss. Or he could spill the beans right now – but then he'd serve time for the assault and lose the rest of the money. Was it worth a try? If it didn't work he could still do the dirty on Waring. He folded his arms and tried to look unconcerned.

'You're trying to frame me,' he insisted. 'I can't tell you nothing 'cos I never done nothing. My nose is broke and I gotta see a doctor.'

The detective gave a long, slow smile then got up, crossed to the door and opened it. He called, 'Get us both a cup of tea, constable, will you? It's going to be a very long night!'

By eight o'clock Maisie was beginning to worry. She thought that Charlie might have gone round to see Annie, but she didn't want to suggest that to Hester. Had he had second thoughts, she wondered. When the doorbell rang she jumped to her feet.

'That'll be him!' she cried and rushed along to open the door.

Disappointment. A young lad stood outside. Maisie guessed he was around nine years old.

'Ma says Annie's bleeding and you'd best come.' He held out his hand. 'She said you'd give me a penny.'

'Bleeding? Oh my Lord! What's happened to her?'

He shrugged. 'Don't know. Ma never said.'

Maisie saw the way he avoided her gaze and a horrid suspicion began to grow. 'Has there been an accident? Was Annie knocked down?' Or was this what she thought it was? 'What else did your ma say?'

'She's bleeding . . . more than most. That's all.'

Maisie hesitated. What on earth should she say to Hester?

'And who is your ma?' She fished in a pocket and found a penny.

'They call her Auntie. Everyone calls her that.' He watched the penny.

Maisie groaned as her worst fears were confirmed. She said, 'Where is Annie?'

'She's still at our house. She's very poorly.'

'Wait there for me.' Maisie went back into the front room. 'I'm sorry, but . . . but a friend's been taken ill. I have to go, but I shan't be long and Charlie will be back at any moment. There's food in the larder. Make yourselves a sandwich. I'll be back as soon as I can.'

Hester said, 'Is there anything I can do to help?'

'No! That is, I'm sure I can manage.' She fled before Hester could ask any more awkward questions and followed the boy at a half-run. She rarely chose to be out at nights especially in winter. Tonight the gas-light reflected brightly on the snow and there were other people in the street, some carrying shopping, others pulling small children on home-made sledges. Three boys threw snowballs at anything that passed and an elderly woman, grumbling under her breath, scattered salt over her doorstep. There was a chill in the air, but Maisie was oblivious to everything but the urgency of her visit.

The boy finally stopped at a small terraced house and knocked on the door saying, 'This is it.'

His task finished, he held out his hand for the reward, then darted off, swooping, hollering and kicking snow in all directions, like a dog released from its lead. A woman, presumably Auntie, opened the door. She was small and shapeless and looked tired and dishevelled. Her apron was stained with blood and Maisie's heart fell. She stepped inside the hall which was littered with boxes and baskets on to which clothes had been tossed at random. There was a strong smell of disinfectant and something worse which Maisie failed to recognize. Was it blood? Her stomach churned.

Auntie said, 'Don't you go blaming me now, for I won't have it. They come to me in tears, wanting to be rid of the child and won't take no for an answer. She may be your friend but she brought it on herself and no one can say otherwise. She's in here.' Pushing open the door to a small back room, she stood back to let Maisie pass.

'Annie!' Maisie rushed to the bed where Annie, pale and drawn with pain, was lying flat on the bed with her feet raised on a pillow. She still wore her day clothes, but these had been pulled up to allow Auntie to attend to her.

On seeing Maisie, Annie gave a heartfelt cry and began to sob hysterically.

'I'm sorry, Maisie! I'm sorry. I didn't know how it would be . . . and now she says it has gone wrong and it's my fault.'

''Tis your fault, you wicked creature.' Auntie stepped closer, glaring indignantly. 'Who else can you blame? Unless it's your fancy man.' She sniffed.

Maisie said soothingly, 'It's nobody's fault. Things happen, Annie.'

Auntie turned on her. 'Young people these days have no idea how to behave. None at all. I see it all around me. I see the results of their wanton behaviour.'

Annie cried, 'We didn't mean any harm.'

'Well, harm's what you've got!'

Maisie wanted to pick Annie up and take her away from there, but she didn't understand exactly what had happened or whether it was safe to move her. Somehow the beginnings of the child had been removed – that much she knew. Or thought she knew. How had this 'gone wrong'? Was Annie still pregnant? She glared at Auntie. 'How bad is it? Has she lost a lot of blood?'

'A fair amount. I've stuck the sheets out in the yard. What a mess!' She planted her hands on her hips and glared at Maisie. 'And what a hullabaloo she made. Sobbing and screaming. I thought we'd have the neighbours round, hammering on the door. "D'you want the child or not?" I asked her. "Yes or no?" ' She shook her head in disgust. 'I've had women younger than her make half the fuss she made!' She rolled her eyes. 'I'll be glad to see the back of her and that's the truth.'

Maisie eyed Annie doubtfully, turned back to Auntie and lowered her voice. 'Is she fit to be moved? I mean, could she walk home or would she start to bleed again?'

'Course she can't walk. Not for an hour or more I reckon, but then she might manage it.' She flung out a hand. 'She's all yours. I've done my part. You find a way to get her out of here, that's all I want.'

Looking at Annie, Maisie's worries multiplied. Suppose her brother found out the truth – he might blame her for not keeping an eye on Annie – not that it was her responsibility and she would tell him so. Suppose Hester found out – what would she think? Would she think less of Charlie? Suppose Charlie blamed himself. Suppose he was mad with Annie.

She said tentatively, 'Could you make her a cup of tea, please? It might—'

'Cup of tea? No I couldn't!' Auntie glared at them, her voice full of righteous indignation. 'What do you think this is, a tea shop? She can have a glass of water – like it or lump it!'

Auntie flounced out of the room. Within seconds she was back again with the promised water which Annie drank eagerly.

Auntie folded her arms over her chest and added, 'And don't even think of going to the police because I'll deny it. Oh, yes! That's the thanks I get from some folk! They come here begging for help, saying their husbands will duff them up, and when I do my best by them what do they do but turn round and accuse me of all sorts of things.' She shook her head, despairing of mankind and young women

in particular. 'I don't know why I bother and that's the truth.'
She glared at Maisie who seemed to wither under the look.
Well, I can't stay here all day. I've got more important things
to do!'

When she'd disappeared for the second time Maisie
remained at the side of the bed holding Annie's hands.

Annie whimpered and her face crumpled. 'What's Charlie
going to say?' she asked desperately. 'He'll never forgive
me. I know he won't.'

'He doesn't have to know,' Maisie said, her face grim.
'We'll say . . . We could say it happened naturally. D'you
think it's possible?'

'I suppose so – but then what does Charlie know about
these things anyway? Oh, Maisie, I'm sorry I got you into
this. I didn't mean it to go wrong.'

'I know.' She was thinking desperately. 'You just lie there
and calm down while I work out a way to get you back to
your room.'

Hester sat alone in Maisie's front room and watched the
hands of the clock tick round. An hour passed, then five
minutes, then ten minutes more. What had happened to the
sick friend, she wondered. Perhaps she had been rushed to
hospital. A thought struck her. Maybe Maisie's friend was
male. She might well have an admirer although she hadn't
said so and neither had Charlie.

She shrugged. It was none of her business. Once she and
Charlie were married it would be, because then the 'admirer'
might become her brother-in-law. There would be other
relatives and friends and they would all be part of Maisie's
new life. More time passed and she became restless. Tired
of the relentless clock, she went upstairs to the room Maisie
had said would be hers. She sat on the edge of the narrow
bed and stared round her, vaguely aware of the scent of
polish. There was a home-made rug beside the bed, a
chamber pot underneath the bed. She turned back the covers
and discovered clean but thin sheets and well-worn blankets. The chair beside the bed had a clean towel draped
over the back of it and there was a wash stand with a jug,

a bowl, and a piece of soap in a saucer. It was a far cry from her rooms in Chalker Street, but she sensed that Maisie had done her best and made a point to remember to praise the little room as soon as Maisie returned.

'Where are you, Charlie?' she cried aloud. She felt tired, lonely and unloved, and was tempted to throw herself down and give way to tears of self-pity. That, however, would be the very worst thing she could do. She remembered the first time they had arranged to meet in the Verandah Café and she had turned up too late. She had let him down on that occasion, but he had never reproached her. Now he was letting *her* down, but she was sure he would have a very good reason. She had to trust him – and she must not give way to her emotions. It would be too unkind to greet Charlie with red eyes.

Maybe she would make herself a sandwich. Forcing herself to her feet again, she went downstairs and found the kitchen. It was neat as a pin, she thought with approval. The table was scrubbed clean, a kettle simmered on the stove, the window shone and the floral curtains appeared newly ironed. Had Maisie done all this for Charlie or for her? Oh, dear! Now she was flattering herself.

The walk-in larder was lined with shelves and that brought a smile to her lips. Had Charlie made them? She tried to imagine him at some time in the future, putting up shelves in their own flat and that cheered her up immensely.

The bread was in a wooden bin and she found a lump of cheese. Butter was available but it was cold and unspread-able. It all seemed too difficult. Hester lost her appetite and closed the larder door. She would wait for Charlie and Maisie to return. Seeing Charlie would make everything all right. Her appetite would return and the vague headache that now lingered would vanish at the sight of him.

Lost in happy dreams, she was startled by a ring at the front door. Flying down the passage she fumbled with the lock. 'Charlie!' she exclaimed, all her doubts and insecur-ities disappearing like mist as she opened the door.

'Miss Barnes?'

Shocked, she stared at a policeman. 'No. That is, she does

live here, but she's gone to see a sick friend. I'm expecting her back at any moment. Would you like to wait?'

He hesitated then removed his hat and followed her inside. 'It's about her brother,' he confided, removing his helmet.

Hester froze. 'Her brother Charlie? What's happened to him? Is he all right?' She sat down heavily, one hand on her heart.

He hesitated. 'I should speak to a relative.'

'I'm his fiancée. Does that count? I've just come up from London for the wedding. Where is Mr Barnes?'

'His fiancée? Is that so?' He gave her an appraising look.

'Yes. The banns have been called already. Surely you can tell me.'

After a short hesitation, he said, 'I'm afraid Mr Barnes was set upon, miss. He's in the hospital. Now, now!' he added, seeing her jump to her feet. 'There's no cause for alarm. He's not dead.'

For a moment, cold with shock, Hester could only stare at him fearfully. 'But his injuries,' she stammered. 'How serious are they? And who would set upon him? That is, he lives here, he was born here, everybody knows him! Are you sure it's him?'

'Quite sure, miss.'

'Oh, dear! When can I see him? When can *we* see him?'

If only Maisie had not been called away. Hester felt that she needed someone to share the problem.

The policeman frowned. 'You'll have to speak to the doctor or the sister. They'll tell you all about it. But don't you worry – we've got the man who did it. Not a local man, that we do know because he wasn't known to the victim. Robbery gone wrong – that's what I heard.'

Hester sat down as the ominous words repeated themselves in her head. *Robbery gone wrong.* 'What do you mean, gone wrong?'

'Well, that's what we call it when there's a bit of a bashing instead of just the robbery. Like the victim fights back and gets a mauling.'

'Oh God! A mauling. Poor Charlie. Is he badly hurt?'

'It was rather nasty, miss. But . . .'

They both turned as they heard a key turn in the lock of the front door.

Maisie was a pitiful sight, pale and drawn, her hair dishevelled and with blood on her clothes.

Hester began to feel as if she were in a nightmare. 'Maisie, what's happened?'

Maisie was staring at the policeman in horror. 'It wasn't what you think,' she stammered. 'The woman was . . . that is, she is a qualified doctor but something . . . Annie's going to be all right so there's no need to . . .'

The policeman turned enquiringly towards Hester, who said, 'This is Maisie Barnes, Charlie's sister. A friend of hers had an accident.' To Maisie she said, 'Charlie was set upon and hurt and he's in the hospital and we need to speak with the doctor.'

Maisie's eyes widened. 'Charlie? I thought this was about . . . Charlie's *hurt*? Oh, no!' For a moment she stood in a dazed confusion then made a huge effort to pull her wits together. 'Let's go then.'

Without a word Hester and the policeman followed her out of the house, where Hester asked the policeman for directions to the hospital. They thanked him for his help, he left them, and the two women were on their way. There were no convenient buses so they were forced to walk and Hester found it difficult to keep up with Maisie, partly because she was unused to walking any distance and partly because Maisie's stride was longer than hers. As they hurried through the streets, Maisie told her about Annie's hopes of an abortion.

'It went wrong, but don't ask me how,' she said angrily, making no attempt to choose her words carefully or soften the blow for Hester's benefit. 'I suppose you realize that if you hadn't come on the scene, like you did, the banns would have been called for Annie and she'd be marrying him instead of you. She'd have had no need to do anything so stupid!'

Hester, out of breath and stunned by the revelations, reacted angrily.

'So it's all my fault, is it?' she demanded. 'Let's not

blame Charlie or Annie. I'm the stranger so it has to be *my* fault.' Already terrified by the attack on Charlie and shocked by the knowledge that he had made Annie pregnant, Hester was in no mood to suffer Annie's accusation. 'I suppose if I had been a local woman or a friend of yours, it would be different.' She was falling behind and had to raise her voice. A woman passing by on the other side of the street, turned to stare and Maisie turned long enough to hiss, 'Keep your voice down, can't you?'

Hester ran to catch up with her and grabbed her unceremoniously by the arm and swung her round until they eyed each other furiously. 'I'll have you know,' cried Hester, 'that I came up here to marry Charlie because he wouldn't consider anything else. And if you don't approve then that's unfortunate but marry him I will – regardless of you or Annie!'

Maisie wrenched her arm free, her eyes glittering furiously. 'He might think you're wonderful, but I don't and I like Annie and she's been faithful to him and . . . and now look what's happened to her!'

Stung by the unfairness of Maisie's attitude, Hester refused to back down. 'And look what's happened to me,' she shouted. 'I've given up a wealthy lifestyle with a big house and servants, not to mention a generous financial settlement by his aunt – and all because I love your brother above everything else.' She snatched a quick breath. 'He's head over heels in love with me! And all I get is abuse from you. All I can say is, if this is the way you treat people, you must make a lot of enemies, Maisie Barnes!'

Appalled by this unexpected attack, Maisie burst into tears. For a moment Hester regarded her dispassionately, but then her anger slowly faded. She reminded herself that Maisie was Charlie's sister and she had no wish to come between them. Charlie loved Maisie and she, Hester, would do well to love her also. For better or for worse, this was Charlie's world and she had promised herself she would fit in. Gently she pulled the other woman into her arms and Maisie didn't resist.

'Hush, Maisie. Tears won't help. I'm here now and we'll do this together.'

'I'm sorry,' Maisie said, sobbing. 'I'm so sorry. I shouldn't have said all that. Please don't tell Charlie. I'm just so tired and frightened and nothing's going right.' She found a handkerchief and wiped her eyes. 'I didn't mean any of it . . . at least not all of it, it wasn't fair on you. I don't want to like you, but you seem very nice.'

Hester said, 'Let's get to the hospital and see Charlie. Everything else can wait.'

Maisie nodded. 'And you won't say anything?'

'No. We've plenty of time to talk . . . and get to know each other. Let's just go and see Charlie now.'

They both hurried on and by the time they reached the hospital Maisie seemed more together.

The doctor, a Doctor Peterson, was not exactly forthcoming. 'Not because I'm holding anything back, but because the outcome, I'm afraid, is very uncertain.'

'In what way? What are you saying?' Maisie looked baffled.

From the moment she entered the hospital, her confidence had waned again. 'I hate these places,' she had confided to Hester under her breath.

Hester decided to take a firm line. 'But Mr Barnes will make a good recovery?'

Doctor Peterson hesitated. 'We are hopeful, but it's difficult to be sure at present.'

'Why is that?'

'Mr Barnes is not always fully conscious. He drifts in and out. That's because he received a blow to the back of the head and until he recovers fully and can talk to us properly he—'

Maisie cried out, 'You mean he can't *talk*!'

She glanced at Hester who was equally shocked.

Hester said, 'He spoke to the police.'

'A few words, that's all. A few lucid flashes.' The doctor gave them an encouraging smile. 'I have seen patients recover from worse injuries. Mr Barnes was punched and kicked and he has broken ribs and a fracture to his lower left leg.'

Hester was grateful that they were sitting down. Somehow,

against all the odds, she had expected Charlie to be out of hospital in a few days. It was now looking increasingly unlikely. 'Can we see him, please?' she asked.

'I'm afraid that isn't a good idea.'

'I won't leave until we've seen him.' Aware that Maisie glanced at her, she amended, 'We both need to see him. Just a glimpse. We won't disturb him.'

Reluctantly he nodded. 'But be prepared for a worrying sight. He is in a bad condition.'

Hester forced back sudden tears. This was not how she had imagined their reunion. She must remain strong, she told herself.

Abruptly she stood up and reached out a hand for Maisie, who said shakily, 'We'd like to see him, whatever he looks like.' Hester knew she had already suffered much anxiety over Annie.

Dr Peterson shrugged, rose from his chair and led the way from his office to the ward. Their first glimpse of Charlie was worse than either had expected.

'Oh, Charlie!' cried Maisie, appalled by what they saw.

Charlie was stretched out in the bed with his arms straight by his side outside the blankets. His broken leg, hidden by splints and bandages, was raised on a wire contraption and bandages hid much of his head and face. He lay with his eyes shut, white and still. His face was puffy and his split lip had been carefully stitched.

Hester stared at him and felt the tears press against her eyelids. 'Is he asleep or unconscious?' She hardly recognized her own quivering voice.

'Unconscious.' To prove this the doctor leaned forward and said loudly, 'Your sister is here, Mr Barnes, with your fiancée.'

Charlie gave not a flicker of comprehension. Hester felt her hopes shrivel. Would he ever recover? Would they ever marry? Tears filled her eyes as she stared at him. This was the ruin of all their plans. Echoing Maisie's earlier words, she whispered, 'Oh, Charlie!'

But Hester's shock suddenly gave way to anger, which deepened so fast that her tears dried before they could be shed.

Turning to Maisie, she said grimly, 'Whoever did this to him is going to pay a dreadful price!'

Mrs Carradine was intrigued to receive a letter from Hester.

> *I am writing to apologize for my abrupt departure a few days ago. I was beginning to feel drawn towards Hilsomer House, and was losing confidence in my ability to find my way to Charlie's home in Liverpool. I suddenly realized that if I didn't leave, I might never make the move and I was determined to be with Charlie.*

'Oh, you foolish girl!' Edith exclaimed. 'You will live to regret that decision.' She sighed. What on earth have you let yourself in for, Hester? she thought. Struggling on the pay of a ship's steward with Lord knows how many children!

She read on, her mouth pursed in disapproval.

> *However, I hated leaving you without a goodbye as you have been very kind to me and I will always remember that with gratitude.*
> *Now however, I write with very sad news for my fiancé was attacked on the day I arrived here. He suffered a severe beating and is seriously ill in hospital.*

Attacked? Heavens! What is the world coming to? Edith had only a vague memory of the steward, but the thought of him being assaulted disturbed her sense of fair play. She had always been disgusted by mindless violence. 'Poor Hester,' she murmured. *What a sad beginning to their relationship.*

> *You would be shocked if you could see the terrible injuries that he received. He is still drifting in and out of consciousness and the doctor fears he may yet lapse into a coma. The police have arrested the man who did it, but he claims he was paid to do it by someone*

*who had a grudge against Charlie. The police are still
questioning the attacker and are determined to find
the person behind it and bring them both to trial. The
motive is a total mystery as Charlie's sister says he
has no enemies. Meanwhile, Charlie remains seriously
ill. I would be grateful if you would remember him in
your prayers.*

*I would be grateful too, if you do not discuss this with
Alexander until he has heard about it from me. I shall
be writing to him shortly to ask for his understanding.
I wish you both a happy Christmas – your daughters
also – and hope for a happier New Year for all of us.*

*Yours faithfully,
Hester Shaw*

Edith read it through again and then clasped her hands,
closed her eyes and whispered a quick prayer for the young
man's recovery. Not that she wanted Hester to marry him
but no doubt the young woman had taken it badly and was
deeply unhappy and bitterly disappointed by the unexpected
turn of events. If Barnes died, of course, Hester might recon-
sider and . . . but no. She mustn't think like that. Most
unchristian, she reproached herself sternly.

After a few moments' further thought she decided to do
as Hester Shaw requested. She would not speak of Mr Barnes
to her nephew until he had heard the news from Hester
herself. For one thing, she had no wish to spoil Christmas
by the sharing of bad news and – if she was honest – she
was secretly afraid that her nephew might gloat. With an
effort she decided to put aside all thoughts of Hester Shaw
and her young man. Tomorrow was Christmas Eve and she
would be with Dorcas who would also remain in ignorance
of the assault. With enough goodwill, they could still enjoy
the festive period. What a strange Christmas it was turning
out to be.

Later that evening, however, when Alexander called in on
her unexpectedly, he caught sight of a letter on the mantel-
piece and recognized Hester's handwriting on the envelope.

Taken by surprise, his aunt handed it to him with a shrug. As he read it he felt as if he had been punched in the stomach. For a moment, as panic enveloped him, his aunt's elegant sitting room swam before his eyes and he sat down heavily on the ottoman. He had heard nothing from Hester. The news of the beating was expected, but the details of Fitch's arrest shook him to the core. He felt a sweat break out on his skin as the significance of the disaster struck home.

Aware that his aunt was watching for his reaction, he forced himself to calm down and drew several deep breaths before glancing up at her. 'If she has written to me, the letter hasn't arrived,' he said. 'Probably lost for suitable words. Excusing a betrayal can never be easy, can it?'

Edith looked at her nephew in surprise, disappointed by his reaction. 'But isn't it dreadful? Mr Barnes being set upon like that! Like him or loathe him, one cannot help but sympathize with the man. It was a most reprehensible act.'

'Very unpleasant,' he agreed, 'but bear in mind Hester does exaggerate. It was probably nothing more than a disagreement. Men of his type are prone to fisticuffs at the slightest provocation. Probably fell out over a game of cards or got drunk!' His heart was pounding and he brushed a hand across his forehead to remove some of the perspiration before his aunt noticed it. 'Probably deserved it.'

'But Hester says Mr Barnes is not fully conscious and may slip into a coma! And that it was *deliberate*. Surely, in your line of business, you find that quite alarming.'

Alexander shrugged. 'Barnes has obviously made enemies. It sounds as though poor Hester has chosen what is known as "a wrong'un".'

Would Fitch talk? That was the question that echoed through his mind. If he did he would never see the rest of his money. If he didn't, he would serve his time and then come calling for it. That Alexander could just about bear although he had counted on the matter being dealt with quickly and then forgotten. Being implicated in any way would ruin him. He would be arrested, accused of conspiracy to commit a crime, tried and sent down. A senior policeman in prison. The scandal would make headlines in all the newspapers. Utterly humiliating. And life in prison would be dangerous. He would not live long. He handed back the letter and noticed that his hand was trembling.

Edith said, 'At least they have the man who did it. If Mr Barnes dies he'll hang for murder and serve him right! Nasty little thug!'

Alexander felt like throttling her. Stupid old fool! She was twisting the knife with a vengeance – but then she didn't know the true facts. Calm yourself, he told himself again. There was no need to panic at this stage. There may yet be a way out of it. If Fitch was going to cave in he would have done so already and he, Alexander, would have heard about it. It was small comfort but Alexander was clutching at straws. 'How on earth did they catch him?' he asked aloud, trying to speak normally.

'Does it matter? The good news is that they have him in custody. I must write back at once and say how sorry we are.'

Sorry that Fitch went too far but that's all, thought Alexander. Or perhaps he should have told Fitch to kill him and done with it. Then there'd be no comeback at all. He drew a deep breath and then another and composed his features. His aunt was very sharp and he mustn't allow her to suspect anything.

'Are you all right, dear?' she asked. 'You look rather pale.'

'I don't feel too well. Maybe a touch of flu. There's a lot about.'

'Is there?' Edith shook her head. 'Poor Hester. What a calamity.'

'She has only herself to blame.' The spiteful words slipped out and he instantly regretted them. He should sound more sympathetic.

'Oh, Alexander! That's not at all like you.'

At least he had the satisfaction of knowing that Barnes was suffering. Hester, too. Fitch had earned his money on that score but how had the fool allowed himself to be caught? Hester hadn't explained that part of it.

'I doubt they'll have a very happy Christmas,' he said,

softening his tone slightly. 'She should have stayed here with us.' He shrugged again. 'I really thought Hester had more sense.'

'That's because you're a man,' his aunt said tartly. 'Only women understand matters of the heart. Poor Hester. If he dies she'll be alone in a strange town.' She glanced up at him. 'Do you think she'd come back to you?'

'Do you think I'd take her back?' Stung, he was once again scornful. 'No, I wouldn't! She's shown herself to be superficial and heartless and I want no more to do with her.' He felt it was safer to talk about Hester and let the details of the attack fade.

They fell silent. Alexander crossed to the sideboard and poured himself a large brandy. He must be on his own to think this through, he thought. He needed time to cover his tracks and limit the damage that the fool Fitch had caused. He'd survived some tough times and taken some serious risks to reach his present position and he certainly didn't intend to let Fitch bring him down.

'I must go,' he told her, 'I've some catching up to do. A bit of work that can't wait.'

'Oh, poor Alexander!' She tutted. 'You work too hard. You should take a break. It's Christmas Eve tomorrow. Will you join me at Dorcas's? You know you'd be welcome – your first Christmas without poor Marcia. You don't want to be on your own.'

'She hasn't actually invited me, Aunt Edith, so I don't imagine she'd welcome me with open arms!'

'She's jealous, that's all. She and Evelyn are both a bit jealous of our rather special affection for each other.' She smiled. 'But Evelyn will be going to her mother-in-law's as usual and you shouldn't be all alone. Think about it, dear.'

But that is exactly what he did want, he thought irritably. He wanted to be alone with his problems, without interference from well-intentioned women. There would be other Christmases and he would be happy to miss this one although he could see there was no chance of that happening.

* * *

Ten minutes later he was back at Hilsomer House, where he let himself in and breathed a sigh of relief. At last Hester's letter to his aunt had given him some advance warning of possible difficulties and for that he was immensely grateful. He was also determined, for some reason he didn't comprehend, that Hester should never understand his part in Barnes's downfall.

Leaning back against the closed front door he considered possible ways to divert attention from himself. Obviously if accused – if named by that rat Fitch – he would emphatically deny any connection with him and would swear on the Holy Bible to that effect if necessary. He allowed himself a thin smile. Rank gave him power. He could beat this threat if that is what this affair was to become. He could bluff his way through, for God's sake! He was not inexperienced in these matters.

He had, however, forgotten about Sergeant Harrow.

Eleven

Next morning, Christmas Eve, it was decided that Maisie would go round to see how Annie was while Hester visited Charlie. Wrapped warmly against a light fall of wispy snow, and with one of Maisie's shawls lending extra protection to her head and shoulders, Hester crunched her way towards the hospital, studying the surroundings with interest, aware that these streets and these people were part of her new life.

It was a far cry from London, she admitted. The streets were meaner, the people less fashionably dressed. There were fewer hansom cabs and more men pushing barrows. Her ear was gradually becoming accustomed to the Liverpool dialect which reminded her of Charlie. It seemed to her that the people were cheerful – there was laughter and good-natured 'ribbing' – and she sensed a feeling of solidarity that she had never experienced in London.

When she reached the hospital and made her way up the stairs to the men's ward, she found a few last touches being made to the Christmas decorations. A cheerful young nurse was laying holly along the windowsills. Three children from another ward were helping one of the ward orderlies to hang small baubles on a large Christmas tree. With a rapidly beating heart, Hester made her way past the other beds, wondering what she would find when she reached Charlie. No doubt he would be wondering about her – she must be cheerful and very positive with no mention of the worrying time she had spent waiting for his letter or the anxious train journey and subsequent disappointments. And not a word about Annie! However, before she reached the

bed where she had last seen Charlie, she was waylaid by
the sister.

'Very good news, Miss Shaw!' she cried. 'Mr Barnes has
regained consciousness and is asking to see you.'

'Asking for me? Oh! That's wonderful.' Hester's relief
was huge and she smiled radiantly. 'I can hardly believe it!'

'Your prayers have been answered, Miss Shaw.'

'So it seems.'

'But a word of warning. Your fiancé will tire easily and too
much excitement will not be good for him. The doctor wants
you to stay no longer than five minutes and to try and keep
him calm. Is that understood?'

'I'll do my best!'

She found Charlie propped up against the pillows, and
he smiled when he saw her. Despite the stitches in his lip,
the darkening bruises, the swollen jaw and the bandages
round his head, the love in his eyes shone through. He still
loved her, she thought, weak with relief.

'Charlie,' she whispered. 'Oh, my darling Charlie!'

Drawing up a chair, she sat down. There was nowhere
on his poor battered face where she could plant a kiss without
the risk of hurting him so she picked up one of his hands
and kissed it long and hard.

'You came,' he said. His voice was husky and faint and
she leaned nearer to hear him properly. 'Sorry . . . didn't . . .
meet you.' He looked at her with such delight in his eyes that
it made her laugh.

'You look terrible and happy at the same time,' she told
him. 'It's bizarre but . . . dearest Charlie, I was so afraid.
I thought you were going to die! That beast of a man! But
we mustn't talk about that. The sister says you have to stay
calm. And I am only allowed five minutes when I can hardly
bear to let you out of my sight!'

He squeezed her hand. 'You're . . . all I need! You got
my letter?'

She shook her head. 'It didn't arrive, but I expect it was
the Christmas rush – but I came anyway. And here I am –
and I'm here to stay!'

'Still love me?'

'Of course I do! Do you love me?'

He nodded but she could see that even that small movement was an effort.

He said, 'Will we still . . . be married?'

'Oh, yes, Charlie! As soon as possible. I'll talk to the vicar and explain what has happened.'

Charlie was staring at her with such a rapt expression and Hester realized that the same expression must be visible on her own face.

He closed his eyes tiredly, but kept a tight hold on her hand.

Hester said, 'I'd love to kiss your mouth, but you're so swollen and bruised it would hurt you. But your hand is just as dear to me.' She kissed it again.

The sister hurried past and mouthed, 'Time's up.'

Hester groaned. 'I have to leave you to rest,' she said, 'but I'll come back tomorrow.'

'Promise.'

'I promise.' Slowly and reluctantly she stood up. It was agony to leave him – such a short reunion – but she was terrified of doing anything that would slow his recovery. 'Don't go away,' she teased.

'No . . . chance!' He tried to smile but the damaged mouth made him grimace instead.

As she turned to go the doctor entered the ward and, catching her eye, beckoned her over. Outside the ward he told her that a detective was waiting to speak with Charlie, but they had refused to allow it yet. 'When he is stronger,' he said. 'They do need to know as much as he can tell them, but we have to put the patient's wellbeing first. It was a vicious attack and it seems they want to make further arrests. I gather there was another man involved. They may well wish to speak with you.'

'I don't know anything about it,' she said, surprised.

'I'm just warning you. They insist that sometimes people know more than they think they do and can recall certain things under judicious questioning.' He smiled suddenly. 'But as for your young man, he must have a strong constitution. It was a very close call and we were not at all sure he would survive.'

Hester's expression hardened. 'I'd like to find the man who did it – and do the same to him! Not very Christian, maybe, but that's how I feel. The last time I saw Charlie he was a normal, cheerful soul . . .' She bit her lip, unable to go on.

The doctor smiled. 'The moment he regained consciousness he spoke to the nurse, trying to discuss your wedding. He was half delirious and in some pain, but he was asking if you could be married in the hospital. He's so impatient.'

'And could we?'

He shrugged. 'It's most unusual but it might be possible at a later stage. His leg is the biggest problem – it was a bad break.'

'I'm very grateful for all that you are doing for him, doctor.' She hesitated. 'Do you have *any* idea when he can come home?'

He grinned. 'I was waiting for that question, Miss Shaw. The answer is it will be several weeks and may even be months – and he may never totally recover.' He was considering his words carefully, she noticed. 'His head injuries are quite severe and to tell you the truth, we are amazed at his progress so far. He will almost certainly limp, but thankfully there seems to be no paralysis despite the bruising along the spine. Keep praying for him, Miss Shaw, and we will do our best. You know what they say – time is a great healer. Now you must excuse me.'

Hester walked home, her feelings very mixed by what she had learned. The hospital staff were being positive, but Charlie was certainly not out of the woods yet. The doctor seemed to be hinting that the man she loved might never be the same Charlie Barnes! Not that she cared for herself, she would marry him whatever happened – it was impossible to think about life without him, but for Charlie . . .? Suppose he could never return to his job on the *Mauretania*. She wondered just how much it meant to him to be at sea and it dawned on her that although she adored him and always would, she knew very little about him. But then Charlie knew very little about *her*.

It doesn't matter, she said to herself. We've got all our lives ahead of us in which to find out!

*   *   *

Christmas morning dawned bright and clear, but as Alexander awoke he groaned with frustration. His aunt would be putting in an appearance later in the morning, intent on supervising the cook who wasn't looking forward to what she deemed 'needless interference'.

'Young Mrs Waring always left everything to me,' she had protested in an uncharacteristic outburst, when Alexander broke the news. 'I've cooked here for I don't know how many Christmases without a word of complaint from anyone. And she'll be here to supervise breakfast? What does Mrs Carradine think she can teach me about cooking scrambled eggs? As for the main meal I could cook it with my eyes shut! Your wife, Mr Waring, understood that the kitchen is *my* place and left me to my own devices, but your aunt seems to think . . .'

Mercifully, at that point, she had run out of breath and Alexander had muttered something suitably soothing and had promised to try and keep his aunt busy elsewhere. He had decided to ask her to go through the linen for him, to see if anything needed mending or to be replaced. He would say that poor Marcia hadn't been up to it during the last months of her illness and he didn't feel the housekeeper would make such a good job of it. He was hoping this subtle flattery would do the trick.

He got out of bed and did his exercises while his thoughts turned towards Fitch and Charlie Barnes and the possible consequences. He would refuse to discuss it with his aunt insisting that this was Christmas Day and they must put all their problems aside and enjoy it. After his initial shock his confidence had returned.

'Look on the bright side,' he told himself, as he searched for a suitable tie – preferably one that his aunt had given him. 'You're a free man.'

He would sort out the Fitch business and then he could relax. Marcia was dead and Hester had fled into the arms of a worthless man. She would eventually see the error of her ways, but by then she could plead on bended knees for a second chance – without any chance of success. He would be making advances to a pretty little nurse, with or

without his aunt's approval. Young Della Telson was ripe
for the picking, he thought as he took a last look at himself
in the large swing mirror.

'Happy Christmas, Alexander!' he said to his reflection,
pleased with himself and the world. He felt cautiously sure
that he would soon be in control of his future and he awaited
the start of the New Year with a growing sense of excitement.

At half past nine his aunt arrived, fluttering and cooing
with festive good wishes and an armful of presents which
she placed on the table in the sitting room.

'I do hope you sent Hester a card,' she said. 'I left the
address for you.'

'I tore it up. I want to forget her. Whatever hopes you
may have harboured I must disappoint you.' He bent to kiss
her, thus delaying her reply.

'Tore it up? Oh, really, dear, that is so like you! Ever
since you were a child you have never learned to deal with
disappointment.' Patting his arm, she smiled. 'But we won't
talk about it any more. Let's concentrate on enjoying
Christmas Day. Marcia would have wanted us to be cheerful,
wouldn't she?'

'I doubt it, Aunt Edith! She would want me to be punished
for my liaison with Hester! Oh, didn't you know? She was
aware of her existence and took pleasure in trying to make
me feel a cad.' He exulted inwardly at the expression on
her face. 'For the past few years our marriage was somewhat of a sham!'

For once his aunt was lost for words, he thought, as he
settled her on the ottoman.

'Well, she hid it very well. So she knew. How dreadful.'
She gave him a deeply reproachful glance.

He said, 'Marcia the martyr.'

The cook knocked and entered. 'Good morning, Mrs
Carradine. Happy Christmas.' She turned quickly to
Alexander. 'The dinner's underway, Mr Waring, sir, and
should be ready by two o'clock as planned. Breakfast is on
the sideboard, but the scrambled eggs won't be moist if you
leave them too long. Is there anything else?'

'No, thank you, Cook.'

In the dining room Alexander sat down, his spiteful mood giving way to one of resignation. Somehow he would get through the day. He had had his revenge and it was undeniably sweet. There had been nothing between him and Fitch in writing so there was no chance of problems in the future. Not that he expected any. Fights were common enough and no one was safe on the streets. It was a fact of life. Who was going to worry about a ship's steward?

Urged on by his aunt, he opened the presents. 'Leather gloves? My word, Aunt Edith, they're smart. Thank you. And what's this? A box of handkerchiefs. Splendid!'

'Handkerchiefs are always useful.' She waited hopefully.

'Oh, good gracious!' he exclaimed. 'I haven't given you your gift. Do forgive me. This has been such a difficult Christmas . . .' He faltered and tried to look woebegone and thought that Edith's face softened a little. He regretted tormenting her. She was always so determined to think well of him and he had made it almost impossible.

He fetched a large box from behind the ottoman and placed it carefully in her lap. 'Happy Christmas, dear!' He leaned down and kissed the top of her head.

'This looks intriguing!' Her elderly fingers struggled with the large ribbon bow and then began to tear at the paper. It always touched him to see how impatient she was when she was excited – just like a child. He had spent a lot of money on her and saw it as an investment. He needed to be in her 'good books' because he wanted her to approve of Della. There was a lot of money at stake after all. As his aunt folded back the tissue paper the telephone rang. Edith lifted out a wonderfully soft cashmere cardigan in delphinium blue.

'To match your eyes!' he told her.

Before she could utter a word of thanks, Alexander excused himself and hurried into the hall to answer the telephone.

A voice he wasn't expecting said, 'Is that you?'

A wrong number! 'Who is this?'

'It's me, Harrow! I have to speak to you.'

Anger fired up within Alexander. 'I thought I told you . . .'

'Are you alone? It's rather delicate, if you know what I mean. Rather private.'

Alexander's eyes narrowed and he felt a jolt of unease. He would have to brazen it out. 'Private? What are you talking about? We have nothing to say to each other.'

'It's important.' The sergeant's voice was very low. 'Are you alone?'

'As good as. Look, we have nothing to say to each other. Do you understand?' After a disconcerting silence Alexander asked, 'How did you get this number?'

There was a long pause. 'Ways and means! You'd know about that.'

A knot of real anxiety now throbbed in Alexander's temple. 'If you've something to say, say it – or get off the line! It's Christmas Day, for God's sake!'

A long pause drove Alexander almost to the point of frustration. Surely the fool wasn't drunk.

'It's about that little job. Know what I mean? Seems it didn't go to plan and our lot have got Fitch and they smell blood. Talking to his drinking pals, searching his place. You know the drill.'

'Searching his . . .!' Now he was thoroughly frightened. The money! The first payment! Where had Fitch hidden it? Alexander closed his eyes and a wave of nausea swept through him. He had to know the worst or he was going to be vulnerable.

Before he could decide how to play it, Harrow spoke again, his voice stronger. 'It's like this – I reckon I'm going to get reporters sniffing round – like blooming bloodhounds they are. Gentlemen of the press! Gentlemen. Hah! You know what they're like. Offering money for information they can use in their newspapers.'

Oh God! Worse and worse! The little sod was blackmailing him. Alexander tried desperately to think, but his brain seemed numb and his heart was racing uncomfortably in his chest. What did one do when faced with a blackmailer? Go to the police, of course – but he *was* the police! What should he do? Think! *Think!*

'You still there?' The voice was relentless. 'I mean, I don't want to tell them anything. You know me, but . . . my memory could be a bit weak. That would be convenient, wouldn't it? Know what I'm getting at?'

Alexander ground his teeth with fury. Bitterly he regretted using Sergeant Harrow to get to Fitch, but that was in the past and couldn't be undone.

'Listen to me!' he snapped as forcefully as he could. 'Do not mention my name on the telephone. Not ever! Have you got that?' He raised his voice. 'Do not mention my name! Ever! To anyone!' He took a deep breath and tried to calm himself. 'And never phone me again. If you do I promise you'll regret it.'

Harrow went on as if he hadn't spoken. 'I mean, you're a wealthy man but I'm just a sergeant and a bit of extra cash would be very handy.'

There was now a distinct whine in the sergeant's voice and Alexander swore under his breath. What he wanted with all his heart was to strangle the greedy little blighter and silence him for ever, but that seemed unlikely to happen. So what *was* to be done, he wondered. Suddenly Alexander saw his whole career crumbling – and all because of Charles Barnes. And Hester, of course, because it was Hester who had brought Barnes into the equation.

A timid cough made him turn and he found his aunt standing in the doorway looking at him nervously. Hell! He had forgotten all about her. Covering the mouthpiece of the telephone, he said, 'It's nothing, dear. I won't be long.'

'Who is it? Is something wrong?'

'Nothing's wrong. Go back in there.' He jerked his head towards the sitting room. 'I'll be with you in a minute.' As she hesitated he added her to the list of people with whom he would like to deal harshly, but, to his relief, his aunt withdrew as instructed.

Alexander drew another deep breath to steady himself. He would have to deal with this later. He uncovered the mouthpiece. 'I'll see to it. Do you understand me? It's Christmas and this is most inconvenient. I can't talk now.

We . . . I have visitors. My wife died recently and I still have arrangements to make. The funeral and so on. I'll contact you. Do you understand me?'

He waited in vain for an answer and then the line went dead. Before rejoining his aunt, Alexander sat down on the stairs and put his head in his hands. He tried to recall his side of the conversation. How much had his aunt overheard? He would have to bluff it out. Forcing a smile, he stood up and glanced in the mirror. Yes, he looked as bad as he felt. Badly shaken and furiously angry. He would never have expected Harrow to turn on him. But then he had trusted Fitch to give Barnes a beating, not half kill him! He smoothed his hair, tugged down his waistcoat and eased his collar.

Walking back to the crumpled wrapping papers and presents he said cheerily, 'So sorry, dear! Would you believe it? I'm off duty, it's Christmas Day and some blithering idiot decides to land me with all his insecurities. If he can't do the job he should leave the force and become a green-grocer or a milkman.' He laughed. 'I'll have his guts for garters when I get back into the office!'

'So it's nothing serious? I thought . . .'

'Serious? Only for him! Now, hold the cardigan up, dear, and let me see how it suits you.' She was still regarding him anxiously and he ploughed on. 'I thought it the same colour as your eyes. A lovely cornflower blue.'

'You said you were busy with Marcia's funeral.' She looked puzzled.

'Oh! That was just to shut the man up. He isn't to know it's been and gone. I think Marcia would forgive me for that small lie.' He smiled as she held the cardigan against herself. 'Yes! A perfect match.' He leaned forward and kissed her. 'Happy Christmas, dear.'

She laid it reverently over the arm of the ottoman. 'It must have been very expensive. You do spoil me, Alexander.'

He crossed the room to pour himself a brandy. While his back was towards her he took a large gulp and then topped it up. He needed to be alone with his thoughts. Turning back he said, 'Will you excuse me for a few moments. I have to make a few notes before I forget. It will only take about ten minutes.' He pointed to a small present as yet unwrapped. Smiling he said, 'It's a small extra for you. It will give you something uplifting to sustain you while I'm upstairs.'

The book contained biblical quotations – one for each day of the year. It was the sort of thing his aunt professed to like. As she picked it up, he hurried from the room with his brandy and almost ran upstairs and into his study. He was trembling as he threw himself into the familiar leather-backed chair and closed his eyes. The familiar surroundings gave him a sense of security, but he knew it to be false. He was in deep trouble, he acknowledged, and had behaved in an ill-restrained fashion. He had forgotten his mantra which was 'Pause first, act later'. His feelings against Barnes had led him to act first and he was going to regret it later. He should have thrown Hester out when he first learned of her obsession with the young steward. Trying to punish her lover had been a mistake, but he had done it because he thought he could get away with it. He had the power and the connections and the nerve to take revenge. But he had been too confident and that meant he had misjudged Fitch. The fool had gone too far and if Barnes died, he, Alexander, could be found guilty of conspiracy to murder. How could he have been so careless?

Now the worst scenario had happened and he would need all his skill to evade the retribution he deserved. No point in relying on Fitch or Harrow. They would both finger him. He would need all his cunning, skill and courage to fight off the threat. If he couldn't find a way through this, the rest of his life would not be worth living.

Wednesday, 25th December – What a dreadful day this has been. A Christmas Day to forget. Thank heavens Hester Shaw was not involved. I hardly know how to write down my suspicions, but I feel sure poor Alexander is in some kind of trouble. When he was a boy he would bring his troubles to me, but now he is politely resisting my efforts to help him. He had a weird telephone call this morning while we were unwrapping our presents and whoever it was upset him quite dreadfully. I think he was bullying him because Alexander sounded very worried and then angry, and when he saw me at the door he tried to pretend it was nothing important but I know it was. He was lying to me!

He went upstairs for ten minutes to finish a report but didn't come down again until Cook announced lunch. He had been drinking and was in a hateful mood. He hardly spoke to me and snapped at Mrs Rice, saying she had ruined the meal which wasn't true. Poor Mrs Rice ran out in tears. When I made to follow her out and comfort her, Alexander screamed at me to sit down and mind my own damned business! I was glad that Marcia wasn't alive to see him in such an emotional state. I wish he would confide in me because as things stand, I don't know how to help him. I shall keep my eyes and ears open. He may think me an old fool but I shall make it my business to know what is going on.

I don't think I shall ever want to wear the beautiful cardigan he gave me – it would bring back too many unhappy memories.

Three days later Hester returned from the hospital looking serious and at once sat Maisie down.

'We have to talk,' she said. 'We have to make some plans for the future and Charlie has to be at the centre of them.'

Maisie nodded. 'I've been thinking the same thing, but I didn't like to bring it up over Christmas. We both know the main problem is going to be . . .?'

'Money!'

'Exactly. You and I have to face facts. You kept house for your brother who was earning a weekly wage. I was keeping house for Alex and he was keeping me financially. Now neither of us has anyone to earn for us.'

Maisie sighed. 'We have no idea when Charlie will go back to work – if he ever can – so I've been thinking I'll

get a job. There's bound to be something. There's always
work at the laundry where Annie works. Her friend Ginnie
has just left and they've said she can have her job in the
ironing room. So if Annie takes that job I could have her
present job. It's hot and steamy work but it's regular and
it would pay the rent of this place and a bit over.'

'I used to be a children's nanny,' Hester told her, 'until
my employer forced his way into my bedroom and then
lied about it, blaming me! I could try for something similar.
I can also play the piano a little and could give lessons to
beginners – if we had a piano.'

'And we haven't!'

They both laughed.

Hester frowned. 'D'you know any rich people with young
children I could teach privately? Maybe I could advertise
somewhere.' She brightened. 'If a family had a piano I could
go to the house and teach there.'

Maisie said, 'The big snag is – who's going to look
after Charlie when he comes home? If we're both out at
work . . .'

'I spoke to the doctor again and he still won't commit
himself about when Charlie can come home, but he did say
in a few weeks we might be able to marry in the hospital.'

Maisie stared at her. 'And you didn't think to tell me!
Hester Shaw, you amaze me. That's wonderful news.'

'I'm sorry. I was more concerned about our day-to-day
living expenses. I have ten pounds left from the money
which Edith Carradine paid me to be her travelling
companion. I shall put all that towards whatever expenses
you have with this house and our food – and there's the
coal! Oh, dear! I realize now how spoiled I was when I
was with Alexander. He paid for everything. I'm not really
used to dealing with money, but it's high time I learned.'

Maisie steepled her hands. 'There's something else.
Annie's not much good at writing, but she's determined to
write a letter to Charlie to tell him about the baby and what
she did, to say sorry. She's not expecting a reply and she's
not expecting him to go back to her, but she says she wants
to "wipe the slate clean". That's how she put it – but she

doesn't want to upset you. You wouldn't mind, would you, Hester? She's been through a lot and she's very unhappy. I said I thought you'd understand.'

'I don't mind, Maisie. I feel very sorry for her. She's never going to want me as a friend, but I don't see her as an enemy. I can see why she loves Charlie.' She smiled. 'I can't see why anyone *wouldn't* love him.'

A knock at the front door interrupted the discussion and Maisie went to answer it.

A policeman said, 'Miss Shaw?'

'No. I'll . . . It's not about my brother, is it? Charlie Barnes? He's . . .'

'Indirectly. I need to speak with Miss Shaw. In private.'

'You'd better come in.' She sent him into the front room and called Hester.

As soon as the two of them were seated, the policeman introduced himself as Detective Constable Blewitt who was making some enquiries into the attack on Charlie Barnes. 'I understand from the hospital,' he began, 'that you and Mr Barnes are engaged to be married if he recovers.'

'*When* he recovers,' she corrected him. 'That's right. We are.' She regarded him warily.

'We also understand from an informant that you recently lived with Alexander Waring of Scotland Yard.'

Hester frowned. His manner was beginning to alarm her. Why was it any business of the police who she had or had not lived with?

'I don't see what right you have to question me about Mr Waring. And who is your informant?' In an attempt to hide her nervousness she was sounding uncooperative and realized, with a sinking heart, that she was making a mistake.

'You will see, Miss Shaw. I'm sorry to have to tell you this but we have information to suggest that the attack upon Mr Barnes was not random but was in fact *ordered* by Mr Waring.'

Now Hester stared at him blankly. 'I don't quite understand,' she began. 'How could he . . .? Why would he? None of this makes sense. I thought you'd already caught the man who did it.'

'We have, Miss Shaw, but we now understand that he was merely the hired assassin, so to speak. It certainly does look that way. Could jealousy be a motive, do you think?'

'I don't understand,' Hester stammered. 'At least . . . Are you saying someone paid this man to attack Charlie?'

He nodded.

'And you think that man was Alexander? Oh, that can't be right.' She shook her head. 'Mr Waring is a very civilized man. He would never . . .' She swallowed. Her throat was uncomfortably dry. 'He would never do such a thing! Who says he did?'

'The man who attacked your young man. The man we have in custody who admits to the crime. A certain Matt Fitch. He claims that he was paid by Waring to give Charlie Barnes a beating and—'

'Wait!' she cried incredulously. 'You think Alexander *paid* a man to hurt Charlie? I don't believe it. I know him. He wouldn't do such a thing.'

'Miss Shaw, we need to know if you can think of anything to corroborate Fitch's statement. A telephone conversation, perhaps? A letter he tried to hide? Any slip of the tongue that gave you cause to suspect any wrongdoing?'

'No! Never! That is, I can't recall a single thing that worried me.'

'His wife might have had doubts. She might have been able to help us but I understand she died recently.'

Hester nodded. 'She'd been ill for a long time. I never met her.' Tuning out the man's voice, she stopped listening to him as she tried to reassure herself that Alexander was the man she knew; the man she had once hoped to marry. Surely she knew him better than they did. Alexander had his faults, but at heart he was honourable, she told herself. She had trusted him. Lived with him. *Slept* with him. 'There must be some mistake,' she said at last. Wild-eyed she looked at the detective for a hint that this wasn't happening. 'This man Fitch must be lying!' she said firmly. 'He's trying to pin the blame on to . . .' She faltered to a stop, chilled by the look of pity on the detective's face.

'I'm afraid not. Matt Fitch has the money to prove it.

I'm sorry, Miss Shaw. We found it when we searched his room and have now been forced to widen our investigation.' He sighed heavily. 'The case now has all the hallmarks of a major scandal. Firstly Mr Waring is a highly respected police officer and secondly the victim might have died from his injuries. We understand Mr Barnes's health is not entirely stable. If he should take a turn for the worse then it would be murder. It may be attempted murder. Or conspiracy to murder. You do see the need for great discretion here.'

Hester nodded but her mind was reeling with terrible possibilities. Suppose for a moment that this *was* true and Alexander had decided to punish Charlie. A terrible idea was forming in her mind – that if Alexander had done this to Charlie, then indirectly, that made it her fault. Charlie falling in love with her had brought on the attack and his terrible injuries! That unbearable thought overwhelmed her and, as she cried out in protest, a weakness overtook her and she felt herself sway forward into a welcome darkness . . .

When she opened her eyes again, Maisie was waving a small bottle of *sal volatile* under her nose and Hester came round to find herself lying on the floor with a cushion tucked under her head. She was coughing and spluttering with tears running down her face. As her memory returned, she cried out again.

'Come on, love,' Maisie urged. 'It's going to be all right.' She put an arm round her and helped her on to a chair. 'You had a shock, that's all. I'll make us a cup of tea.'

Hester looked round. 'Where's the policeman? He said such terrible things about Alexander. It can't be true . . . can it?'

Maisie shrugged. 'Don't ask me. I daresay we'll know all in good time. I sent the policeman packing. Said you'd had enough for one day and was in no state to carry on. He's coming back first thing tomorrow, but we're to say nothing to anyone. He was determined. Very hush-hush, he said. We have to be discreet. That was his word. Discreet. Now sit up and lean back – that's the way. I'll make the tea and then you can tell me everything. Or whatever you can tell me. It all sounds very dramatic.' She paused. 'Cheer up, Hester! Whatever it is we can beat it. We're tougher than we look.'

She bustled out leaving Hester sick at heart and trembling. She would share everything she knew, she decided. She and Maisie and Charlie were in this nightmare together. Somehow they would have to learn how to survive.

Twelve

Edith woke up at ten to five on the morning of Sunday, the twenty-ninth of December. Immediately all her fears came rushing back and she lay awake weighing up what she ought to do about her nephew. She knew he was a grown man and that she had no influence on him any more, but she still loved him like a son and felt that somehow she might be able to help him. Who else could he turn to for support? Marcia was gone – not that she would have been much use. 'Weak as water!' Edith sniffed disparagingly.

Marcia had always taken the line of least resistance and would have been no help at all. Struggling into a sitting position, Edith stared round her bedroom which was familiar but full of night shadows. The moon still shone fitfully but Edith lit her bedside candle, put on her spectacles and reached for her diary. Carefully she reread the last few entries, trying to glean any clue from what had happened over the last few weeks. She knew that before her abortive trip to the doctor in New York all had seemed as usual. It was just around Christmas that matters had turned rather sour and difficult.

Perhaps something had happened while she and Hester were on the *Mauretania*. She had always worried about Alexander's chosen profession. It was dangerous and he must have made enemies along the way. Maybe a villain from his past was threatening him. Possibly a man he had put away had re-emerged from prison vowing revenge. Was her nephew's life in danger? The thought sent a cold shiver through her. Surely he could arrange protection for himself, if that were the case. Unless he was too proud to ask for help. That was probably it. He thought he would look weak if he asked for help and was trying to deal with the problem alone.

Unless he was romantically involved. She gasped. Suppose he had met another woman. But then he'd have no problem because Marcia was dead and Hester had found someone else. She shook her head and ruled out that idea. Unless the woman was married and the husband had found out and was threatening to give him a hiding or report his behaviour to his superiors. She considered the scenario carefully but rejected it. Alexander was a very attractive man, but he had more sense than to risk his career over another man's wife. He was no fool.

She closed the diary, annoyed at her inability to discover the truth. And then another notion took hold of her – Alexander was seriously ill and was secretly fighting for his life!

Oh Lord! she thought. Was that it? He'd be reluctant to upset her and would keep the bad news to himself, but naturally he'd be edgy and moody. But how would that explain the telephone call he had received on Christmas morning? She frowned, trying to recall any words or phrases she had overheard. He'd been speaking to someone – Sergeant Somebody – and he'd shouted at him not to mention his name to anybody. Later he'd said he'd 'see to it'.

She was now wide awake and it was too late to try and go back to sleep so she decided to get up. She would make herself a cup of Bovril – that was always heartening. Later she would go round to Hilsomer House and demand to know what was troubling him. Somehow she would coax or bully the truth out of him. In all probability he would be glad to get it off his chest. Feeling somewhat happier, she climbed out of bed and made her way to the kitchen. She smiled as she filled the kettle. Only a few more hours then she would know the worst and they would both be feeling a lot better.

The hansom cab dropped Edith at the door just after ten and she marched up the steps, gathering herself for the coming storm. She would tell him that she would not leave the premises until he had told her the truth. Straightening her back she listened for the maid's footsteps, but it was Mrs Rice who opened the door. Not with her normal smile of welcome but with a distraught expression.

'Oh, Mrs Carradine, thank goodness. Come in, do. We're all at sixes and sevens! Such dreadful goings on!' Ignoring Edith's demand to be more explicit, she headed back to the kitchen where Rosie, the maid, pale and upset, was sitting at the kitchen table sipping a mug of tea. Mrs Rice, by comparison, was red-faced and distinctly flustered.

'What on earth is happening here?' Edith snapped, her tone sharpened in apprehension. She was right. Alexander had been hiding something from her.

She looked at Rosie and asked, 'Why aren't you working? You're not paid to sip tea.'

'Because I've got the sack!' Her mouth trembled and she looked to Mrs Rice for help.

'Well, if my nephew has sacked you, you obviously deserved it.' Edith sat on the chair Mrs Rice provided for her and said, 'I'll have a cup of tea, please, and a biscuit. I didn't have any appetite for breakfast.' Perhaps, since Marcia's death, her nephew had been having trouble with the staff. Too strict, maybe, or not strict enough. Maybe the sergeant he had been talking to on the telephone was Rosie's father and they were arguing about her being dismissed. Edith felt marginally more composed. If that was all it was, she had worried for no good reason. Turning to Rosie she said, 'What have you done, you silly girl?'

Rosie's eyes widened. 'Me? I haven't done nothing! Mrs Rice knows. Nor has she. We've both got the sack.' She began to cry.

Edith accepted her tea, added sugar and stirred it relentlessly. She made no attempt to drink it as she sat silent, trying to hide her dismay at this new revelation. So this was it, she thought dully. Either Alexander was not coping without Marcia or he had suddenly taken leave of his senses. She stood up.

'I'll speak with Mr Waring. Where is he? In his study, I daresay.'

As she moved towards the door Mrs Rice said, 'He's nowhere, Mrs Carradine. That's the trouble. He's gone. Packed a few things, called a cab and walked out on us.' Taking pity on Edith, she said, 'Come back and sit down. It's not good news, is it? Sit down and take a few sips of your tea.'

Edith wasn't used to taking orders from a servant, but suddenly her legs felt weak and she made her way unsteadily to her chair and sat down. 'This is most . . . You say my nephew has *gone*?' She frowned. 'There must be a simple explanation. You must have misunderstood the situation.' Please tell me you have, she begged inwardly. Aloud she said, 'I can assure you Mr Waring has not walked out. That is utter nonsense. Where would he go? He would have told me.' She was annoyed to hear a shake in her voice. Show no weakness in front of the servants, she reminded herself. Her mother had drummed that into her when she was a very young woman about to be married. 'Take your time, Mrs Rice, and tell me what has happened.' She sipped her tea, watching the housekeeper over the top of the cup.

Mrs Rice glanced at Rosie who said, 'I went up to make the bed as usual and he wouldn't open the bedroom door even though he's usually in his study by the time I go up and—'

Edith said, 'I want to hear it from Mrs Rice. Your turn will come, Rosie.' She knew it made no difference who told her, but she had spoken to Mrs Rice and the girl must not be allowed to take liberties, whatever the circumstances.

Mrs Rice tutted and began her version. 'When Rosie came down and said where should she start because Mr Waring wouldn't let her in I thought it odd but sent her to do the bathroom instead. I was cooking breakfast – you know, ma'am, how Mr Waring likes his Sunday breakfast. Always two fried eggs and three rashers of best back bacon done crispy—'

'Please! I'm not interested in his breakfast.' Edith added another spoonful of sugar to her tea and began to stir it furiously.

The housekeeper continued. 'Then he came hurrying

downstairs and I thought better get the bacon – oh, sorry!
He came into the kitchen and said, "No breakfast, thank
you. I have to go away in rather a hurry. Something unexpected." ' She raised her eyes to the ceiling as if to improve
her memory. 'Oh, yes, then he said, "I've left a note for
my aunt. I shall be away indefinitely so here is your pay.
A little extra in lieu of notice and because you'll have to
find new employment." '
    'Did he explain the circumstances?'
    'No, ma'am, he didn't. I was so shook up I never thought
to ask him and anyway he was off out the door. I followed
him along the passage to ask him what was going on, but
he must have telephoned for a cab because it was waiting
for him and he turned back and saw me at the front door
and he didn't even wave goodbye.'
    Still sniffling into her handkerchief, Rosie saw her chance.
'I got on with the bathroom like I was told and then I
wondered whether to strip the bed and—'
    'What's that?' Edith turned to her.
    Mrs Rice said, 'Forget the bed, Rosie. Forget all of it.'
Her voice rose with a hint of hysteria. 'After all these years
devoted to the family, we're not needed here any more.'
She, too, appeared to be on the verge of tears.
    Edith wished she could join them but tears were far from
her eyes. She sat, dry-eyed, her throat tight with fear.
Something terrible was happening to Alexander and she
was too late to help him. Perhaps he had become mentally
ill under the pressure of work at his office or had suffered
a breakdown because of Marcia's prolonged illness and
recent death. He had gone. Indefinitely, he'd said.
    'He must have said why or where,' Edith said desper-
ately. 'He must have said something. Try and remember
anything else he said.'
    'He left you a note. Maybe that will—'
    'Oh, yes! The note.' Edith seized upon the idea. 'Rosie,
run up to the study and find the note and bring it down –
and hurry.'
    When Rosie had gone, Mrs Rice said, 'Mr Waring gave
us each three weeks' wages but we'll have to start looking

for work elsewhere. It's a good thing you came round because we were wondering what to do.' She hesitated. 'I live here, Mrs Carradine, so I'll have to find another live-in position. I don't suppose you know of anyone.'

'Not at the moment, but I'll think about it and ask my friends and my daughters. In the meantime, if you've been paid for three weeks you can go on living here and keep an eye on the house. Do a bit of cleaning . . . I can't believe Mr Waring has gone for good. But by all means look for another post in case he doesn't return.' Did that sound reasonable, Edith wondered. Was it likely? In her heart she didn't think so but better to 'keep a lid on things'. No point in alerting the neighbours. Certainly no point in starting unsavoury gossip.

Mrs Rice asked, 'What will you do? Call the police? They find missing persons, don't they?'

Edith smiled. 'My nephew is not missing, Mrs Rice. He has chosen to leave Hilsomer House and . . . Ah! Here is the note. Thank you, Rosie. I suggest you remake Mr Waring's bed with clean sheets before you do anything else.'

The note was short but for a moment her eyes misted over at the sight of the familiar handwriting.

Dear Aunt Edith,

Do please forgive me for what I have done. I know it will hurt you. The police will almost certainly call at Hilsomer House in the near future and they will explain what has happened. I have to try and start a new life somewhere else – hopefully abroad. I've been such a fool but I hope you can find it in your heart to remember me with at least a small measure of your earlier fondness.

Sadly, your loving nephew,
Alexander

Through her deep confusion and fear, Edith heard Rosie leave the room, shooed out by Mrs Rice. She read the letter again, searching for clues but there were so few. With a sudden clenching of her fist, she screwed up the letter.

Mrs Rice eyed her hopefully. 'Well? Does he explain what's happened?'

Edith thought rapidly. It would be best to tell the servants as little as possible without actually deceiving them. How little would satisfy them, she wondered.

'No,' she said at last. 'He says only that he is going abroad for a few years. He . . . he's given up his job and . . . and plans to make a fresh start. And that he's sorry he didn't tell me but it was a sudden decision.' Avoiding Mrs Rice's eyes, she tried to smile as she tucked the offending letter into her pocket.

'Make a fresh life doing what, I wonder?'

Mrs Rice has put her finger on it, thought Edith. The letter raised more questions and answered none. And the police might call. She would have to warn her.

'Alexander says the police might call during the coming days. If they do . . . you must say you know nothing about it and send them round to my flat. I don't want you to have to worry about any of that. Just say he left hurriedly and you don't know when he's coming back. What's the matter?'

Mrs Rice was shaking her head. 'I couldn't pretend I don't know anything. I couldn't lie to the police – I'd get into serious trouble.'

The poor woman was right, of course. Edith sighed. 'I have it. I'll move in here for a few days then I can deal with them. That seems sensible, don't you think?'

Mrs Rice's frown faded. 'Oh, yes! That would be wonderful. I mean, you'll know what to say to them. I wouldn't – and he's your nephew.'

Edith decided not to take offence at what seemed like a slur on Alexander.

'Finish the breakfast,' she said. 'I'll eat it and then I'll go home for a few clothes and personal items.'

Her face cleared. She was going to need help to survive whatever lay ahead and it suddenly seemed a good idea to get in touch with someone else who knew Alexander well. After church she would write to Hester Shaw.

*   *   *

Eleven o'clock found Edith Carradine kneeling in prayer at her usual church, praying for Alexander to come to his senses and return to Hilsomer House. She had recovered from her initial shock and her natural resilience had returned. She now felt reasonably confident that whatever the problem was, she could help him. As the congregation rose to sing the final hymn, she slipped from her seat near the rear of the church and tiptoed out. The good Lord would understand, she knew, that she had important things to do. She had made Him aware of the difficulty and would now expect him to offer her strength of purpose and clarity of thought.

Entering Hilsomer House twenty minutes later, she was pleased to see that Mrs Rice looked more her usual self and that Rosie had stopped crying.

Calling them both into the kitchen, she said, 'I shall make all efforts to find my nephew, but if I don't succeed you may both rely on the fact that I shall write each of you an excellent reference on behalf of Mr Waring. That will make it much easier for you both to find alternative positions.'

She then went upstairs to the study and sat at Alexander's large desk to write to Hester Shaw. After much soul-searching she decided to be completely honest.

My dear Miss Shaw,

I write with a heavy heart to acquaint you of certain facts concerning Alexander. For reasons I do not understand, he has left Hilsomer House abruptly and has given the servants three weeks' money in lieu of notice. Naturally I am shocked but not yet despairing. With God's help he may eventually return – depending, no doubt, on his reasons for leaving.

He left me a note which explains nothing but I suspect some kind of breakdown. He told the servants to expect a call from the police. I find that horribly ironic. When I know more I will contact you again, but I think you should possibly be prepared for a similar visit, depending on how far-reaching their enquiries prove to be. I hope everything goes well for

you with Mr Barnes. When you marry, if you wish to
invite me to the wedding, I shall be pleased to accept.
  In haste, your friend,
  Mrs Edith Carradine

She found a stamp and sent Rosie to the nearest pillar
box but before she returned, the police arrived in the shape
of a constable and a detective inspector.

Ten minutes later the three of them sat in the study where
the constable was searching through the various drawers
and cupboards, having been given permission to do so by
Edith. Detective Inspector Raffey was asking questions and
writing in his notebook while issuing instructions to his
constable.

Edith was recovering from the shock of what she had
been told – that her nephew was wanted by the police for
incitement to a crime and that his victim was none other
than Hester's young steward from the *Mauretania*.

'Is Mr Barnes going to live?' she asked, her voice queru-
lous.

'They think he'll live, but there may be permanent
damage.'

'And his broken leg?'

'He'll always limp. That's what the doctors say.' He spoke
in a matter-of-fact tone, as though nothing would ever
surprise him. She found that irritating. DI Raffey studied
his notes, frowning at what he had written. He was tall and
thin with frizzy hair and small eyes. He spoke quietly but
appeared wrapped up in his note taking and rarely gave
Edith a direct look. 'So you do not think Waring has another
home anywhere where he might have gone?'

'Not to my knowledge.'

'Any friends or relatives who might be harbouring him?'

Edith stiffened. 'He has friends and relatives and he might
be *visiting* them, but as for *harbouring* – the answer's no.'

They were already treating him as a criminal, she thought
resentfully, even before he had been charged or tried. What
had happened to the democratic way – innocent until proved
guilty?

The constable closed the final drawer and shook his head.

DI Raffey said, 'Talk to the housekeeper.'

The constable left the room.

'What are you looking for?' Edith asked.

Without bothering to answer, DI Raffey asked, 'Does your nephew own a boat?'

'Good Lord, no!'

'Does he have friends or relatives abroad? France, perhaps?'

'Not to my knowledge.'

She wanted to say that even if she knew she wouldn't tell him but that would be pointless. If this silly business ever came to a trial she would offer herself as a character witness and they would never accept her if she had antagonized the investigating officer. Instead she tried to hold herself together and maintain her dignity.

The detective picked up a diary the constable had found earlier and gave it his full attention.

'What do you know of this Hester he refers to?'

'Hester Shaw lived in a flat belonging to my nephew for several years.'

'So he has another house or flat? When I asked you earlier, you denied it.'

It was true. She felt a moment's panic. 'I always thought of the flat as hers, not his. He lived here with his wife and . . . and visited Miss Shaw.'

'But he paid the rent?'

'I suppose so. It was none of my business.'

Edith was asked to give the address and did so. 'But she isn't there now. She is in Liverpool.'

'You do see, Mrs Carradine, how this looks. Waring keeps a mistress, the mistress finds another man and Waring is overcome with jealousy and wants revenge – on both of them. He arranges to have the other man beaten up. He does it because he can. He's a senior policeman and thinks he's above the law – a fatal mistake. He thinks he can get away with it, but it blows up in his face.' He smiled for the first time. 'That's what comes of relying on scum like Fitch. You'd think a man in Waring's position would have had more sense.'

The same thought had occurred to Edith, but she had resisted it as disloyal in the extreme. She said nothing, her lips pursed, her expression giving nothing away. In his note Alexander had wanted her to forgive him but she didn't think she could. If this were all true, what he had done was a most terrible thing and Mr Barnes, an innocent man, had suffered for her nephew's wickedness. Because that's what it was – a vile and wicked act. She wanted to believe that Alexander had somehow been framed by his enemies, but part of her found the facts plausible. The question in her mind was – if Alexander had hated Barnes that much, could he have done this? If this Fitch character had *killed* Mr Barnes it would be even more serious because then it would be a hanging matter. And poor Hester! Edith wanted to cry but she had been brought up to show self-restraint and now she was denied the release that tears would have brought.

The constable returned. 'The housekeeper says he kept a gun in a box beside his bed but it's not there. Only the box.'

'A *gun*!' Edith's hand flew to her mouth as she choked back a cry. Alexander had kept a gun. How had she not known that? And why had he taken it with him? Who was he going to shoot? Not Fitch, surely. He was already in custody. Would he shoot at the police if they tried to arrest him? How desperate was he?

The two policemen exchanged meaningful glances and suddenly Edith wanted them both out of the house. The strain of trying to remain composed was becoming too much for her. She abandoned her upright stance on the edge of the armchair and allowed herself to lean back against the cushion. She felt smaller and more vulnerable as she did so, but somehow she must convince these men that there was no way they could intimidate her into admitting anything that might incriminate Alexander.

Rosie knocked and was admitted. To Edith she said, 'I usually go home at this time and Mrs Rice doesn't need me so . . .?'

DI Raffey said, 'You can go for now. Thank you for your help.'

What had Rosie told them? Edith wondered nervously.
It seemed the servants knew more than she did.

'Take this back to the station.' He tore a page from his
notebook and handed it to the constable. 'They'll need to
search this address, too, and the sooner the better – and talk
to the landlady if there is one, or the neighbours. We can't
afford to miss anything. This case is going to be very big!'

Turning his attention back to Edith, the detective inspector
towered over her. 'So you last saw him when?'

'Christmas morning.'

'And why did you come to his home yesterday?'

'Because he seemed upset by a phone call he received
Christmas morning. I wanted him to confide in me. I thought
he might be ill or . . . or having a breakdown. His wife had
only just died. He seemed worried. Not himself.' She was
aware of a great weariness. 'I've told you all this before,
when you first arrived.'

To her relief he snapped shut the notebook. 'I think that'll
be all for today, but we may need to contact you again. If
your nephew should contact you, you are duty bound to
report it directly to me at the police station. Failure to do
so means you are interfering in a police investigation and
that is a serious matter. Are you clear about that?'

She nodded.

'I'll see myself out. Oh! Do I have your home address?'

'I gave it to the constable.'

'Thank you, Mrs Carradine, for your cooperation.'

After he'd gone Edith still sat in the chair, waiting for
the churning in her stomach to stop, but before it did so
Mrs Rice came in with a brandy. Neither woman spoke
until the door was almost closed. Then Edith said, 'Pour
one for yourself, Mrs Rice!'

Edith closed her eyes. It finally occurred to her to wonder
what Hester Shaw would think about it all. An unhappy
smile twisted her mouth. An invitation to her wedding to
Mr Barnes now seemed extremely unlikely.

Three days later Hester sat beside Charlie's bed and broke
the news of Alexander's disappearance and the alleged

reason behind it. The doctor had agreed that she might safely pass on the information as his occasional lapses into confusion were becoming rarer.

The police were waiting to be admitted so that they could speak with him and Hester felt that their interrogation would come as less of a shock if he already understood the main points of the conspiracy. As she spoke to him she couldn't avoid making the comparison between the Charlie she had first seen in the bar of the *Mauretania* and the man she saw before her. His curly brown hair was completely hidden beneath white bandages, the alert grey eyes were dulled by the medication he had been given and his cheerful voice with its Liverpool twang was painfully slow, allowing little of his cheeky talk and sweet compliments. But, she reminded herself, he was still alive and for that she thanked God daily in her prayers.

Hester had made the account of Alexander's involvement as simple as possible and Charlie appeared to have understood her.

'So, Charlie,' she said, 'will you ever forgive me? I can see how it looks – that it's because of me and you that you were attacked. Well, actually it's because of me. Alexander didn't really want me, but he didn't like me falling in love with you. I had no idea he could be so violent – or that he cared for me enough. No, it isn't even that he cared. You stole something he believed he owned. He couldn't bear it.' She stopped, searching his face for his reaction.

Charlie squeezed her hand. 'Not . . . your . . . fault,' he insisted. 'Don't . . . blame you . . . falling . . . love . . . me!' He managed a grin. He still had difficulty speaking, but the doctor believed that it would improve with time. 'The leg's mending,' the doctor had told her. 'He'll soon be up and about.'

They both knew this was an exaggeration, but Charlie was thinking very positively, refusing to think that he might not make a complete recovery. Nobody disillusioned him although the long-term prognosis was not entirely encouraging. As soon as the leg bone had healed they would allow him up for a short time each day and the doctors would

design exercises which would strengthen the leg muscles.
The trauma to his brain was what worried the doctor.

Hester showed Charlie the cutting from *The Times* newspaper, outlining the case and describing Alexander who was
'on the run and believed to be carrying a firearm'.

'A gun! I can't believe it,' Hester repeated. 'I knew him
all those years and trusted him completely.'

'You . . . were . . . wrong.'

'And Marcia, his wife! Thank goodness she isn't alive
to be caught up in the scandal. I wonder where Alexander
has gone . . . and poor Mrs Carradine! She's a funny old
thing and can be difficult at times but she adored him.'

The bell was rung to announce the end of visiting time,
and Hester kissed Charlie's hand by way of goodbye. She
longed to fling her arms around him, hold him close and
smother his face with kisses, but that was out of the question and would remain so for some time.

'Don't forget I love you,' she told him, her throat tight
with the familiar sorrow of leaving him again.

He smiled. 'You . . . only . . . one . . . me.'

'And you're the only one for me. Aren't we lucky?'

He nodded as Hester blinked away tears. Lucky they had
found each other and lucky that so far no one had been
able to tear them apart.

She said, 'Is it all right if Maisie comes in tomorrow
instead of me? She is longing to see you and has been so
patient. I feel unkind, keeping you all to myself.'

He nodded and she could see that he was tiring. A nurse
appeared beside her with a thermometer in her hand.

'Isn't he doing well, Miss Shaw? A model patient.'

She popped the thermometer into his mouth and prepared
to update the notes which hung at the end of his bed.

'I must go,' Hester told him. 'Happy New Year, Charlie!'

As Hester made her way along the now familiar corridors,
she thought of the people caught up in the events of the past
weeks. Edith Carradine, Alexander – even Annie Green.
Especially Annie Green. Why, she wondered, had the price
for her happiness with Charlie come at so high a price?

*   *   *

Charlie watched her go for as long as he could, because it was difficult and painful to turn his head. He lived for her visits, but he hated to see her so worried. It was Waring's fault, and that made him hate Waring with a deep passion. He had prayed every night that something bad would happen to him and he was pleasantly surprised that the Lord had heard his prayers and had set the might of the law on him. Serve him damned well right! The man was evil. While in a hating mood, Charlie hated the knowledge that his beautiful Hester had lived with the brute, but there was no way of undoing the past. He hated the fact that Annie had suffered because of him and that presumably she must hate him. Charlie was sad, too, about the baby she had 'lost' and had searched his mind for a way to put that right. The solution still evaded him. He hadn't shown the letter to Hester because he knew she'd be unhappy about it.

The nurse removed the thermometer and glanced at it. 'Still doing well,' she told him. 'So, when's the wedding? Going to hold it here in the hospital, I hear.'

'No . . . better . . . church. Do it . . . properly.'

'Well, wherever you hold the wedding, Miss Shaw will be a very pretty bride!'

Beaming, he gave a small nod, and she moved on to her next patient.

Yes, Hester would make a wonderful bride, he reflected, immediately cheered by the prospect. And she would be a wonderful wife and mother. Three children? Maybe four. His smile disappeared.

In his bedside cupboard there was a letter he had decided not to show to Hester. It was from Chalky and he knew the contents by heart. Chalky had spoken to the boss about when Charlie was well enough to resume work. A steward with a limp and a possible speech problem would have no place on the *Mauretania*, but, as he was well-liked, they would find him another position if he wanted to resume working on board the ship. Perhaps a job in Stores. It was a blow to Charlie's hopes of a decent career. Stores led nowhere and had none of the buzz and glamour of work in the bar – and it would pay less. So maybe four children would be too many on his pitiful wage as a store hand. The prospect dismayed him but he forced aside his doubts. There were compensations. He had survived the revenge Waring had planned for him and would live to see the man brought to justice. Ruined, in fact! And although Charlie was gentle at heart, he was looking forward to watching Waring go through hell while he, Charlie Barnes, shared the rest of his life with his beloved Hester.

Thirteen

The hansom cab rattled along at a sluggish pace, drawn by a tired horse. The cab driver was also tired and reckoned it was long past his bedtime. He often worked until the early hours, but he had started earlier than usual and the day had been busy and his chest was playing him up again. His lungs had never taken to cold, damp weather and he had often thought of moving to Australia or California but never could get the fare together.

'Not a star in the sky tonight, guvnor,' he remarked, hoping for a response from his fare. He'd picked him up at Waterloo station thinking it would be a short and sweet fare and he'd get off home with a bit of extra cash because his passenger had offered to pay double the normal price and that was not to be sniffed at.

'No. Too cloudy,' the passenger replied.

Encouraged, the cabby pressed on. 'I like a bit of moonlight myself.'

No answer. Miserable sod, thought the cabby, resigned. A bit of chat never hurt anyone and it passed the time. Still, they were nearly there. He'd heard half past eleven strike so maybe he'd be home by one. It was New Year's Day and his wife would nag – until she knew about the bit of extra money. That'd bring a smile to her face. He grinned and whipped up the horse. 'Get up there!' he shouted, to impress his fare. The horse ignored him as usual.

'Ten more minutes and we'll be there,' he promised cheerily. 'Soon be tucked up in a nice warm bed.' He chuckled to show it was a joke but the gentleman remained silent.

True to his word, ten minutes later, he reined in outside

a large house and jumped down to assist his gentleman fare who handed over the promised money and bade him a terse, 'Goodnight.'

'Goodnight, guvnor, and a happy New Year!'

Alexander watched the cab disappear into the darkness then turned and walked up the steps to the front door. Taking out his key he turned it carefully in the lock, opened the door slowly, then stepped inside and closed it quietly behind him. Why was he bothering? he thought, with a shake of his head. There was no one here. Mrs Rice and Rosie were gone. They would find other work, he reassured himself. His aunt would help them. He stood in the hallway, waiting for his eyes to acclimatize themselves to the dim light which filtered through the glass fanlight over the front door. He was pleasantly surprised that the house still had that lived-in feel. A certain warmth remained despite the inclement weather. He toyed with the idea of removing his overcoat but decided against it. He stood for a moment with his eyes closed then slipped his right hand into his pocket and fingered the pistol.

Alexander went up the stairs thinking about Marcia and wishing he had been more patient with her during her various spells of ill health. As he walked along the landing towards his study he remembered Hester and regretted that she must now thoroughly despise him. Once inside the familiar study that he had always thought of as his sanctuary, he recalled his aunt and her many kindnesses and wished he could thank her instead of inflicting more anguish. Lastly he thought with relish of the expression of horror on Harrow's face the previous night, just before Alexander shot him.

He sat down at the empty desk, put the pistol to his right temple, and, for some reason he didn't understand, waited patiently for the clock in the hall to start striking midnight. After the third stroke he whispered 'Oh God!' as he pulled the trigger.

Seven hours later Mrs Rice splashed cold water over her face and neck and dried herself with the towel. 'It is 1908!'

she said with amazement. She had always lived each year
in the fearful belief that it might be her last so that each
New Year came as a pleasant surprise. Crossing to her
calendar she put a line through the first of January and
stared at the second. 'Thursday, the second of January! Well,
well! Thank goodness last year is over.' She sighed. It
seemed that in the blink of an eye her life had changed.

She struggled into her clothes and went downstairs to
relight the stove and begin preparations for Mrs Carradine's
breakfast.

Outside there was a rough wind blowing, but much of
the snow had melted and the slush had been cleared away.
From behind the kitchen door, Mrs Rice took down Marcia's
apron and put it on with a brief whispered prayer for her
ex-mistress's soul. She had taken to wearing it 'in memory
of' her departed mistress and liked to think that, should
Marcia Waring glance down, she would approve. Not that
Mrs Waring often ventured into the kitchen, but in the early
days she had sometimes decided to try out a recipe given
to her by a friend. Mrs Rice had convinced herself that,
now that Marcia Waring was dead, someone else might as
well get some wear out of the apron. It would be a pity to
waste it.

'Poor woman,' she said, tutting at the wasted life. No
children and an unfaithful husband. What good had all that
money done Marcia Waring? Kneeling in front of the stove
she arranged paper and kindling wood, piled on small coals
and lit it.

Upstairs she could hear the old aunt pottering about in
her bedroom. Mrs Carradine would soon be downstairs,
poking her nose in everywhere – but at least she, Mrs Rice,
didn't have to sleep alone in the house. She had also seen
a marked difference in the old lady's attitude. It seemed as
though her nephew's shame had reduced his aunt in some
way. Mrs Rice occasionally felt sorry for her.

Steps sounded on the stairs and Mrs Carradine appeared
in the kitchen. She said, 'Happy New Year, Mrs Rice. A
new day, a new year.'

'That was yesterday, ma'am. Today's the second.'

'Really? I'm beginning to think my mind is wandering.'
She sat down.

'Hardly surprising, Mrs Carradine. You've had a lot on
your plate recently. But now we've got a brand new year!
Something to look forward to.' She smiled cheerfully.

'Just a few stewed apples, Mrs Rice. I'm not very hungry.'

'Should I serve it in the dining room? Mr Waring . . . oh,
sorry! That is, he liked to eat there . . .'

'Yes, yes. The dining room.' She sighed deeply. 'I didn't
sleep well. Something woke me from a deep sleep – I was
dreaming about Alexander when he was a boy.' She smiled
faintly. 'We were so close. When he went off to his prep
school. I went with him on the train because his parents
couldn't take him. They led such busy lives. He was only
nine and trying hard to be brave . . .' Swallowing, she
frowned at another memory then rubbed her eyes. 'What
was I saying, Mrs Rice?'

'You didn't sleep well, ma'am.'

'Oh, yes! Something woke me and I sat straight up in
the bed, wide awake. I listened but didn't hear anything.
When I looked at the clock it was exactly midnight. Did
you hear anything?'

'No, ma'am, nothing, but I do sleep heavy. Like a log,
my ma used to say.'

The old lady shrugged. 'Some time I have to speak with
the family lawyer, but not just yet. Too many unanswered
questions . . . I shall start going through the house later
today. There is so much to sort out. I hardly know where
to begin. All Mrs Waring's clothes, for a start – and
Alexander's desk.'

Mrs Rice hesitated. 'I think most of his stuff's gone from
the study. The police took a lot away when they searched
the house. I do know they cleared his desk and . . .'

'Yes, yes!' Mrs Carradine interrupted her. 'I take your
point. No need to go on like that. We all know what's
happened. God knows we do!'

There was an awkward silence. Mrs Rice went to the larder
and produced stewed apples, sugar and cream and put them
on a tray which she carried through into the dining room.

Mrs Carradine said, 'Where's Rosie?'

'You gave her the day off. Her mother's having a baby.'

'Did I?' She shrugged. 'A baby, did you say? How many's that?'

'There are six children. Rosie's the eldest. All girls.'

'I hope the police didn't take the photographs as well. They can be so heavy-handed. There were some photographs I value. Some taken while Alexander was at school – one on sports day, I recall. He had just won the hundred yards race and he was so proud!' She smiled. 'Beaming and holding up the cup. And another, one of my favourites, taken sitting on my lap at a picnic. He was only four, bless him, and still had his curls. He was such a lovable little chap. I'll try and find them. You might like to see one or two.'

Mrs Rice tried to look enthusiastic. 'That would be nice.'

Stifling a yawn behind her hand, Mrs Carradine stood up. 'Breakfast calls,' she said. Halfway to the door she turned back. 'There's one photograph of the three cousins, Dorcas, Evelyn and Alexander. Sitting together on the beach at Ramsgate. They all had buckets and spades, but Alexander had a larger size than the girls because, as he insisted, he was a boy! He pleaded so sweetly that I couldn't resist him although it didn't please my daughters. I knew why it was important to him – he wanted to build a bigger sandcastle, you see.' She laughed. 'Method in his madness, you might say!'

Devious little devil, Mrs Rice thought, but simply smiled. She watched Mrs Carradine as she left the kitchen and thought how quickly the spring had gone from her step. The past few weeks had done the old lady no favours.

After a simple lunch of soused mackerel, Edith remembered her promise to Mrs Rice and began to look for the photograph album. With an effort she recalled that it was red leather and somewhat faded from years of handling. It wasn't in the sideboard where she expected to find it, nor was it in the cupboard under the stairs where some of Alexander's things were kept with a few of Marcia's.

She found tennis racquets, a pair of hiking boots, a box of Christmas decorations which Marcia had made, several board games, a croquet set and various other odds and ends – but no album.

Perhaps it was in Alexander's bedroom – or the study. With a sigh she made her way upstairs, trying to visualize exactly where it might be. The study had plenty of shelves and cupboards plus the old trunk in which he had taken his school things to and fro. She smiled. He had been so proud of the new trunk with its brass locks and leather straps . . .

Opening the door she stood for a moment totally un-affected by the scene that met her eyes. Her sight registered her nephew, but her mind was unable to grasp how he came to be where he was. He was leaning forward, his head on his desk, seemingly asleep, but when she spoke to him he failed to answer. For an awful moment the scene was entirely unreal and she suspected she was losing her mind. Alexander had left days ago so how . . .

'Alexander!' she repeated. If only he would lift his head and smile the way he did . . . then everything would be all right. But deep inside she was being forced to accept that this was not going to happen and that something was terribly wrong. She began to tremble then took a small step forward and then another.

'Oh, my dear!' she whispered.

The blood had spread out across the desk and had dripped off on to the carpet.

'Blood,' she whispered and her legs almost gave way. Could she believe what she saw, she wondered. Her nephew rested there so peacefully, it seemed a shame to disturb him by prying further. But, of course, she must.

Softly, tremulously, she walked round the desk and saw the pistol which had fallen from Alexander's dangling hand.

'Oh, darling! What have you done?' she asked. 'My dearest boy!' She shook her head slowly from side to side, while her hands, overlapping, were spread across her chest. 'What *have* you done?' She laid a hand on his head but withdrew it quickly and stared in horror at the sticky red mess on her fingers. Lifting her gaze she noticed small red spatters on the wall behind his chair.

Shocked into a cold stillness, Edith watched Alexander for what seemed for ever – until the world began again and she was able to draw a long shuddering breath and then another. Still gasping for air, she turned and stumbled from the study on to the landing where she clutched at the balustrade to support herself.

'Mrs Rice! Please come!' Her voice was hoarse and very weak. She tried again. *'Mrs Rice! Please!'*

'What is it, ma'am?' Mrs Rice appeared, holding up floury hands. 'I'm just rolling a bit of pastry for . . .'

'Leave it! It doesn't matter.' Nothing would ever matter again, Edith thought, a sob rising in her throat. 'You have to come up.' As Mrs Rice came up the stairs, wiping her hands on a damp cloth, Edith warned her, 'I'm afraid . . . It's not very pleasant but . . . There has been a bit of an accident.'

Within half an hour of the telephone call to the police, the street outside Hilsomer House was full of policemen and newspaper reporters who were augmented by a crowd of interested bystanders who refused to be dispersed. Harried by frustrated constables, the crowd simply moved to another vantage point. Edith and Mrs Rice had been seen by a police doctor and allowed to leave. They had been taken to Dorcas's home where she made them as comfortable as she could and provided warm sweet tea and small lemon cakes by way of light but nourishing refreshment.

For a long time Edith said nothing, reliving the moment when she finally accepted that Alexander was lost to her, but suddenly she recovered enough to tell her daughter a few details. Talking about it brought home the dreadful reality, but she felt that keeping it all inside her head would drive her insane.

'Thank heavens for Mrs Rice,' she said generously. 'She was such a comfort. So calm and . . .'

Mrs Rice said, 'After my first scream, maybe. I was that shaken up I'm afraid I couldn't stop myself.'

Dorcas nodded. 'It must have been a terrible shock for both of you. I'm so sorry. Poor Alexander.'

Edith nodded. 'My first thought was to call a doctor, but I knew it was much too late. He must have come into the house after we went to bed and I did hear that noise that woke me up. It must have been the gunshot. I didn't think Alexander would want the police around with all that mess, but Mrs Rice insisted we had to notify them. I thought we should clean up a bit before they arrived but Mrs Rice . . .'

'I thought we had to leave it as it was because they call it a crime scene and have to take fingerprints and things like that because there might have been another person involved and not suicide and . . .'

Dorcas said, 'It seems so unkind to call suicide a crime. I mean, it's a very personal thing and I'm sure Alexander isn't a criminal.'

Edith closed her eyes. 'In fact that's exactly what he is, dear. Or was, God rest his soul. The police say he killed a man down in Devon somewhere. He was blackmailing him – the man, not Alexander. It sounded rather complicated but it's all to do with poor Mr Barnes in Liverpool.'

Dorcas looked puzzled. 'But how on earth could that be? It doesn't make sense.'

'I know that, Dorcas, but there were two men involved . . .' She shook her head. 'Don't ask me to explain. It's making my head spin.'

Mrs Rice said, 'Then perhaps Mr Waring did the sensible thing by . . . by what he's just done. Better than hang—' She stopped abruptly in mid word and glanced apologetically at Edith. 'Sorry, ma'am. I don't know what I'm saying. I'm that upset.'

Edith was clasping and unclasping her hands. 'The policeman – the senior man – said Alexander did the decent thing in the end. He's hoping to hush it all up. It would look so bad for the force. One of their own senior men.'

'Not much chance,' said Dorcas, 'with all those reporters outside. I know we never thought Alexander was capable of such bad things but . . . but he has killed a man and sent a thug to injure another man. I wonder what poor Hester will make of all this when she hears. She must have loved Alexander once.'

'Of course she did.' Edith glared at her. 'He was charming, considerate, well-respected . . . until now. You talk as though your cousin is – *was* – some kind of monster. He was a very good man but for some reason he snapped. Maybe something went wrong inside his head.' She sat up a little straighter in the chair.

'Maybe he had a tumour like that opera singer that went mad and had to be committed. We'll probably never know.' She looked at her companions hopefully, to see if they would accept this version of events.

Dorcas said, 'We *will* know, Mother, because there'll be a post-mortem and they can find out about tumours and suchlike.'

'Well, there you are. Poor Alexander!' Edith embraced the possibility.

'Let's hope so,' said Dorcas, but she sounded unconvinced.

Mrs Rice said, 'Mrs Waring was always on to him to get a new carpet for the study. Good job they didn't with all that . . . Oh!' She clapped a hand over her mouth and, afraid to look at Edith, glanced apologetically at Dorcas.

Edith gave her a withering glance which the housekeeper missed and Dorcas said quickly, 'I'll make another pot of tea.'

Weeks passed and Alexander's body was finally released for burial by his family on the second of February, after most of the publicity had been forgotten. To avoid the press, the family had decided to bury him in the Hampshire village where he was born. Hester had been invited and had discussed the matter with Charlie who said generously that she should go 'for the good times'. By this time, Charlie had been allowed to leave the hospital after reassuring his doctor that between Hester and Maisie, he would be well looked after.

Very few local people realized that the funeral arranged for that particular day was that of *the* Alexander Waring who had featured in most of the country's newspapers throughout the first week of January.

The temperature had dropped suddenly during the previous night and the few mourners left their footprints in two inches of crisp white snow as they made their way to the newly dug grave in a remote and untidy corner of the churchyard. The service had been very short with no music and the vicar made it clear by his attitude that he resented the family's choice of Alexander's final resting place. Dorcas, Evelyn, Edith and Hester were the only mourners. Mrs Rice had refused to return to Hilsomer House and Edith had helped her to find a new position. Rosie had returned to her parents to help look after her mother and the new baby.

As they watched the coffin being lowered into the icy ground, Hester ignored the vicar's rushed prayer and uttered one of her own, asking God to forgive Alexander for the wrong he had done and to bear in mind the good things also.

Afterwards they hurried to the small public house nearby where they had arranged for hot tea and sandwiches before the family set off on their return train journey to London, and Hester made her way back to Liverpool. Hester and Edith parted with a shy kiss.

Edith said, 'I shall think of you often, Hester. Perhaps I could be kept informed as to Mr Barnes's progress.'

'Most certainly,' Hester agreed. 'I want the two of you to be properly introduced one day. Better still, you must come to the wedding. You could book into a nice hotel and enjoy yourself. Charlie remembers you from the ship and sends his regards. He did ask that you should be invited to the wedding.'

'He did?'

'Because, if it were not for you making the journey on the *Mauretania* and taking me as your travelling companion, I should never have met him. We owe you a great deal.'

It seemed to Hester, as she waved them off at the station,

that the worst must be over. She was to discover in the weeks that followed, that indeed it was.

Wednesday, 3rd June, 1908 – I received an invitation today to Hester and Charlie's wedding and will be delighted to write and accept.

At last, the solicitors have decided how they will settle Alexander's estate, but we still have no idea when it will be finalized. These things take months if not years. It seems that Alexander did not update his original will. He has left Hilsomer House to Marcia, but since she has predeceased him the house will be sold and the value of the property will be added to the estate and dealt with accordingly. It seems that Dorcas, Evelyn and I are the sole beneficiaries except for Hester. Alexander had very generously left her the flat they shared and I shall suggest to her that she allows me to find a suitable tenant so that the rent will supplement her income until she decides to sell the property – which may be sooner rather than later. Who knows? If Mr Barnes is unable to earn as much as he would have done in his former employment, this will prove to be a very suitable form of compensation (albeit by a circuitous route!) and hopefully Mr Barnes will not discourage his wife from accepting it. I shall write to her on the subject as soon as I have more details from the solicitor and can be more precise.

The more I learn about Charlie Barnes, the more I like him. He made no fuss about allowing Hester to attend Alexander's funeral and I was very touched by that.

On Saturday, the eighth of May, 1909, almost a year later, Edith stepped down from the train and was immediately hailed by Hester who was waiting on the platform with a small baby in her arms – the large perambulator which Edith had insisted on giving to them as a present for their first child waited at home for another occasion. Young Adam Charles Barnes was two weeks old and a lively, healthy boy with Hester's red hair and what Maisie proudly called 'the Barnes lungs'.

As soon as the two women had greeted each other, Edith took her first look at the new arrival, who was sleeping peacefully inside his blanket.

'Oh, my! He's wonderful,' she told Hester. 'It's a long time since I've seen such a young child and I feel quite privileged.'

'I'm sorry Charlie isn't here to carry your bag, but the ship docks tomorrow,' Hester explained as they made their way along the platform towards the barrier. 'He's getting the hang of Stores and is so thrilled to be back at sea again. It was his greatest worry. Of course he misses being with Chalky and the other stewards, but at least he's on the *Mauretania* and that's what matters to him.'

Outside the station they joined the queue for a cab and were eventually rattling through the streets at a smart pace. Hester stole a glance at the old lady and thought she looked tired but doubtless the journey had fatigued her. Edith had made the journey so that she could attend Adam's christening, but there was another reason and this had worried Hester. Ignoring Edith's advice to retain the London flat, Hester and Charlie had decided to sell it and buy a home for themselves in Liverpool. The price of houses was much lower there and they had bought a very nice three-storey house, near to Maisie. With no rent to pay, they were also able to let out the top floor as a separate flat and thus add to Charlie's wages.

Edith had made no attempt to hide her disappointment at their decision, but now she was to see the house for the first time.

'Are you sure you want to stay in the hotel?' Hester asked her. 'You know we have a spare bedroom.'

Edith shook her head. 'I love hotels,' she admitted. 'I always have, ever since I was a child. It's the anonymity. No one knows anything about you. It's a wonderfully secret feeling.'

'Maisie is looking forward to seeing you again,' Hester told her, 'although we're both a bit tired. We went to a friend's wedding on Saturday – Annie Green became Mrs Stanley Holler, and Maisie and I made all the refreshments. Forty guests!'

'Forty guests! Good heavens!'

'We made vol-au-vents, sandwiches, sausage rolls, a large cake, jam tarts . . . oh, yes, and also cheese straws and salmon patties.'

Edith turned to look at her. 'So, you have a nice life, dear – your beloved Charlie, a home, friends and family – and now your baby son. Who could have foreseen all this eighteen months ago?'

Hester smiled. 'And we have you – a very dear friend.'

Edith blinked back tears and Hester guessed they were for her nephew – she would never recover from his shameful death. Hester searched for the words of comfort that could never be enough, but before she could speak the cab was slowing down outside her house. At once, the past, with all its joys and woes, faded from her mind. With Adam in her arms, she stepped carefully down on to the dusty pavement where future joys and woes now beckoned.